I'M
HERE
TO
HELP

I'M HERE TO HELP

CLAIRE LUNN

bookouture

Published by Bookouture in 2025

An imprint of Storyfire Ltd.
Carmelite House
50 Victoria Embankment
London EC4Y 0DZ

www.bookouture.com

The authorised representative in the EEA is Hachette Ireland
8 Castlecourt Centre
Dublin 15 D15 XTP3
Ireland
(email: info@hbgi.ie)

ISBN: 978-1-83618-259-7
eBook ISBN: 978-1-83618-258-0

To both my mother and mother-in-law, who would never stoop so low.
And Mum – thanks for trying to find me all the lemon-flavoured food.

CONTENT WARNING

This book features emotional abuse and sexual assault. If this is potentially sensitive for you, please read with care.

PROLOGUE

NOW

It's now or never.

They'll be gone for a good couple of hours, maybe the whole afternoon, if I'm lucky. I doubt I'll ever get a better chance than this.

If I wait any longer, it could be too late.

I head for the inside door that leads to the garage. I shove my feet into my shoes and grab our coats. The realisation that I should have bought new ones along with our new clothes strikes me, but it's too late now. I can buy new coats later.

It's cold in here. It's always cold in here. Russ talked about getting some heating installed, but never got around to it. I'm grateful for that today, as the drop in temperature soothes my growing nausea. My car is a little electric Toyota, perfect for running around town. I now wish I'd asked Russ to leave me the BMW, simply because that has more space to manoeuvre in. Tiny cars may be good for calming your climate change worries, but it's almost impossible to squeeze myself into the back so I can put Olivia in her car seat. Usually she'd jump in there herself and all I'd have to do is secure her straps, but she's still so sleepy I have to manhandle her into the seat myself.

'Mama, what we doing?' She yawns and rubs at her eyes. My heart surges towards her. Make no mistake, I would die for this child.

Hell, I would kill for this child.

I tell her we're going on a little drive, and she smiles sleepily at me as I finally snap the buckles in place.

I take a moment to wipe the sweat from my eyes. It may be cool in here, but I'm boiling hot again. I'm running on pure adrenaline right now, and I know I'm going to pay for this big style later. My stomach is churning as Sprout, obviously feeling the flood of stress hormones, continues to thrash around in my belly. I take in a few deep breaths and rub at my bump in an effort to soothe the baby, but I've been playing this game long enough to know what's coming next. It's always better to get it over with than fight it, so before I get into the driver's seat, I throw up with practised ease into an empty paint pot. My whole body shudders as it purges, my head swimming alarmingly.

But I can't stop now. It's taken me over half an hour to get to this point. They could be back any minute.

I dump the rucksack in the passenger seat and use the clicker to open the garage door as I settle myself behind the wheel. The door rises, inch by torturous inch, and I find myself begging it to open faster. The sudden glare of sunlight momentarily blinds me, leaving me groping for my sunglasses. In a heart-stopping moment, another car pulls up outside. I grip the steering wheel, preparing to run over anyone who might try and stop me, but it's only a delivery driver. With shaking hands, I put the car in drive and inch my way out of the garage. I have to keep it together. No point getting this far and then crashing the car at the top of the road.

'Okay. We're doing this,' I mutter under my breath. 'We're just driving. Nothing more. Just... go.'

I indicate left and pull out of our driveway. Apart from the delivery driver, there's no one to be seen. Unless they've hired him to spy on me, I think I might have made it.

I think I might be free.

But I can't get too cocky. Getting away from the house with Olivia is only half the job. Now I've got to get out of town, judge the roads, see which one might be the safer option. Ideally, I want to be on a train before they've even realised I've gone.

I decide on Woolerton. It's a little bit further away, but it's a larger station with more frequent trains running. Plus, I can take the old ring road. It's usually pretty deserted, meaning I shouldn't get caught up in traffic. It also doesn't have any cameras on it. The more distance I put between myself and home the more my shoulders relax, and I stop white-knuckling the steering wheel.

I look into my rear-view mirror, relief welling inside me. Olivia is watching the world flash by, one of her froggies clamped to her tiny chest.

'Well, Pumpkin, we might just be—'

But before I can finish, the world explodes around me.

I'm thrown forward in my seat. The seatbelt bites painfully into my chest and bump, enough to make me cry out. A small part of me wonders why the airbag hasn't deployed as my face hits the steering wheel. Pain detonates across my nose, my eye sockets, my jaw.

In slow motion, I try to raise my head. Blood runs from my nose and mouth. There's an ear-splitting wail from behind me: Olivia, hysterical. But there's nothing I can do. It's as if someone has poured iced treacle into the gears of reality, slowing the world to a sluggish crawl.

All I can do is to focus one last time as someone approaches my shattered window before I lapse into unconsciousness.

'Oh dear, oh dear. What are you doing, Frankie?'
I can't reply.
They've found me.
At least I tried.
At least I tri—

PART ONE

ONE

SIX MONTHS EARLIER

Frankie

I don't want to be here.

And it's not just because I've been dragged out by my mother-in-law. It's windy and wet, that drifting rain that doesn't so much fall as cling, making me feel uncomfortably damp. Add this to my nausea, and I'm feeling pretty miserable. I trudge after Petunia like a sulky teenager into Socrates, a jewellers that holds some sway over the Yachting Club set.

After the chill damp of outside, Socrates feels like entering a sauna perfumed with cedar, leather and something sharply antiseptic. I gulp in a breath, hoping it might settle my stomach. Instead, it makes me feel dizzy. I reel a little and clutch at the door-frame to steady myself.

A clipped voice chimes.

'Is madam—'

But before the fussy-looking man behind the counter can finish his question, Petunia interrupts him.

'She's fine. Come along, Frances.'

Right, you can do this. You can. How long does it take to pick out a watch? Ten minutes? Twenty? Then Petunia will take you home. Sure, Amanda will leave you with Olivia, but a day of CBeebies isn't going to wreck her. Just breathe.

Judging by the way his eyebrows furrow, the man is concerned. Probably more for his ridiculously priced stock than for me. I force a weak smile.

'I'm fine. It's nothing, don't worry.'

I join Petunia, who is looking at watches with prices that make my eyes water. All of them are huge, shining brightly under the harsh lights of the cabinets that house them. My stomach gurgles and my head throbs; all I want to do is lie down, go to sleep, anything but deal with the glare of LEDs on glass and gold, the hideous smell of the unnaturally warm air and that strange hum the watches make as they all tick the wrong time, all of them except one lying about how long I've been here, and how long I have left.

'I think this one,' Petunia says, pointing through the glass at one of the gold carbuncles. I swallow before I speak, hoping that might help calm my roiling stomach.

'It's nice,' I say, even though it isn't.

I want to go home.

Petunia, forever a beacon of empathy, rolls her eyes and tuts heavily.

'For goodness' sake, Frances, you could at least try to pretend to be interested. We need to get your husband something nice. Something meaningful. That's why I brought you along.'

That's not why she brought me along and she damn well knows it – she brought me along so she can show me how she's still in control of her son's life, despite him being a married father of one, and how I'm nothing more than a vessel to produce grandchildren for her – but I let it slide. On any other day I might show a bit of fight, but not today. Today, I feel like I've been hit by a train. I lean against the glass cabinet. It feels cool. I try to surreptitiously rest my forehead against it, hoping it might make me feel better, but the fussy man behind the counter clears his throat. I can feel him glaring at me, so I quickly straighten up. I've left a slight smear on the glass. What is wrong with me? Oh my God, what if it's norovirus? That was going around Olivia's nursery a couple of weeks ago. But she's never had any symptoms. Does norovirus spread asymptomatically? Or is this something new—

'Frances!' Petunia is looking pretty furious, so I do my best to focus. I offer her a smile, but it feels like more of a grimace.

'I'm sorry,' I say. 'I'm really not feeling all that well. If I'm honest, I feel quite sick—' As if to prove my point, a wave of nausea hits me, causing me to gag a little. 'Look, I'm going to have to find a bathroom, then I need to go home.'

'But what about Russell's birthday present? I want to make sure we're prepared.'

It takes all I have not to scream that Russ's birthday is not for another two weeks and I know this is yet another one of her power moves designed to remind me who is actually the most important woman in his life.

'Petunia, I'm really sorry, but I can't—' I clap my hand over my mouth. Okay, what did I eat yesterday? Maybe that's it. Better than norovirus. At least that's not contagious.

'For the love of God, why didn't you say anything earlier?'

I want to protest, to say that I did, but as I open my mouth, I feel the heave and before I can stop myself, I've thrown up all over my mother-in-law's shoes.

The room falls silent. Even the watches seem to have stopped ticking.

Petunia looks down at her feet in sheer horror.

I wipe my mouth with the back of my hand and shrug.

It's the little wins, you know?

TWO

It wasn't norovirus.

In fact, it wasn't any illness at all.

As it turns out, 'morning sickness' is a bit of a misnomer. 'All-encompassing vomit hell' would be a much more accurate description, but I doubt the NHS would go for it.

'Mama! Mama! Look what I got!'

I hate to admit it, but I have to force the smile on my face as Olivia charges into the living room, Petunia in tow. I really wish we didn't have to rely on her help, but Russ has to work and there's no way I can keep up with the tiny ball of energy and mischief that is my three-year-old daughter. I shuffle myself until I'm sitting up, acutely aware that I'm still in my dressing gown, to see Olivia holding up yet another stuffie. Chocolate rings her mouth.

'Oh my, who is this?' I say, trying to keep the animosity out of my voice. From the outside, this might look like a doting grandparent indulging their only grandchild, but I know it's really a carefully placed depth-bomb, specifically designed to undermine me after I asked Petunia not to buy Olivia everything she asks for and not to give her chocolate during the week.

What makes it even worse is that Russ was the one who intro-
duced the chocolate rule – he's spent the last couple of years
fitting gastric sleeves and performing bariatric surgery at a
private hospital, so he likes to keep our sugar consumption
down to the minimum. Not that Petunia cares. She's all smiles
and agreement to his face but does whatever the hell she wants
behind his back, safe in the knowledge that whatever she does is
more likely to cause an argument between us rather than end
up with him confronting Mummy Dearest.

'Oh dear.' Petunia wrinkles her nose as she enters the living
room. I feel my blood pressure spike. 'You didn't get much done,
did you? And are you really still in your dressing gown? I
thought that was the plan. I took Livvy out for a few hours to
give you some time to get on with things. Look at the state of it
all. Poor Russell, coming home to this.'

Olivia's bouncing her new toy off my arm, singing a song
about frogs. There's a wild look in her eyes, the one that only
young children on a serious sugar-high have. It takes everything
I've got not to snatch the wretched thing off her and hurl it at
her grandmother.

'I'm not feeling very well—' I start.

'Oh, we're still going with that, are we?' Petunia folds her
thin arms over her bird-brittle chest. It's crossed my mind a few
times that it would only take a quick shove down the stairs to get
her out of our lives, even temporarily, and each time the thought
pops in there, I feel a little less bad about it. 'You do know that
pregnancy isn't an illness, right? I threw up every day when I
was pregnant with Russell and Amanda, but there was no
lazing around for me. I had to suck it up and get on with it.' She
affects a sigh. 'I ask you, Millennials these days. So fragile.'

'Well, my doctor doesn't see it that way. She says I have to
be careful, or I could end up hospitalised, and Russ agrees with
her.' I don't know how I manage to keep my voice so steady. 'I've
been signed off work for a reason.'

'Well, so says you. In my day we just had to put up with it. My poor Russell, being forced to live like this.' She begins to gather up random items and place them in random places, a pantomime of helping me clear up when we both know she's doing the exact opposite. 'And what's this? Takeaway?' I groan inwardly as she fishes out a grease-stained white box from beside one of the chairs. 'What about all the casserole I gave you? You can't be through all of that?'

'Russell fancied a Chinese, and given I'm not able to eat anything like that, he ordered it from The Zen Wok...' I trail off. I don't know why I bother. It's pointless trying to justify anything to someone who is determined to see the worst in you. 'We still have some casserole in the freezer,' I say, neglecting to tell her we still have *all* of it in the freezer as her casserole has always been terrible, and the mere thought of it is enough to make me heave.

'Mama, can I have a 'nana?' Olivia says in a sing-song voice. Before I can remind her what the magic word is, she wanders off towards the fruit bowl, so I just nod. She grins back at me, showing me all of her adorable little baby teeth, and selects the largest one. 'You open it?' She waves it in my direction and begins to make her way back towards me, but before she can reach me, Petunia has already swooped in and snatched it from her.

From the moment that banana leaves Olivia's hand, I see the toddler-rage well in her eyes; in her desire to one-up me again, my mother-in-law has made a grave mistake.

'Here, let Gran do that for you—'

But she can't finish, because Olivia lets out a feral howl, screaming about her 'nana and how Mama has to do it not 'Gwamma'.

To anyone else, this would just be one of those things. Olivia once had a meltdown because I cut her sandwiches into triangles after she'd asked me to do just that, thus confirming that toddlers are both dictator-level unreasonable and don't know what triangles are. But it's okay, because they're toddlers.

To Petunia, however, this is just yet more evidence that I am the worst mother in the world, despite all of this being her doing. She harrumphs and accuses me of coddling, muttering that she must get it from my side of the family as Russell never behaved like that when he was small.

Olivia climbs into my lap. I finish peeling the banana for her and I feel a little thrill when Olivia sniffs and says, 'T'ank you, Mama,' as I hand it back to her.

Petunia purses her lips and folds her arms again, a sure sign that she is on the defensive. She gives the room one last distasteful look and I know she's going to tattle to the rest of the family how I keep her Russell (never Russ, which is what I call him, because that's 'common') and her precious grandchild living in squalor. Sticky with banana, Olivia asks her grandmother if she would like some 'nana too; it's everything Petunia can do not to sneer at her.

'Well, I'm off,' she says. I can hear her clenching her teeth. 'By the way, that lovely rose by your front door is looking half dead. You need to take better care of it.'

And with that, she's gone. No goodbye, no kisses for her granddaughter. At first I'm annoyed at this – she shouldn't punish Olivia because she doesn't like me – but when Olivia asks if she can watch some *Peppa Pig*, I realise she hasn't even noticed.

And that's probably for the best.

THREE

EIGHTEEN WEEKS PREGNANT

I don't like how many people are in my living room. I'm not sure why most of them are here. I find it hard enough to concentrate through the nausea when it's just me and Russ; quite why his parents and sister are here for this I don't know, but I am suspicious, to say the least.

'This is Jasmine,' Russ's sister Amanda says. She's the spit of her mother, tall, thin and full of sharp angles, like she's made of pins. Many consider her beautiful – she was a model in her youth – but I think her severe dark bob and the slash of red lipstick she always wears just make her look cold. She is, however, needle-sharp in the intelligence department, meaning I have to be very careful around her. Nothing – and I mean *nothing* – escapes Amanda's notice.

Next to her, a young woman in her early twenties smiles and says 'hi'. She is physically the complete opposite of Amanda, with ash-blonde hair that tumbles over her shoulders in those beach-waves that all the young women on Instagram seem to have, and her make-up is professional yet subtle. I'm not sure what to make of her, but if she's coming with a Petunia-

shaped stamp on her forehead I'm already making up excuses as
to why I don't want her in my house.

When no one else speaks, I manage to conjure up a 'hi'
back. For some reason, this feels like an intervention rather than
a job interview – a job interview that I'm supposed to be in
charge of, I hasten to add.

'I'm Frankie, I'm Olivia's mother.' I cringe a little inside,
because of course she knows who I am; that's the reason she's
here. 'It's nice to meet you.'

'Um, yes, I... I'm Jasmine.' Her hesitation has nothing to do
with confidence and everything to do with me stating the
bleeding obvious. 'Pleased to meet you.' Jasmine holds out her
hand, ready for me to shake it. This catches me off guard; such
an old-fashioned gesture from such a young woman feels
vaguely wrong, and it's only when I notice everyone is looking
at me funnily that I realise I'm the one being rude.

'So, I take it my sister has told you of our... issues,' Russ says
after I've shaken Jasmine's hand. He looks almost as uncomfortable as I feel, and I still can't work out why he's agreed to this.
Having some help around the house while I'm feeling rough
would definitely be welcome, but a live-in nanny? I'm not so
sure. It might be usual in the kinds of circles Petunia and
Amanda move in, but to me it feels alien, like you're cheating
somehow.

Before Jasmine can say anything, Petunia jumps in.

'Yes, of course we've explained the situation. Jasmine's the
perfect solution. She already has experience working with children and wants to become a child psychologist—'

'Oh, you want to be a child psychologist?' I say, earning me
an eyebrow raise from Petunia, shocked at my sheer nerve in
interrupting her.

'Yes,' Jasmine says, smiling widely. 'I have a first-class
degree in psychology, and my dissertation was on the effect of
extended childcare on children and their relationships with

their caregivers, so this would be the perfect opportunity for me—'

'Indeed, this really is the best solution,' Petunia says, unceremoniously cutting Jasmine off. 'I'm not even sure why there's a discussion about it here.'

'Mum...' Russ says in a low voice.

'What? We've all said it. Frankie can't cope. Jasmine needs a job. We know Jasmine's family, so it's not as if she's going to mess us around. Better than employing God knows who from some terrible agency. I just don't see what all the fuss is about.'

I bristle and shoot Russ a Look, but I don't say anything, because it's pointless. Sadly, they are right. I *am* struggling. And if it gets any worse, I've already been told I might have to stay in hospital, and I don't want that, not one bit. If I end up in hospital, the most likely outcome is Petunia will be looking after Olivia, and I don't need her dripping poison into my daughter's ears twenty-four hours a day. It's bad enough when she takes her out for a short trip – it can take days to re-set the behaviour clock. Plus I don't have the energy to deal with both Petunia and Amanda. When they tag-team, there's no winning; they steam-roller me no matter what I say, pregnant or not. My only hope in this is Russ. When Amanda told him about Jasmine he wasn't that keen, but after he went out for dinner with his family, he suddenly came around. Said his mother was right, and that it was the perfect solution to our issues. At the time I thought it was just Petunia wearing him down, but now Jasmine is sitting in front of me, an unpleasant sense of unease trickles through me.

Jasmine is, to put it bluntly, gorgeous.

She isn't very tall but she is the right kind of curvy, with just a hint of cleavage peeking over her otherwise demure collar-line. Her skin looks soft and dewy and her eyes are a sparkling blue-green, far more striking than my muddy brown. Next to Jasmine, I look and feel like an old heifer, which I realise isn't fair, because it isn't Jasmine's fault that I'm unwell. It isn't Jasmine's fault that I struggled to lose my baby weight. It isn't Jasmine's fault that she's young and beautiful. Hell, all women in their early twenties are beautiful by default, even if they don't realise it. It also isn't Jasmine's fault that Petunia probably invited her to that dinner, getting her hopes up. And it certainly isn't her fault that Russ agreed to this meeting.

'I've already explained the situation completely,' Amanda says. She's sat bolt upright, like she's at a shareholder meeting rather than in her brother and sister-in-law's home. 'She knows about your condition, how they're concerned it could progress to hyperemesis gravidarum if it doesn't ease soon and how the GP has recommended you should rest. She's also aware of the blood pressure spikes you've been having and how you need to keep stress to a minimum. I think it's perfectly reasonable to suggest that this is probably what's best for the family as a whole.' Amanda makes a circle motion with her hands, again like she's in a meeting rather than a domestic setting. 'Obviously we all know Jasmine' – *Except me*, I think to myself. I don't know Jasmine – 'She's Helen's daughter, of course.' I catch a glare from Petunia, as if to say that I have no reason to be concerned; she's known Jasmine all of her life, so there really isn't any need to protest at all. Amanda carries on. 'All of this is basically just a formality to make sure everyone's on the same page, you know? Good.'

Amanda continues to drone on, laying out the facts of our situation and how I'm not coping, as if to say – why am *I* being so bloody difficult? And, yes, I won't lie, she does make a good point. If Jasmine wants to cause trouble, it's not just her job on the line. Lifelong relationships could also be ruined.

Apart from the fact that Petunia is the one who has organised all of this, I have absolutely no reason to feel this hostile towards Jasmine. Maybe I *am* the problem. I've always found it hard to ask for help. My mum always said I was far too independent for my own good. When I moved down South permanently to be with Russ, I pretended it was all fine, even though I was leaving the only real support network I'd ever known behind. And now look at me: sick and being bullied into a decision I'm not sure I'm ready to make. For all they know, my morning sickness could clear up next week – I'm in my second trimester, and it usually tails off during that. I take in deep breaths through my nose and swallow, fighting to focus. Is it me, or is it hot in here? The room is stifling; with so many people in it, the air isn't circulating. A familiar feeling in my chest stirs. My stomach bubbles. My throat constricts.

I'm going to throw up, and there's nothing anyone can do about it.

'Excuse me,' I blurt out and all but hurdle everyone's legs as I make a bid for the downstairs bathroom. I don't make it, but thankfully there is a plastic bucket on the floor of the hallway outside. It's a good job Duplo is so easy to wash.

'Oh dear, is Mama being sick again?'

I glance up from my makeshift sick bucket, willing my stomach to settle enough for me to answer. My father-in-law, Filippo, is standing on the stairs, holding Olivia. He'd offered to go upstairs and watch her while the rest of us 'interviewed Jasmine'. He doesn't have much of a stomach for conflict, and often ducks out of such engagements. Even though this can be irritating, especially when I'm caught between Petunia and, well, *everyone*, I can't help but like Filippo. He's so chill, so charming. I often wonder exactly how he came to marry Petunia – and how the hell he has managed to stay with her for so long.

He ambles downstairs and sets Olivia on the ground. She stomps over to rub my back. She's seen Russ do it so many times over the last couple of months, it's inevitable that she would copy him.

'Dere, dere, Mama,' Olivia says. 'It okay.'

Tears well in my eyes. It's not supposed to be like this. I'm supposed to be preparing Olivia for a new sibling. I'm supposed to be excited. We're supposed to be having fun. Instead, I'm a miserable grouch.

It's not fair.

Filippo fetches me some kitchen towel, and I wipe my mouth and blow my nose.

'Uh oh! Mama sick onna Leggos!'

Olivia points into the bucket, looking cartoonishly horrified.

'Yeah, I'm sorry, Pumpkin. Mama was sick on your Lego. But it's okay – I'll rinse it and we'll pop it in the dishwasher.'

'Oh dear Lord, not *again*. Frances, the bathroom is right there.'

I pick up the bucket and close my eyes, trying to steady myself before turning around to face Petunia. I should have known she'd follow me, and now she's scolding me like I'm a dog who's peed on the carpet one too many times.

'Mum, she can't help it.' Russ pushes past his mother to check on me. A pathetic wave of gratitude breaks over me. At least he's taking my side this time. 'If it is hyperemesis, it's no joke.' A soft hand rests on my shoulder. 'Are you okay?'

'Ridiculous,' Petunia hisses, and stalks back off into the living room.

The gratitude is chased away by a stab of jealousy. Jealous that his life hasn't changed. That he's not the one feeling completely broken, an alien in his own skin. We weren't even planning on having a second child, despite his bloody mother insisting it was cruel not to give her a brother. And yet here I am, my already ruined body going in for another round.

... But I don't say any of this. And not just because I know my marriage is in trouble, and that it has been for a while. If it hadn't been, I'd have stood up to her. But Petunia has this way of worming under my skin, playing my nerves like she's plucking at a harp. I'm not sure if she's causing trouble because she genuinely wanted a grandchild, or she was hoping the arguments having a baby can cause would split us up for good. No, the other reason I keep quiet is that I can see Jasmine standing behind Petunia, her eyes almost comically wide with sympathy, or at least what I think she thinks might be sympathy. To be honest, it looks more like horror.

'I hope you're good with vomit,' is all I can say to her before I trudge off to the bathroom, closing the door behind me.

FOUR

I splash cold water on my face in the hopes it might help me feel more human. It doesn't. My face is still puffy and the network of broken capillaries around my eyes look even more prominent than usual, making me look like I am wearing a delicate lace mask. According to my GP, it's one of the signs they look for when it comes to diagnosing hyperemesis. They call it a 'butterfly mask', because if you squint hard enough, it kind of looks like a large butterfly has landed on your face, spreading its wings over your eyes. In some women it's simply hyperpigmentation, but in my case, it's all down to burst blood vessels because I'm throwing up too much.

Needless to say, I hate it.

After emptying out the Duplo box, I pour a load of disinfectant over the sick-covered bricks and leave them to soak. Then I swish a bit of mouthwash around my mouth and steel myself to face everyone's judgement.

There's a soft tap at the door.

'Honey, are you all right?'

Russ is using his reasonable, soft voice, the one he uses with nervous patients and now his wife, because deep down I think he knows he's the one responsible for all of this. Despite society's obsession with blaming women for unplanned pregnancies, they don't happen without at least *some* male input, after all.

I shake my hair back and re-tie it into a struggle-bun. It's kind of sad. Once upon a time, I'd brush it first. Now, I simply don't care. I have no one left to impress.

'Yeah, I'll be out in a sec,' I say, proud at how bright I sound.

'That's good. Olivia's talking to Jasmine. They seem to be getting on really well.'

My heart sinks.

'You didn't wait for me?'

'Well, it was kind of hard. Jasmine was in the room and Olivia asked who she was, and it seemed a bit stupid to lie to her, so...'

So I get to miss out on witnessing my daughter's first reaction to the woman who is going to be entrusted with her safety? I don't get to see if she's apprehensive, or guarded, or horrified, or whatever? Typical.

A plume of anger rises within me, and I have to take a few good, deep breaths to steady myself before I open the door. Russ stands there, smiling like I've just come round from surgery, and I kind of want to smack him in the face for it.

'You couldn't have waited?' I keep my voice low.

'Frankie... what? Why are you making an issue of this?' He looks genuinely confused, and a little hurt, as if all of this is my fault, that I'm the one in the wrong.

'I thought we were doing this together.'

'We are, aren't we? I took the morning off work to do this.'

'Oh, so, what, I'm now expected to thank you for being so generous with your time?'

'Frankie... what's gotten into you? You're being so unreasonable—'

'*I'm* being unreasonable? I'm not the one who arranged this!'

For a split second Russ's calm facade slips.

'Oh, right, because you were doing so well on your own—'

'No, Russell. Stop it. You don't get to use that against me – your mother does that enough—'

'You keep my mother out of this,' Russ hisses.

'If she'd let me, I'd gladly comply, but given she's the one who's always sticking her oar in—'

'Is everything okay?'

Both Russ and I snap our heads round to find Amanda lounging in the doorway. There's an air of triumph about her, leaving me in no doubt that she's heard every single word of our whispered argument and is looking forward to running off to Mummy Dearest and tattling on me.

'Hey, little sis, yeah, everything's fine,' Russ says, as sunny as can be. 'Frankie's feeling really drained, and I think maybe we should pick this up another day?'

I stare at him, physically forcing my mouth not to gape. Oh no. No, no, no. He's not going to use me as an excuse to escape a difficult situation that he arranged.

'No, it's fine, everyone's here now so we may as well finish this,' I say, with far more bite than I intended. Amanda's eyes widen, then narrow. *Yeah, well, judge away.* 'Everyone's witnessed me throwing up, and given that is the main reason we're in this... situation' – it takes everything I have not to say *mess* – 'I say we just crack on with it, yeah?'

Russ tenses beside me, but I don't care. I have had enough of his family's bullshit, and they're going to play the game by my rules from now on.

Back in the living room, everyone is calm. Petunia is sipping her coffee and Filippo is checking his phone; on the floor, Olivia is sitting in Jasmine's lap while she reads her a story. Some of the fire within me leeches away. Even I can see from this little interaction that Jasmine is a natural with children. Everything from the tone of her voice to the easy way she holds my daughter's tiny body makes it clear that her desire to work with children is a genuine one.

'Mama!' Olivia screeches as I enter the room. 'Is Ja'min and we reads a story!'

I manage a weak smile.

'That's so cool, Livvy. What story is it?'

I already know, because there's only one story Olivia wants read to her right now.

'Is *Froggies' Day Out!*'

'Now, there's a surprise,' Russ says, sounding amused. He slips an arm around my waist. I glance at him; it's as if we were never on the verge of an argument only moments ago. Even after all these years, appearances still very much matter. 'She loves that book.'

'Well, it's a great story, isn't it, Olivia?'

Olivia nods her head vigorously.

'The froggies have fly ice-cream and they have a big pond and all their friends and they dance!' She throws her arms into the air, her eyes shining. She misses smacking Jasmine in the nose by mere millimetres, but Jasmine doesn't seem to mind; she's too busy laughing with Olivia, bouncing her on her knees.

I have to admit, even I find that adorable.

The rest of the makeshift interview goes much more smoothly after that. Sure, it still bothers me that all of this was essentially set up without my involvement, but I can't deny it – Jasmine seems pretty adorable and, more importantly, capable. When things draw to a close, Russ tells Jasmine we'll ring later to let her know of our decision. She leaves with Amanda, who now looks insufferably smug. A short while later Petunia and Filippo also leave. Instantly, the weight of the room lifts, and I feel like I'm able to breathe again.

'Well, Pumpkin – did you like that?' Russ scoops Olivia up into his arms. She whoops with joy, and then giggles as he tickles her. I can't help but smile. This is how it's meant to be. 'Do you want Jasmine to come and stay here to help look after you?'

'Ja'min come over again?' Olivia looks delighted by the prospect.

My smile freezes.

'Uh, I thought we'd discuss that together before asking?'

Russ sets Olivia back down on the ground.

'Why?' he says. 'Olivia's the one she'll be looking after, so her opinion is important.'

'Yes, I know, but maybe we shouldn't get her hopes up before we've had a chance to discuss it.'

'Come on, Frankie. Is there any discussion to be had? You saw her with Olivia. Sure, I agree that she should have a probationary period to ensure she settles in, but I don't think we're going to get anyone better.'

'Maybe, but that's not the point—'

'Darling, I don't understand you sometimes. Is your need to hate my family so strong that you're willing to look a literal gift horse in the mouth?' Russ laughs, as if that might soften the blow of his words.

'I don't hate your family! I just... I wish I had more of a say. I'm going to be seeing her a lot more than you are, and she's going to be living here, with us. Call me paranoid, but I think we need to take some time to consider this properly before we welcome a stranger into our house.'

'She's not a stranger, Frankie. She's Helen's daughter—'

'And I barely know Helen, let alone her daughter!'

'Is Ja'min coming back? Is Mama mad with Ja'min?'

I drop to the sofa, exhausted.

'No, sweetheart, Mama is not mad with Jasmine. She was very nice.'

'She like the froggies. I like the froggies.'

'I know.' I sigh. The momentary clarity I am gifted after an episode of sickness is wearing off, and the fog is returning. 'I just need to talk to Papa about it, that's all.'

Russ sits next to me as Olivia rushes over to her toy box and pulls out her favourite frog plushie, because where other little girls are obsessed with dollies and puppies, my daughter simply adores frogs. She then wanders back over to me and holds the frog up to my face.

'Froggy hugging Mama,' she says.

Tears gather in the corners of my eyes, but I refuse to let them spill. I pantomime hugging Froggy back – even though she has a few, they're *all* called Froggy – and stroke her hair.

Russ puts his arm around me and pulls me closer to him.

'We could do a week's trial,' he says, and kisses the top of my head. 'Just a week. And if you don't like it, we can at least say we tried.'

I nod, exhausted.

A week. I can do a week.

FIVE

Russ is at work when Jasmine arrives. He said he tried to get time off but couldn't because they were swamped and it would mean cancelling surgeries, which he doesn't like doing unless it's a dire emergency, so it's up to me and Olivia to settle her in.

'I don't know how much Russ has told you, but you're at the top of the house,' I say as I climb the stairs, far more slowly than I usually would. By the time I get to the top, I'm fairly puffed and my head is a little swimmy. 'It was designed as an office, but we also use it as a spare bedroom. There's a small en suite up there that you're free to use. It only has a shower, so if you want a bath, you'll have to use the family bathroom downstairs.'

Jasmine follows me up, beaming. She hasn't brought much with her, just a small suitcase. She probably doesn't want to seem over-keen or make any assumptions over how long she's staying here.

'After university accommodation, that sounds like heaven,' she says. Her voice is far more steady than mine as we breach the top of the stairs. I open the door to the space that was once an attic and gesture that she can go in first, but that's more to buy some time for me to catch my breath than out of any form of politeness.

'Oh my God, it's so nice!' Jasmine exclaims. And it is. The room isn't huge, but there's a big dormer window that lets in all the light, and the soft, buttery yellow we've painted the walls means the room feels warm all year round. Russ has moved all of his office stuff downstairs to make room for a small chest of drawers and a wardrobe, and the bed may not be king-sized, but it's plenty big enough for one person. I've even added a few houseplants, because everything is better with houseplants.

Jasmine sets down her little suitcase, her eyes shining as she turns to me.

'Thank you so much, Mrs Minetti,' she says. 'I just love it.'

'It's nothing. And, please, call me Frankie. Mrs Minetti makes me sound like my mother-in-law.'

Jasmine titters at this. I'm not sure if she's just being polite or if she's tactfully acknowledging just how awful Petunia can be. It's not as if she hides it, after all.

We regard each other for a long moment, both of us smiling and nodding, unsure of what to say next. I've never done anything like this before – the closest I've ever been to any kind of live-in situation was when my nan got herself a lodger and that only lasted three weeks because, as it turns out, lodgers and vulnerable old people don't mix, no matter how many reassurances they give you that they're not going to try and sell all your nan's valuables on eBay.

'Anyway,' I say, far too brightly, 'I'll let you settle in. I don't know if Russ has gone over the house rules with you yet' – I wince internally, but it has to be said – 'but we can do that later. I'm also not sure how you want to play meals at the moment. Of course, you're welcome to eat with us, but I understand if that might feel a bit awkward, especially as the evenings will be yours after looking after Olivia all day. But, like I said, we can talk about that later.'

'No, that all sounds perfect,' Jasmine says. 'Umm, thank you for the opportunity to do this. I can't stress how much this will help me in my chosen field. I'm hoping to specialise in the younger end of paediatric psychology, so Olivia's the perfect age for me.'

I'm not quite sure how to take that. Olivia's the perfect age... for what? But I don't make a fuss. I'm sure she simply means that Olivia's age is the age group she's interested in working with, and not that she's going to use her as some kind of personal guinea pig. I just nod and take myself back off downstairs again, peeking in at Olivia as I pass by her bedroom door. She's still fast asleep, napping like an angel. Not for the first time, I'm left wondering why she can't sleep this well at night.

Back in the kitchen, I make myself a cup of ginger tea. I don't particularly like it, but everyone says it's supposed to alleviate the symptoms of morning sickness and I'm desperate. I take a sip, grimace and then wander into the nook, a small back room that we've made into our designated 'messy' room where Olivia can get all her toys out without worrying about people – Petunia specifically – turning up and judging. I try to make myself comfortable, but I feel strangely on edge.

There's a stranger living in my house.

Sure, it might only be for a week, but it doesn't change the way I feel.

We've never had a stranger stay over. Family, of course. Friends, definitely. But we've always drawn the line at friends of friends, and Jasmine isn't even that. I don't even know what she is to us, to be honest. It's funny: had she been a young man seeking work experience with young children to help him become a paediatric psychologist, or nurse, or whatever, we'd probably have asked him if he was out of his mind. But we don't do that with young women. Sure, there are lots of statistics to support why this is the case, but it's still weird.

I glance up at the ceiling, trying to imagine what Jasmine might be doing up there. Unpacking, probably. Or maybe she's sitting on her bed, having similar thoughts to me. She has, after all, just agreed to live in a stranger's house.

Of course, I read her CV. A good crop of GCSEs and top A levels from a small but well-regarded local private girls' school. A first-class psychology degree. She's only just been accepted for her master's in child psychology and she's already talking about maybe stretching to a PhD. In many ways, she has more in common with Russ than I do.

The baby monitor beside me crackles, followed by a small yawn and a declaration of 'Froggy!'. Then the pitter-patter of tiny feet as Olivia gets out of bed. I close my eyes, willing my body to move, but every part of me feels heavy with fatigue. I take in a deep breath to steel myself for the gargantuan challenge of standing up, knowing that this is only going to get worse as my pregnancy develops. I'm not all that big yet – showing, but not waddling, as my GP said. There are more footsteps on the landing, and even though we have a sturdy stair gate, I don't like it when Olivia is upstairs unsupervised. I've imagined her climbing over the gate and tumbling down the stairs one too many times.

I'm halfway up when I hear Olivia say 'Ja'min!', followed by her running. For some reason, my heart thumps and starts to race. By the time I'm at the top of the stairs, I'm red-faced and sweaty, but it has nothing to do with exertion.

The door to Olivia's room is open, and I can hear Olivia chattering away as I approach it. She's sat on Jasmine's lap, telling her about her froggies again. When she spots me in the doorway, she jumps up, her excitement plain.

'Mama, Mama, it Ja'min!' Olivia says, running over to hug my legs. 'Ja'min here!'

'Yes, darling,' I say. 'It is Jasmine.' A strange prickly feeling settles in my chest. At first I think it might be anxiety, but it's more insidious than that.

It's jealousy.

This girl has been in my house for no longer than half an hour, and she's already acting like Olivia's mother. Like *me*. I haven't even given her a proper house tour yet – the plan was to settle her into her room, give her some time to orientate herself, help her log in to the Wi-Fi and then show her around the house. By that time, Olivia would be awake and I would be able to see how they interact from the start, given I'd missed that the other day. And now I've missed it again.

Not that Jasmine realises she's already overstepped her boundaries. She's beaming again, a wide Hollywood smile that shows off her perfectly white, perfectly straight teeth.

'I heard Olivia get up, so I thought I'd save you the journey,' she says. 'But I guess you wouldn't have known that, huh? Routines, hey? They're so hard to break.'

'Yes, they are. You've jumped right into yours, though, haven't you?'

'Well, I just thought I'm here now, so may as well get stuck in. Sorry if I overstepped...'

Her smile falters a little, and it looks like she's genuinely contrite. Olivia looks from me to Jasmine and then back to me again in the most unsubtle way only toddlers can get away with. That's when I realise. I want to be mad at Jasmine. I want her to mess up. And that's not fair. I let out a sigh, my shoulders slumping.

'It's okay,' I say. 'It's just... it's a lot to get used to. My pregnancy with Olivia was fine, and I'd hoped that this one would be too, that I'd be able to do everything myself, but that hasn't happened. And I won't lie, I'm struggling with it a bit.'

'I get it,' Jasmine says. Olivia has run back to her and is currently pulling her by her hand, over to her toy chest, no doubt keen to introduce her to all of her toy friends. 'I can't even imagine how it feels to experience what you're going through. I'm not here to replace you. I'm just here to help. And you're giving me a place to live while paying me, so I thought it best to get stuck in. But if you want me to back off for today, I totally understand.'

'Ja'min, Ja'min, look! Look at my froggies!'

She turns her attention back to Olivia, who is currently cramming frogs into her waiting arms. It looks like whatever misgivings I might have, Olivia has definitely made up her mind. She doesn't share her frogs with just anyone, after all.

'You like your froggies, don't you?' Jasmine says.

'Yeah, I like froggies, I got dis one from Mama and Papa and he's the biggest froggie and then the purple one, he's from the forest, and—'

'Shall I go?' I ask. But Jasmine can't reply. She's too busy being buried in frogs, so I leave them to it.

SIX

I don't go back downstairs. Instead, I lay on my bed listening to Olivia and Jasmine in the next room. There are no tears, no wails of 'Mama!' when she realises I've gone, just her constant chatter and the occasional comment from Jasmine when she's allowed to get a word in edgewise.

I close my eyes, allowing the sunlight that filters in through the blinds to warm me. I have to give her a chance. Whether this is only for a week or ends up being for the rest of my pregnancy, I have to remember that she's here to help, not to replace me. Russ is only agreeing to this because, despite all of our problems, he loves me and wants the best for me and our little family. If anything, this proves how much he cares.

So why do I feel so wary?

I tried not to Dr Google my feelings, but it's hard. The lure of the iPad is strong, and last night, I crumbled. I couldn't sleep and Russ's snoring was driving me to distraction, so I got up, made myself a cup of chamomile tea and did some mindless Mummy surfing.

The thing with having kids is, there is no manual. They literally give you a tiny bundle of helplessness after what is probably the most life-changing thing you can do and basically say, 'Yep, off you go, try to keep it alive!' – and that's it.

You're effectively on your own.

I don't think I slept at all for the first three months of Olivia's life. Every night was spent watching her, leaning over her crib every five minutes to ensure she was breathing. That heart-stopping panic when you don't think you can see their little chests moving is like nothing I've ever experienced. And then there's the feeding. Breastfeeding looks so simple until you actually try to do it. Turns out, babies don't know what they're doing any more than you do, and I lost count of the amount of times I nearly gave up. The excruciating zap of pain that comes with every bad latch (your fault), the worrying about whether you're producing enough milk (your fault), whether your diet is affecting them negatively (your fault), and don't even start on the horrors of navigating things like going out in public... all I can say is Mother Nature really knew what she was doing when she invented oxytocin. It is, as they say, one hell of a drug.

It turns out, it's just as hard dealing with toddlers, and in the end I made a vow. No more Dr Google. People only want to talk about the negative stuff. Remember what the midwife said: no one is going online to share their deepest, darkest secrets because they're happy and having fun. Looking up problems online is as toxic as comparing your life to someone else's Instagram feed – just don't do it.

But that is easier said than done.

Olivia is still chattering away. It sounds like she's set up a frog tea party, which is just about her most favourite thing to do. I can hear Jasmine making yummy sounds as she pretends to eat the toy food Olivia is inevitably forcing on her.

A lump forms in my throat, and a tear escapes the corner of my eye.

I'm not sure if I'm upset I'm not in there, or relieved that this might just work.

. . .

The next thing I know, the light in my bedroom has changed and I'm feeling a little chilly. Momentarily disorientated, I sit up too quickly, which makes my head swim and my belly twinge. I take in a few deep breaths and try to will the sleep-fog away, only for it to be replaced with a bone-deep anxiety.

I fell asleep.

I fell asleep with a *stranger in my house*.

The sickness I'm feeling now has nothing to do with my condition and everything to do with guilt and fear. How could I? Jasmine hasn't been here five minutes yet – anything could have happened. Is Olivia okay? Has she hurt herself? Has Jasmine kidnapped her? Assaulted her? Oh my God, my poor baby girl, I'm literally the worst mother in the world—

A high-pitched squeal of delight breaks through my self-recrimination, followed by a laugh and a cry of 'Found you!' I struggle up off the bed and totter out into the hallway beyond; Olivia is facing the wall with her pudgy hands over her closed eyes, counting. Or, at least, doing her best to count.

'One, twoo, fweee, five—'

'What are you doing, Pumpkin?'

She lowers her hands and glances over at me.

'No, Mama, I counting and then I find Ja'min.'

'You're playing Hide and Seek?'

'Yeah, hide and go peeking.'

'And Jasmine is hiding?'

'Uh-huh. I counts to ten and then I go find her.'

With that, she goes back to her counting.

'One, two, fwee, five—'

'Four,' I say, absent-mindedly.

'I know, I got it right. Five, six, seven, uh...'

'Eight.'

'Ten! Imma coming ready or no!'

And she's off, first running into her bedroom, then into the small back bedroom we use as a store room. There's another delighted squeal followed by 'You found me!' from Jasmine, then even more laughter.

I lean up against the wall, my worry now completely replaced by a guilt so heavy I find myself sliding down to the floor.

This is what I should be doing with Olivia. It should be me, making her laugh like that.

And I used to. Until I fell pregnant, I would roll around on the floor with her, play froggies, throw her up into the air until she was breathless with unbridled toddler joy. It hits me how long it's been since I played with her properly, and how long she's had to make do with entertaining herself. How much I've relied on the TV as a babysitter.

'Are you okay?' Jasmine wanders out of the spare room, her face the very picture of concern.

'Oh, yeah, of course, just felt a bit dizzy, you know? I think I got up a bit too quickly.'

Jasmine's expression changes from concerned to something that might be sympathy, might be condescension. Olivia toddles up behind her, asking why Ja'min stopped playing.

'It's all right, sweetie,' I say. 'You can go back to your game.'

'Is Mama bad tummy 'gain?' It breaks my heart to see my baby girl's expression morph into an exact replica of Jasmine's. 'Poor Mama.' She reaches out with a pudgy hand and strokes my hair. Tears betray me as I try to get a hold on myself.

It shouldn't be like this.

'Shall we make Mama a cup of tea, Olivia?' Jasmine says, her voice deliberately upbeat.

'Yes!' Olivia jumps with her arms stretched above her head, as if making herself taller adds to the emphasis of her words. She's so stinking cute sometimes.

'Thank you for offering,' I say, 'but I haven't even shown

you around the house.' I struggle up to my feet, using the wall as a brace. Jasmine offers me her hand, which I take. 'I'm okay. Just have to take things slowly.' I blow out a long breath and rub at my belly. 'I'm sorry your start has been so chaotic. I didn't mean to fall asleep. I'm just so tired.'

'It's fine,' Jasmine says, her voice low and soothing. 'That's why I'm here. You have nothing to worry about.'

Oh, how I wish that was true.

SEVEN

It doesn't take long to show Jasmine the main areas of the house. Once I've wobbled downstairs, I take her to the kitchen first and show her where everything is. I never switch the cupboards up as Russ doesn't like it. He got quite angry when we first moved in together and I swapped around the cupboard we keep the mugs in and the one we'd reserved for crockery. He said it made coming home from a late shift unnecessarily difficult, and that if I want him to wake me up unnecessarily, then continue mucking around with the 'natural order of things'. I didn't even know there was a supposed natural order of things when it comes to the contents of kitchen cupboards, but as I've said to my friends many a time: Russ is a man who knows what he likes, and likes what he knows.

It didn't escape my notice that he'd set out our kitchen in a rough facsimile of his mother's, but I decided this was definitely one of those 'pick your battles' moments and let it slide.

After the kitchen, I show her the basics, up to and including the garage where the fuse box is. I don't bother with upstairs, mainly because she's already been in all the rooms after playing hide and seek with Olivia, but also because I can't face the stairs again, and instead take her out into the garden.

'Oh my God, it is so lovely out here,' she enthuses. 'You have a greenhouse too? Amazing!'

'Do you like to grow stuff?' I ask.

'Oh, yes, gardening is one of my hobbies. My friends call me Grannycore, say that I'm twenty-three going on seventy, but it's just so relaxing, you know? Planting things out and watching them grow... it feels like the garden is giving you a gift.'

I can't help but smile at this.

'Well, you can take over garden duties if you like. Things are a little bit more overgrown than Russ likes, but I can't handle soil or anything that might be contaminated by cats or other wildlife. I said I could wear gloves, but Russ doesn't want me to risk it, so I'm kind of stuck with pruning the roses and not much else. I like to grow things with Olivia so she has at least an idea of where her food might come from. I wanted to get some chickens, but Russ doesn't like the smell and the mess they bring, so tomatoes and strawberries it is.'

'That sounds awesome,' Jasmine says, beaming. 'I love growing herbs and microgreens myself. So healthy, and the flavour of home-grown herbs is out of this world.' She turns to me, looking a little awkward. 'If you like, I could grow that kind of stuff for you? You know, micro kale and spinach sprouts. It's so healthy. I could make you smoothies in the morning. They might help with your nausea?'

I'm momentarily taken aback by this. She's only supposed to be taking care of Olivia; now she's offering to look after me, too. It might only be a small gesture, but I appreciate the thought.

Maybe this might work after all.

. . .

I draw the line at Jasmine preparing dinner. She offered, but it still feels like she's a guest here, and I tell her as much. But then she points out we're paying her, so she's technically an employee, and anyway, she doesn't mind, she likes cooking almost as much as she likes gardening, leaving me to wonder if she actually has any flaws at all.

While I chop onions, I let her entertain Olivia, who is currently showing her what's inside all of the cupboards. Olivia loves this; I usually keep child locks on all the doors, so she's having a whale of a time pulling everything she can reach out of the larder and handing it to her new best friend.

'Up there is the bikkits. Mama keeps them up on the high shelf.'

'Is that so little froggie-monsters can't get them?'

Olivia giggles as Jasmine tickles her.

'Russ isn't particularly happy about there being biscuits in the house. He's been working with bariatric patients for a couple of years and so while we're not sugar-free, he's not keen. I keep a packet of oaties or digestives in there because we always had biscuits in my house growing up.'

'Shhhh, we don't tell Papa 'cos he's not liking bikkits,' Olivia adds, her face solemn.

'Well, your secret is safe with me,' Jasmine says, and winks at Olivia, who grins and covers her face with her hands.

I continue to chop the onions while Jasmine hovers. I can tell she's feeling as awkward as I am, especially now Olivia has wandered off to watch CBeebies; she hasn't had much screen time today, so I turned the TV on in the nook.

'Do you want me to do anything?' Jasmine asks. I consider saying no, but the smell of cut onions has turned my stomach and a huge wave of nausea crashes over me. It doesn't matter how many times this happens, I don't think I'll ever get used to it. I try to mutter an 'excuse me', but all that comes out is a grunt as I drop the knife and make a dash for the bathroom.

It's amazing how well you can aim when you've had a little practice. No puking all over the bathroom for me, oh no. I'm a straight in the bowl, no splashing kind of girl now. My university self would have been so impressed... although maybe not really, given my university self swore she'd never have 'sprogs'.

Funny how life likes to mock our younger selves, really.

There's a tentative knock on the door.

'Are you all right?' Jasmine says. 'I finished the onions. I noticed the recipe book page. Are you making the pomodoro?'

That was the plan, but now I'm not so sure. I thought it would be easy enough – it's just a simple tomato sauce, not a full lasagne or anything – but it looks like my stomach has other plans. I struggle to stand, little flutters in my belly encouraging me up. I have to admit, this often happens after a bout of sickness, and I'm secretly worried it's some kind of warning, no matter what everyone says. Allegedly, sickness is a sign of a good pregnancy.

Allegedly.

'No, it's okay, I'll be out in a minute.'

'Mrs Minetti... Frankie' – Jasmine catches herself before I can complain – 'it's all right. It really is. I'm here to make your life easier, not pile more onto your plate. Oh, sorry, that was insensitive—'

I can't help but laugh.

'Jasmine... you're fine. You've been great. It's just... I wanted to do this one thing,' I say, my voice catching in my throat. This is another thing I can't get used to, the wild mood swings. Sure, I had them with Olivia, but they were nothing compared to this.

Jasmine cracks the door open.

'Sorry, Frankie, it's just hard to talk through the door, you know? Although given the amount of times I did this in club bathrooms, you'd think I'd be an expert. Not that I do it now, of course. I'm not really one for clubbing—'

'Jasmine?' I say, interrupting her.

'Yes?'

'Stop apologising. And it's okay. I did the same at uni. Did the same for quite a while after uni, too.' I rinse my mouth out one last time. 'You're perfectly entitled to go clubbing if you want to. Hell, you should do. Before you know it, you're thirty-one, four dress sizes bigger because you can't seem to lose weight, unable to do anything because everything in existence makes you feel sick.' I try to smile at her, but even I realise it's more of a grimace.

Jasmine gives me a look I have grown accustomed to: one of pity and resignation.

'Do they know what's causing it?' she asks.

'What, the inability to lose weight, or the sickness?'

'The sickness, of course. And you shouldn't be worried about losing weight. You look fine to me.'

So says the girl who looks like she could model swimsuits.

'Nope,' I say. 'I'm just one of the lucky ones. They say it's something to do with hormones, and it might run in families.'

'Oh no. Does anyone in your family have it? Have you asked your mum?'

Her question blindsides me. It doesn't matter how long ago it happened, and I don't think I'm ready to share anything about my parents with her. Not right now.

'Um, no. No, I don't think she did.'

As if sensing my unease, Jasmine frowns but changes the subject.

'Okay, so, if you let me take over making dinner, you can have a lie down. Although it is really early. Do you usually start making dinner this early?'

I can't help but chuckle at that. 'I never used to, but considering dinner prep can now take anything from half an hour to three hours, I like to give myself a lot of leeway. That's why I was making pomodoro: it's easy for Russ to throw in a pan when he gets home. I do all the prep work and if I've had a bad one, he cooks it up. Between you and me, I think he prefers it that way. His dad taught him how to make it "the proper way" and, no matter how hard I try, I just can't get Filippo's recipe to work.'

'Oh, same. I mean, Amanda's Italian food is amazing, but Filippo's is on another level.'

'Have you been out to Nonna's in Tuscany?'

Jasmine's previously sunny disposition momentarily clouds over.

'No... it's not something that's come up. I mean, I've heard about Nonna's cooking, but... anyway, what about Olivia? What does she have?'

I could say something. About her and Helen not being invited to Nonna's. All the family get invited to Nonna's. Except Amanda's. Because while we all know Amanda and Helen are a couple, Russ's family still pretend they're just best friends who happen to live together and that Jasmine isn't basically another granddaughter. I suppose ignoring them is marginally better than outright hostility? But even so, I let it drop.

'Olivia'll have pasta with us. We like to try and include her when we eat. It's important that she eats the same things as us.'

'That's a good mindset to have,' Jasmine says. 'So many children have issues with food these days, mainly because they're fed nothing but mass-produced stuff from an early age. Not that I'm judging anyone, of course – you have to do what you have to do – but when it comes down to it everyone prefers chips, so it's best to get them eating broccoli first, if you get my meaning.'

I do. My mum had a similar philosophy.

It's a shame she never got to meet her grandchildren.

Damn. Why did she have to bring my mum up? Now all I want to do is cry.

In the end, Jasmine finishes up the meal prep, asking when Russ is due home. Today is a day shift, so he should be back by six. He usually texts me if he's going to be late and I haven't heard from him, so fingers crossed. Jasmine then says she'll start cooking at six, and won't listen to any of my feeble protests.

'Olivia can help, can't you?' she says.

'Help with what?' Olivia says.

'Making Mama and Papa some dinner.'

'Yay, dinner!' Olivia scoops up one of her many froggies and does a lap round the nook with him held high, like he's flying. But her pudgy little legs can't keep up with her determination, and before I can warn her, or even begin to think about catching her, she trips, pitching herself face forward onto her wooden toy chest.

There's a moment of utter silence while we all try to make sense of what just happened.

Then Olivia lets out an ear-splitting screech, and both Jasmine and I leap into action.

Jasmine gets there first.

A surge of maternal protection has me pushing her away. She looks shocked, but thankfully shuffles back.

I cradle Olivia in my lap. To my utter horror, her beautiful little face is a mask of blood. The world caves in, and my head feels like someone has just plunged it into a fishbowl. Olivia's still screaming, but it seems muffled somehow. She wriggles in my lap as I try to take in the source of all that blood. A cut, just above her right eye, gapes at me.

My baby is hurt. My baby. My—

'Frankie? Frankie!'

I snap around to find Jasmine kneeling behind me, looking concerned.

'Shall I call an ambulance?'

I look back to my daughter. Her cries have settled into a thin whine as she clutches at me, smearing me with bloody little handprints.

'Frankie? Shall I call an ambulance?'

I give myself a little shake. Have to focus. Think. What would Russ do?

'No,' I say. 'It's just a cut. They won't send an ambulance for a cut. Plus, it'll be quicker if I take her.' I make to stand up, but Olivia tries to climb my body, afraid I'll put her down. I let out an audible wince as something twinges deep within my belly.

'A-are you all right?' Jasmine says. She now looks legitimately scared.

'Yeah,' I say, a little breathlessly. 'Just help me—'

She reaches out to try and untangle Olivia from me, but my daughter is having none of it. She screeches '*Mama, Mama, Mama,*' over and over until I have to beg her to be quiet. Finally, I manage to use the sofa to help haul myself to my feet, my back protesting every painful inch, until I'm breathing hard.

All the while, Jasmine watches me owlishly. Once I'm up, she reaches for my elbow, as if that'll do anything.

'Right, I'll get her in the car. You go to the—' I stop and wince as another pain stabs through me.

'You can't drive,' Jasmine says. 'I'll have to.'

'No, the insurance—'

'Sod the insurance!' Jasmine says. 'It's either that, or we take my car, but I don't know what the exact rules on child seats are—'

'I think we're okay if it's a short journey. Honey, Pumpkin, can you let Mama stand up? Please, not so tight, honey, you're hurting me—' I try to pull Olivia's arms from round my neck, but she's like a small, sticky python constricting tighter the more I try to loosen her. Between the panic and the coppery smell of blood I'm feeling nauseous again. No. Not now. Please. Just let me—

It's no use. I can't put Olivia down, so I bolt for the kitchen sink. Thankfully I haven't had much to eat, and so most of it is tea and bile. I rinse the sink and take a gulp of water straight from the tap, then wipe my mouth with the back of my hand.

'Okay, I'm okay.' I'm panting. I can't help it. 'Let's get going.'

Jasmine is now silent. She scuttles ahead of me, opening doors and making sure the way is clear for us. I can't see if Olivia's cut has stopped bleeding as she won't let me look at it, so all I can do is tell Jasmine where my handbag is, and to use the keys inside to lock up. Then we all pile into Jasmine's Kia, with her driving and Olivia and me sitting in the back.

The journey is a blur. Thankfully the hospital isn't too far away. I hold in a wince as another bolt of pain lances through me.

'Are you all right?' This seems to be the only thing Jasmine can say.

'Just focus on the road,' I reply, taking in deep breaths to try and keep my own nerves as steady as I can.

Finally, I see the sign for Accident and Emergency. Jasmine indicates, and pulls into the correct lane. There's a flurry of beeps as she cuts up the guy who is already there. Her eyes, already wild, widen even further as she mouths 'sorry' to him.

'I'll drop you off at the entrance and then find a place to park,' she says, her voice thick. I can't help but feel for her.

Welcome to your trial period, kiddo.

EIGHT

After all the panic of getting here, we're now trapped in the paediatric waiting room. The triage nurse took a quick look at Olivia's head and said it wasn't anything to worry about, won't even need stitches, probably just some Steri-Strips.

'Head wounds always bleed an alarming amount,' she'd said with a reassuring smile, like I don't already know that but panicked anyway. 'Are you okay?'

I'd tried to give her a reassuring smile of my own, but that's when Jasmine had jumped in, saying I'd been in pain too, and now they want to check me out as well, 'just to make sure'.

I never realised how much 'just to make sure' would feature in my life after I fell pregnant. Before you have kids, there's a definite air of 'what will be will be' to your life; let the chips fall where they may, let the dice roll. But the minute that second little line turns blue? Hello, caution, my new friend.

In the panic, I forgot my phone. Jasmine has hers, but it's out of charge. She was on three per cent and it died on her as she was ringing Russ for me. This means he has no idea we're here. He's going to be so confused when he gets home. All the blood and puke and mess. I hope he doesn't think Jasmine has tried to abduct or murder us.

I told her she can go home if she wants to. Like, proper home, not ours. I haven't asked her if she still wants to work with us. I think it might be a bit too early for that particular conversation, although I wouldn't blame her if she didn't. I'd wager not many first days at work start with a panicky trip to A&E, but here we are. To her credit, she hasn't immediately turned tail and run. Instead, she sits next to me, ramrod straight.

'You really don't have to stay,' I say for the umpteenth time. 'There's nothing you can do.'

'I just want to make sure you're both okay,' she replies, again.

And we're back to an unsettled silence.

'Is this the hospital Russ works at?' she asks.

'No. He's private these days. And anyway, even if he was here, I wouldn't disturb him. It's not like he can dash out or anything.' I let out a long sigh. 'It's going to be fun, explaining all of this to him.'

'You said he usually gets back around six, didn't you? It's gone half five now. Do... do you want me to nip back and wait for him? I mean, I don't want to leave you here on your own, but I can't stop thinking about him coming in and thinking the worst, you know?'

Yeah. I know. It's crossed my mind a few times, too.

'That's a good idea,' I say. 'You can tell him where we are, too.'

'Yeah. That's what I thought. I'll text you when... oh.'

I can't help but offer her a wry smile as she realises I don't have my phone on me.

'How did we survive before mobile phones?' I say, trying to force a little levity to my voice and failing miserably.

She offers me a nervous smile and scuttles away.

Poor kid.

. . .

It's only after Jasmine leaves that I realise I'm now totally stranded. No phone, no wallet, no keys. Day one and everything's already gone to pot. Good work, Frankie.

Olivia is dozing on my chest. The triage nurse told me to try and keep her awake just in case she has a concussion, but you try to keep a sleepy three-year-old up when all they want to do is nap. It's this or a meltdown; I don't think either is helpful if you have a potential concussion. I glance down at the top of her head. Her usually fluffy hair is crusty with blood, and I can see the edges of the cut have started to scab over.

I really need the toilet.

Thankfully, I haven't had any belly twinges since arriving, so I'm hoping that was just a stress reaction. I rub at my bump, hoping the spike in adrenaline didn't upset Sprout too much. Despite the pressure from my bladder, my eyes grow gritty, then heavy. Maybe if I just close my eyes—

'There you are!'

I come to with a start, jolting Olivia awake. She immediately starts whining. There's a good moment when I have absolutely no idea where I am.

'Hello, darling.' A weight lifts as someone peels Olivia off me. My first instinct is to grab her back until reality comes into focus and I realise it's Russ, with Jasmine hovering behind him.

'Oh my God, you're here,' I say. My eyes brim, and I'm unable to stop a sob from escaping. Russ shifts Olivia to his hip, allowing me to bury my face into his armpit.

'What on earth happened?' he asks. 'Jasmine said Olivia tripped in the nook and hit her head on the edge of her toy box.'

'There was blood everywhere—' I say.

'—and you panicked,' Russ says, a little more flatly than I'd like.

I lean away from him, just a little bit.

'As I said, it was a lot of blood.'

'Head wounds like to bleed,' he says.

'The nurse said something similar.'

'Well, as long as you're both all right. Have you been seen?'

'Triaged, yes, but we haven't seen the doctor yet. He said she might need stitches—'

Okay, so the nurse didn't say that exactly, but I still want the doctor to look over her. If anything, the risk of concussion scares me more than the cut does. What if she takes a nosedive overnight? The thought of waking up to find her motionless and cold in bed is too much to bear...

Russ leans back from Olivia. She makes a snuffling sound and tries to hug him closer again.

'No, Livvy, let Papa have a look...'

I know he's doing his job. Not just as a father, but also a doctor. He did his time in A&E. He knows how frantic it can all be. I just wish he was a little... gentler when it came to such things. That he wouldn't look at problems like they were an engine in need of fixing.

'Hmm... it looks pretty clean. Not that deep. A couple of Steri-Strips should do it. Once I've cleaned it out, she'll be fine.'

'But, potential concussion—'

Russ laughs. He actually *laughs*.

'Darling, it's okay. Yes, she hit her head, but the cut is largely superficial. I'll be honest with you, I'm surprised they didn't tell you to just clean it and go home.'

'Well, it was a lot worse earlier—'

Russ leans over and kisses the top of my head.

'Oh, love, you do like to overreact, don't you? Come on. I'll go and have a word at reception, say we're leaving. I would say you could do with a glass of wine, but that's not happening, so how about we order in?'

'But I'd started to prepare dinner—'

'That's nothing to worry about. Sling it in the fridge, we'll have it tomorrow. I feel like Thai.' He turns to Jasmine. 'Do you like Thai food?'

Her eyes flicker from Russ to me and back again. She's wrapped her arms around herself, like that's the only way she can hold herself together. For a moment I wonder if she's going to say no and flee. I mean, I wouldn't blame her. That's exactly what I'd do. Instead, she looks back to me again and smiles. It's not a warm smile, but it's not cold either. It seems... brittle, maybe a little forced. But, then again, after the day we've had, maybe that's only to be expected.

'Yeah. I like Thai,' she says. 'But only if you're sure.'

'What do you mean by that?' Russ says, his voice rich with fake concern. 'After all my wife has put you through, I think buying you dinner is the least we can do.'

'Uh, thank you, but Frankie didn't put me through anything—'

'It's okay,' I say, quietly. 'I'm glad you were there to help.' Of course, had she not been there, Olivia wouldn't have been running around the nook, so you could say it's actually her fault. But I'm not keeping score.

I'm not that petty.

'Great,' Russ says, and before either of us can reply, he strides over to reception, still carrying Olivia. He's in full 'confident doctor' mode and the nurses here seem to be falling hard for it. Not that I blame them. Russ embodies everything a doctor should be. He's suave and sophisticated, his Italian heritage lending him his dark good looks and his private schooling allowing him to feel at home in near enough any given situation. Compared to him, I'm a mouse. Or a shrew.

I still have no idea why he married me, especially since our life together has settled into a rut; a rut that sometimes metastasizes into pointless arguments about how I 'used to be fun'.

But I don't have time to ponder that now. One of the nurses – an older, no-nonsense edition that has probably been dealing with doctoral overconfidence most of her career – is clearly telling him that we should stay and be seen. Russ leans in a little closer and glances back to me, leaving me in no doubt that he's explaining how he'd been at work and that I'd panicked; she's pregnant, you see, and a little loopy at the moment, poor thing, it's not that big of a deal and it's okay, because he has the expertise, if anything changes he'll bring her back straight away, Scout's honour.

And it works. Because it always does.

NINE

It's dark when we drive home. Jasmine is sat in the back of Russ's car with Olivia, but there are no delighted smiles or games of I spy, just silence as Olivia dozes and Jasmine stares out of the window, probably trying to work out a way to say 'thanks but no thanks' to the continuation of her contract.

Once we arrive home, I don't go into the nook. I don't know if the amount of blood in my mind's eye is a construction of my imagination or actual reality, but at the moment, I can't face it. Instead, I run Olivia a bath. She's currently downstairs looking like an extra off *The Walking Dead*, but does otherwise seem perfectly fine. Russ has cleaned her cut and stuck two Steri-Strips over it, telling her that 'Mama was just being silly, it's okay', before rubbing his nose against hers, making her giggle.

I say nothing. It isn't worth it.

Once I get back downstairs I head to the living room and sit heavily on the couch. Olivia is watching TV, snacking on a pile of rice crackers and cut up grapes. She's going to need a proper meal, too, plus the bath – oh hell, the bath! My feet and back are killing me and my head is pounding. I wonder if I could ask

Russ to take over the bath before I flood the house, skip the food and go straight to bed—

'Okay, love, what do you want?' Russ asks. 'Nothing too spicy, obviously—'

'Just a simple pad thai,' I say. I don't have the energy to peruse the menu for anything more exciting.

'You sure?'

'Yes. A small one. I'm not that hungry.'

'Frankie, you have to eat. I know you don't always feel like it, but the obstetrician was clear. If you want to avoid hospitalisation, you need to keep hydrated and you need to eat. And galangal in Thai food is probably as good for nausea as ginger is, so this is practically medicine if you think about it.'

That's a lot of words to say 'I like getting my own way,' but I'm too tired to argue with him so I just nod. If I'm honest, a small portion of chips would probably do me; simple, carb heavy and comforting, with the best ones coming from a grease-trap chippy round the back of a council estate.

'Right, so that's pad thai with tofu for Jasmine, and I don't know... I'd love some satay, but it is high in fat, so I think I'm going to go with the green curry; they do a fantastic job usually...' He wanders out of the living room, tapping at his phone as he goes. I look over to Jasmine, who is perched on the edge of the chair.

'It's okay. You don't have to stay,' I say. 'Are you all right?'

She nods a little too quickly.

'I'm fine. Just... feel like I've been thrown in at the deep end, you know?'

'Yeah, I know. If it's any consolation, none of it was planned. It never is with kids.'

Jasmine laughs at that.

'That is very true.'

'I mean it. If you want to go home you can, we won't judge

you, and I totally understand if you want to back out of your trial—'

'Oh, I think Jasmine has more than passed her trial,' Russ says, as he re-enters the room. 'She handled today like a champ. If you want it, the job is most definitely yours.'

Jasmine looks a little gobsmacked.

I glare at Russ.

'Excuse us for two seconds,' I say as I struggle up off the sofa.

Russ contrives to look as innocent as possible as I all but drag him into the kitchen.

'What was that about?' I ask.

'What?' he replies. He has that wide-eyed, I'm-just-an-innocent-little-boy look that his mother falls for every time, but I know his game.

'Don't pretend you don't know.'

'I literally don't even—'

'Telling Jasmine she's got the job! First you let her meet Olivia when I'm out of the room, then you agree to the trial without discussing it with me first, and now you've told her she's got the job without completing the trial period!' I don't know when or where the tears came from, but they're rolling down my cheeks by the time I've finished. Russ gives me a weary smile and pulls me closer to him; I try to fight it but I'm too tired; too sick; too *everything*.

'Come on, honey, come here. I hate seeing you like this. I wish I could be at home to help you, to take the load off your shoulders, but I can't. I can't be everywhere all at once. I have to work otherwise we'll end up in all kinds of trouble, and with a new baby...' He sighs and kisses the top of my head. Once I would have felt a tingle down my spine, but now it hardly registers. 'That's why I wanted Jasmine to start as soon as possible. Why I want her here now. Not for me – for you. Look at today.

Imagine having to deal with that all on your own—' He stops mid-sentence. 'Did you put the heating on?'

I raise my head from his chest, and sure enough, I can hear the boiler ticking over.

'Oh shit,' I whisper. 'The bath. I was running a bath for Olivia.'

'Oh hell.' Russ releases me and all but gallops out of the kitchen. I can hear his feet thumping on the stairs, followed by the boiler cutting off as he turns off the taps. A few minutes later, he comes back down. To anyone else, he might look quite calm, but I'm not anyone else. I'm his wife, and I know from the way his brows are drawn that I've just fucked up on a colossal scale.

'Is it all right?' I ask.

'It had only started to overflow. Shouldn't affect the ceiling downstairs, but it's pretty wet. I'll just go and get a mop. You go and sit down.'

'I can—'

'It's fine, Frankie. I'll deal with it.'

'Um, is everything okay?' Jasmine has popped her head out of the living room. She's looking concerned again. I think I've lost count of how many times she's asked me this question today.

'Everything is fine, Jasmine,' Russ says before I can get a word in edgewise. 'These things happen.'

I stare at the floor like a chastened child. These things do indeed happen. Just not all in the same day.

In the end, Olivia gets her bath. Russ puts her to bed while Jasmine and I share stilted small talk until our food arrives. I gamely eat as much as I can to show Russ that I really do appreciate him, but he still huffs when I can only manage half my portion. We opt to watch a movie rather than sit in silence. Russ asks Jasmine what she'd like to watch, but I think she's too rattled to choose. After what is probably the second most awkward dinner I've ever had, I brace myself for what I have to do next.

One way or another, this has to be sorted out. I need to know if she's staying or not.

But before I can muster up the courage, Jasmine is already smiling and saying thank you for the lovely dinner, but she'd better be going to bed.

It takes me a moment to process that she means the bed in our house, not that she's leaving.

'That's fine,' Russ says, smoothly. 'Sleep well.'

'Uh, yeah, um, if you need anything in the night—'

'I'm sure I'll be fine,' Jasmine says, and offers us both a little smile.

We wait until she's on the second set of stairs before saying anything.

'She's exactly what we need,' Russ says. 'She could have run, but she didn't.'

'She could have,' I say.

'This could be really good for us. For Olivia.'

'I know.'

'I think we've made the right choice.'

I glance at him as he says this. His words seem to include me, but his tone is distant, his attention fixed on the living room door. A worm of doubt squirms in my chest. He's right. Jasmine is exactly what we need.

So why does this feel so wrong?

TEN

No matter how hard I try, I don't think I'll ever get used to the feeling of someone else living in my house. And then I feel bad, because even I can't deny that the next couple of weeks go by surprisingly well.

After that disastrous first day, it was kind of like the Gods of Parenting took pity on me and decided that I'd been tested enough – for now, at least – and everything else has been pretty much smooth sailing. Jasmine is good with Olivia. She's taken up the slack with regards to encouraging Olivia to learn her letters, and they've planted up a special 'Mama's Smoothies' bed in the greenhouse, filled with spinach, kale, radish and watercress, along with pots of tomatoes, peppers and sunflowers. It is, dare I say, incredibly wholesome and more than I could ever have hoped for.

Unfortunately, with the smooth also comes the rough, and the knock at the door I've just heard is probably the roughest, turning up unannounced for the third time this week.

'Hi, Petunia,' I say, and force myself to smile.

Petunia does not extend the same courtesy.

'This rose is looking ropey,' she says, plucking at the leaves. 'So where is my little granddaughter?'

'Olivia's in the garden, and I've been watering the rose every day.'

'Hmm. You obviously aren't pruning it right.' And with that, she marches straight past me and through the house.

You might think that she'd soften, even if it was just a teensy bit, after everything we've been through. But no; if anything, Petunia is even worse. It's like she's decided that now we have Jasmine, she doesn't need to interact with me anymore. If it was up to her, I have no doubt I'd be out on my ear with Jasmine as my permanent replacement.

I take in a deep breath, hold it to the count of five, then let it out slowly. I haven't been feeling too bad the last couple of days – as it turns out, not having to run around after an energetic three-year-old while you feel like utter crap does wonders for your general well-being – and I'm not about to let my mother-in-law undo all that good work. All I have to do is offer her a coffee, then sit quietly and let her talk to Jasmine. *Keeping her sweet keeps you sane. Don't forget that.*

By the time I'm in the kitchen, the kettle is already on. Petunia refuses to drink instant coffee, so I pull the French press out. I read somewhere that French press coffee might not be good for you, so I offer it to her as often as I can.

'I hope you're not drinking coffee.'

Close your eyes and count to ten...

'No, Petunia, it's not for me. I was getting it out for you.'

Petunia sniffs. 'Why would you do that? Jasmine was going to make a lovely pot of tea.'

'Tea? But you don't drink tea—'

'Excuse me? Of course I drink tea. Just not the tea that you make with those wretched bags. Jasmine's making a proper pot. With leaves.' She folds her arms smugly over her chest, making the array of wooden bangles she is wearing clank like handcuffs.

I smile as sweetly as I can.

'Well, that's nice of her.' I can't help but wonder where these leaves are coming from, given I don't think I've ever bought loose leaf tea in my life. In fact, I don't even think we have a teapot.

'Gwamma! *Gwamma!* Come look!'

Saved by the bell. Or, at least, my daughter.

'It's all right, darling, Gramma is coming!'

She scuttles off, an overgrown spider in designer clothes.

Once Petunia is with Olivia, Jasmine comes back into the kitchen. She's carrying a pretty teapot glazed with grey and blue swirls. She sets it down and reaches for a tin I hadn't noticed before, opens it and spoons out three teaspoons.

'Uh, where did you find that?' I say, trying not to sound accusatory.

'Oh, they're mine. It's okay, I don't mind sharing.'

She fills the teapot up with steaming water, pops the lid on and covers it with a tea-towel.

'Do you want a cup?'

'No, it's okay. I have my ginger tea. The milk in regular tea makes me feel sick.'

I reach into the cupboard above the kettle, searching for my favourite mug. It was Olivia's first Mother's Day present to me. That's why it has olives on it, for Olivia.

It isn't there.

I frown. It went in the dishwasher last night, and I only drink water first thing otherwise I'm in puke-city for the rest of the morning, so where is it?

Jasmine is pouring milk into two mugs.

One of them is mine.

I know it's just a mug. How is she supposed to know it's my favourite? Except we have a whole kaleidoscope of mugs to choose from, a veritable smorgasbord of everything from cheap bucket mugs to fine bone china, and she has to choose mine.

I could ask for it back. Explain that no one else gets to drink out of it.

But I don't. Even in my rising rage, I realise that would make me seem unhinged. Instead I grit my teeth, make my ginger tea and try to decide if I want to go outside with them to be polite or saunter off to the living room to stew by myself.

In the end, being polite wins.

It's really nice out. After the weeks of rain we've had, the late-spring sunshine is a real treat. Every plant in the garden is starting to bud, accompanied by the soft drone of bees as they scout out each one, waiting for the flowers to unfurl just enough to let them in.

'Do I have to say it again?'

It's not so much the words that snap me out of my reverie, but more Petunia's tone. It's the one she reserves for those she deems 'subservient': supermarket workers, refuse collectors, cleaners – you know, all the 'lesser' people she thinks are there to do her bidding rather than actually make the world go round.

Oh, and me. She reserves it for me, too.

I take a fortifying sip of my tea and force myself to look up with a smile.

'Sorry, I was watching the bees,' I say, as sunnily as I can manage. 'It's nice to see them out and about again. Always have liked bees.'

Petunia looks at me as if I've grown an extra head, and then blabbers on again.

'I was asking what time your appointment is tomorrow. For the scan?'

'It's at eleven twenty.'

'Hmm. Did Russell have to take time off for it?'

'Well, yeah, he wants to be there.'

Petunia purses her lips. I can tell that she's struggling with the desire to berate me for ruining his career and to spout how wonderful her son is for doing basic Dad stuff.

'Thankfully Jasmine is here to watch Olivia. Otherwise we would have had to take her with us, and you know what it's like—'

'Wouldn't be the case if you'd gone private,' Petunia sniffs.

'NHS is fine for me,' I say. I'll never forget Russ telling me how much the public health sector has to deal with botched private medical care. Of course, that was before he moved into private care himself. He's changed his tune a little bit recently. 'Plus, the private maternity hospital is a good forty miles away. I don't want to be in labour and still have to drive nearly an hour to be seen. St Catherine's is just down the road, and that makes me feel a bit more secure, knowing that if anything goes wrong, I'll be there in ten minutes, fifteen tops.'

'So, no home birth this time?'

'No. I did ask, but the obstetrician said I'm considered high risk given the emergency C-section with Olivia and the complications I'm having this time round. They said it was safer to come in, and that's fine.'

'Well, now that Jasmine's here, everything should be easier.' She gives Jasmine the kind of smile she should be giving me. The kind of smile I'd secretly love her to give me. Not because I like her, but just... I wish we could be *normal* about all of this.

I had hoped she might have a change of heart when I fell pregnant the first time, but if anything, things soured even more. *Digging her claws in* was the phrase I overheard her say to Amanda once. *Stupid little trollop* was another one. I blame myself, in a way. I should have stood my ground more at the very beginning. Not been quite so ready to appease. Maybe then Russ and I wouldn't have split up. Hell, maybe he wouldn't have had the affair.

She accused me of lying when it all came out, telling people I was making things up to hurt her boy. Then, when I provided actual proof that he was sleeping with that nurse, she switched to how it was all my fault because I obviously wasn't treating him right and he wouldn't need to stray if I was a good girlfriend.

In the immediate aftermath Russ tried to make things right, but I couldn't fight those accusations. I was too young, too tired, too sensitive, so I walked away. And for a couple of years, I really did try to move on. By the time Russ came back into my life, I was older, but, I soon discovered, not much wiser, because when he offered an olive branch, I ended up taking it. He promised his past mistakes were a one-time thing, never to be repeated, then I fell pregnant... and that, as they say, was that. And don't misunderstand me – it was the best thing that could have happened as it gave us Olivia – but I think in Petunia's eyes, I'd locked her son in. Bewitched him into going back. Tricked him into settling. Then there was everything else on top of that: my parents' deaths, the inquest, the shame, my brother moving away... My throat constricts, and I give myself a little shake. Not going to think about that. It's all in the past now.

Focus on the future.

You never know, once Sprout is born, I might be able to convince Russ to move. I'm thinking New Zealand might be nice. Might be able to patch things up with Mike as a bonus. Sure, he's in Australia, but it's still closer than here.

'Anyway,' Petunia continues, oblivious to my turmoil, 'let's go and get some shoes on, eh?'

Olivia throws her arms into the air and shouts 'yay!', then runs into the house, Jasmine following her.

'What's going on?' I say.

'I'm taking Olivia and Jasmine out for afternoon tea.'

'Uh, you are? When did you arrange that?'

'Last night.' She can't help but be smug. 'I thought Russell might have told you.'

'No,' I say. 'He didn't.'

'Oh, well, that's not great, is it? I asked him for Jasmine's number so I could text her to arrange a nice little afternoon out. Of course, it's been lovely to take Olivia out, just the two of us, but she's not the greatest of conversationalists. By the way, you might want to take her to a speech therapist at some point if her speech impediment doesn't improve.'

'What speech impediment?' My hackles, already risen, now bristle wildly.

'Surely you've noticed she can't say her Rs properly? Calling me "Gwamma"?' She visibly shudders, and I've never wanted to hit anyone more than I do her in this moment.

'She's three,' I say through gritted teeth.

'Precisely. She should be growing out of the baby talk by now. Wouldn't stand my Russell or Amanda speaking like babies at her age. Not that I had that issue with either of them.' She catches me glaring at her. 'Now don't look at me like that, I'm just trying to help. For goodness' sake, so sensitive—'

Before I can even think of a comeback, Olivia charges back towards me.

'I gots my shoes!' she pants, delighted. 'I dood them myself!'

'Well, that's nice,' Petunia says. 'And you *did* them yourself, not dood.'

Olivia's small face scrunches up in confusion and looks at me, as if seeking an answer, but to my shame, I don't have one.

'Well done putting your own shoes on, Pumpkin,' I say. 'And they're on the right feet too!'

'Ja'min helped!'

Behind her, Jasmine shrugs and smiles. For a fleeting moment she seems to look a little smug.

'Right, if we're ready, we'll be off.' Petunia stands, clutching her handbag like she's worried I'm going to steal something from it. 'You can relax now. I'm so glad you have Jasmine here – the house looks so much better since she arrived.'

'Well, I haven't done much with regards to the house,' Jasmine says. At least she has the decency to look a little bit embarrassed. 'Just picked up some toys and helped with the dishwasher.'

'Oh, I'm sure you've done much more than that, petal.' Petunia's voice is silky-smooth, the same one she uses with her own children. 'The house hasn't looked this nice, since, well, they moved in.' She gives Olivia an indulgent smile. 'Say bye bye to Mama, darling.'

Olivia runs over and wraps her arms around my neck.

'Bye bye, Mama.'

A lump rises in my throat.

'Bye bye, Pumpkin. Have a lovely time.'

'We is goan to have cake!'

'That sounds lovely. See you later.'

With that, she releases me and runs into the house. Petunia says nothing more.

Jasmine, however, looks back and shoots me a long look as she leaves.

ELEVEN

'Well, I don't know what you expected from her.' Russ takes a sip of wine. He's picked up a nice dry Pinot Grigio, and judging by the condensation rolling down the outside of the glass, it's been chilled to perfection.

I could really do with a nice glass of wine. But I can't. I only have water, or that awful ginger tea.

The things we do for the ones we love.

'I don't know, just not... that.'

'But I don't see a problem, love. They took Olivia out so you could rest. That's the whole point of this. You can't do it all by yourself, so we outsourced it. What are you saying, you don't want that?'

'No, I'm not—' I let out a sigh. 'That's not it. I'm grateful for the help. I really am. It's just... it would have been nice to have been asked. Your mother has never asked me and Olivia out for afternoon tea, but Jasmine's been here for a couple of weeks and now suddenly it's all the rage.'

'Well, if you wanted to go out for afternoon tea with Mum, why didn't you just ask her?' He takes another swallow from his glass, treating himself to a moment to savour it.

I don't answer that. It's not that I can't. It's just that my mum taught me if you can't say anything nice, don't say anything at all.

It's a shame no one taught Petunia that.

'What you have to remember is that while Jasmine is a stranger to you, she isn't to Mum. She's known Jasmine since she was a kid. I only saw her a couple of times growing up, but what with Amanda and Helen being so close, it was inevitable that Mum would get to know her, too. In a way, she's like a bonus granddaughter, I suppose.'

It's interesting that even after all these years, his family still insist on calling Helen and Amanda 'friends'. I hardly know Helen – she's nothing more than a name to me, if I'm honest – but even I know that she and Amanda have been inseparable since Helen's divorce. Some even say Amanda was the reason for that divorce. But nope, according to Russ's family, they're just best gal pals, looking out for each other. Roommates, if you like. Who share a bed and go on holiday together.

'Huh. Doesn't that make Jasmine your niece, or something?'

I can't quite describe the look he gives me at that: all at once disgusted and... worried? No, *hunted*. He shakes it quickly, leaving me wondering if I ever saw it at all.

'Oh no, she turned up way after my time at home. She was a teenager when Amanda and Helen moved in together. To be honest, I don't think I ever exchanged more than a handful of words with her before I went out for that meal with her and Mum and Papa. I'll admit, that's why I was so... cagey about this whole arrangement before.'

'But then you went out for a meal with her and realised she's no longer an awkward teenager, but rather an absolutely stunning young woman?'

I know I shouldn't, but I can't help it. I'm struggling enough with my body, and next to Jasmine I feel like such a frump.

'No! Of course not. I can't even believe you'd go there.

Darling, I lost you once due to my own stupid behaviour. I'm hardly going to risk it again, am I?'

I study my hands and offer him a little one-armed shrug.

'Look, I know you're not feeling great. But there's no need for this, either. It's just not fair on me, or on Jasmine.'

'That's easy for you to say. You're hardly ever here. Your mother just turns up as and when she wishes. And not to see Olivia. No, to see how Jasmine is getting on. It's... weird—'

'Frankie...' There's a tinge of warning to his voice. I know I'm treading on very thin ice, but I can't help myself. I have to get this out, or I'm going to explode.

'It's like... it's like she wants to replace me. She's treating Jasmine more like a daughter-in-law than she ever did me. And I know, she's practically family these days, but this feels... I don't know... malicious. Like she's trying to prove that Jasmine's better at this than I am. And the sad thing is, she's probably right.' I can see he wants to say something, to interrupt me, but I'm now on a roll. 'Yesterday afternoon, Olivia fell over in the garden. Nothing major, just a scrape. Usually she would come running to me, but this time, she went straight to Jasmine. Not her Mama. It's like I've become totally redundant in my own family. First it's my job, then my role as a mother... what next? I feel like I'm... disappearing.' Russ just stares at me as I can't help but spill my guts at him. 'I feel like I'm just a walking womb with no other purpose but to sit and incubate. I can't do anything I actually enjoy because I want to throw up within five minutes of starting. I thought my pregnancy would be nice this time. That having someone to help might free up some time for me to stop stressing and actually start enjoying things again. But instead, I feel worse. I feel... invisible. Like I could vanish and no one would notice—'

'Okay, Frankie, take a breath.' He grips my upper arms, as if he feels the need to physically hold me together. 'Why didn't you tell me this before?'

I tried to, I think to myself. *But you don't like me talking about your mother and how she's spent the last four years making sure I know damn well that she is the only mother in the Minetti family that counts.*

'Because... because it's hard.' My voice hitches. I take in a deep steadying breath, but before I can get myself back under control, Russ has jumped in.

'Of course it's hard. And you have it harder than most.'

I'm not sure I agree with that; it's not like I'm a single mum on benefits living in an eighth-floor flat with no working lift, but I keep the observation to myself.

'The thing is,' Russ continues, oblivious in the way only certain men who feel the need to *fix* rather than *listen* can be, 'your body has gone through huge changes. People think a second pregnancy means broken ground' – I can't help but blink at this, because his phrasing infuriates me – 'but it isn't like that. Each one is different. Unfortunately, you've drawn one of the short straws this time round. But it's not forever. We have the scan tomorrow. Twenty weeks and...'

'Three days,' I whisper.

'Exactly. Twenty weeks and three days. We're halfway through.' *Excuse me?* We're *halfway through?* 'And you never know, the sickness might stop next week. It could stop tomorrow. Not everyone suffers from hyperemesis for the entire gestational period. I know you've overrun the first trimester by a few weeks, but that's not unheard of. I'd argue it's pretty common among women who have morning sickness.' He sets his glass down and pulls me into his arms. 'It will be all right. I promise.'

I could say that I didn't think doctors were supposed to make promises, but I don't. Instead I try to focus on him being physically here for me, because it's becoming a rarity these days. I allow myself to relax and sink into his arms. He has nice arms. Even though he's now over forty, he's always looked after himself. He could easily pass for a younger man. I allow him to nestle my head against his chest and he kisses the top of my head.

'You're not invisible,' he murmurs into my hair. 'Nor is anyone trying to take over your life. We're just doing the best we can in this situation. Remember; this too shall pass.'

I nod as he strokes my face. This is... nice. It's the closest I've felt to him in a while now. Usually he just watches TV and I take myself off to bed. But now... it feels like it used to. That little spark. Maybe it hasn't gone out. Maybe it was just hiding after all.

He rubs at the back of my neck. I lean into it. His lips follow, and a delicious shiver, one I haven't felt in ages, runs through me. I tilt my head, so I can kiss him, then try to swing myself around so I can straddle his lap, but fail miserably. Russ laughs at this.

'I guess that move is another thing that is temporarily off the table, huh?' He has a little glint in his eye, one that I know well. It's been so long since I last saw it. 'You are still beautiful, you know?' he breathes, and then kisses me deeply.

For a moment, I worry that Olivia or, God forbid, Jasmine might appear in the doorway. I think about suggesting we go upstairs, but then I worry that might shatter the moment. I tug at his belt buckle as he runs his hands up my back, over my shoulders, to cup my breasts. In this moment, it feels like those first few giddy years, snatching every opportunity we could to love one another, before the years piled up and my life became his life and his, mine—

My stomach gurgles.

Oh no. You're not going to pull this one on me.

I try to take in a surreptitious breath in the hope of quelling the all-too-familiar churning sensation in my belly, of stopping that awful rising feeling that makes my chest hurt and my throat constrict—

'Are you all right?'

I'm getting really fed up of being asked that.

'Yeah,' I say, as brightly as I can manage. 'It's been a while.'

'It has, hasn't it? I'm thinking over the back of the sofa. If anyone catches us, I'll just say you needed a back rub.'

I nod, not because I'm desperate to be bent over the back of the sofa, but more because I'm worried that if I open my mouth, I might not be able to control what comes out of it.

Russ waggles his eyebrows at me in mock-salaciousness and jumps up from the sofa. I swear, he's worse than any teenage boy. Then he takes my hand and goes to pull me up off the sofa. The moment I stand, my head swims.

Another deep breath, this time through my nose.

I'm not going to ruin this. This needs to happen. To prove that I'm not invisible; that I'm still desirable despite everything...

My gorge rises, and there's nothing I can do about it but mutter 'sorry' and run for the bathroom.

All I can focus on is the sigh Russ gives as I depart.

TWELVE

By the time I come out of the bathroom, Russ has turned the TV on and most of the bottle of wine has been drunk. Even though I can't have a drink anyway, it still feels a little like a slap in the face.

I try to say sorry, but he tells me not to worry about it. It's been weeks – no, make that months – since we've shared any kind of intimacy. I really thought we might succeed tonight. Even though he's trying to project an air of calm understanding, I can tell he's frustrated, in more ways than one.

His phone buzzes, and he chuckles at it.

'Who is that?'

'Oh, just Toby. Arranging his stag and everything.'

'His stag? So he really is going to marry that girl? How old is she again?'

He shoots me a look I can only describe as 'warning'.

'Twenty-two.'

I can't help but pull a face of my own. Toby is an old medical school friend of Russ's. He's also forty-two, old enough to be her father. And she'll be his fourth wife.

None of his former wives have managed to reach thirty

before Toby trades them in for a new model. All I can hope is
that she has a cast iron prenup.

'So where is he going this time?' Russ has been on all of
Toby's stags. One was before he met me, and one was when we
weren't together. The other one was just after we met – a week
in Prague. Back then, Facebook was still all the rage and let's
just say I didn't speak to Russ for a good fortnight after he came
back. I'm not too naive to have thought that lap dances wouldn't
be on the menu. But I don't care what his mates said, what he
was doing in that club with that woman wasn't like any kind of
lap dance I've ever heard of.

'Oh, yes! Knock out. Dubai.' Russ looks ecstatic.

'Pardon? *Dubai?*'

'Yeah, his dad's paying; how monster is that?'

Ugh. I really hate how he regresses into Private Schoolboy
Speak whenever he's with 'the boys'. If I was a betting woman,
I'd put a hundred quid on red trousers being part of the stag
uniform at some point.

'He never has learned to stand on his own two feet, has he?'

'Frankie, I don't know what it is you have against old Trotters. He's a top bloke.'

'His father is a lord.'

'And? Something to aspire to, I'd say.'

I stare at him for a moment, then give in. He will forever be
his mother's son.

'Sure. So when is this magical money-pit stag taking place?'

For some reason, Russ looks a bit shifty, telling me immediately that I'm not going to like the answer.

'Now, before you say anything, it's only a weekend, not a
whole week. We'll fly out on Friday, be back Sunday, maybe
early doors Monday—'

'When is it, Russ?'

'And I only have to pay for the flights, the actual stag itself is
being paid for—'

'Russ...'

He blows out a sigh.

'Late September.'

I blink a few times and make the 'I'm not sure I heard you correctly' face.

'Excuse me?'

'Late September. The wedding is in late October, so it might be early October, you know, if we can't book anything decent or—'

'Late September?'

'Yeah.'

'When our baby is due on September the thirteenth?'

'Yeah, I know, but—'

'And' – I raise my voice, ever so slightly – 'I went overdue with Olivia by ten days, so there's a good chance history may repeat itself, meaning our baby could very well be putting in an appearance in late September.'

'Yes, but—'

I hold up a hand to indicate that I'm not finished.

'You do realise that after I've had the baby, on time or late or whatever, if I end up having another C-section, or even if I don't, I'll be caring for a very new newborn and a toddler on my own while you go to *Dubai* on a stag weekend with your posh mates, paid for by a member of the House of Lords? And you don't see an issue with that?'

'I mean, okay, sure, but it would be the same if I was at work, you know—'

'It really, really wouldn't be.'

'Oh, come on, Frankie – it's Dubai! Once in a lifetime and all that. We've already had to say no to going to Tuscany to visit Nonna this August. And it's just a weekend. I'm sure my mum will pitch in—'

'Oh God, no, don't you dare, no, I am not having that.'

'See? There you go again! I come up with solutions, where

you just want to see the problems. There are ways around this. All newborns do is sleep and cry and shit. It's not as if he's going to remember that his Papa wasn't around for seventy-two hours...'

By the time he trails off, I'm gaping at him. So this is how he views fatherhood? An inconvenience? No, worse than that – boredom. And the problem is, if I put my foot down and say no, he's going to make my life hell. He already hates that I 'won't let him out' in the evenings. I know that Sprout was an accident, but even so...

He snorts and fixes his attention on the TV.

'All I'm saying is I don't see the issue. Mum's there. She'll look after Olivia for you. If your mum was still around she could stay here, help you out, but she's not.'

My heart quickens painfully. How dare he? How dare he use my dead mother as an excuse? But before I can gather myself, he's back at stabbing the TV remote, flicking through the channels like they might provide him with a solution.

'I can't believe you'd say something like that—' I manage to squeak out, but he cuts me off again.

'Darling, I know it's hard. I'm just being practical. This really is a once-in-a-lifetime opportunity—'

'Until Toby inevitably divorces this one and has another stag, of course.'

His expression darkens.

'You really are just determined to see the worst in people, aren't you?'

'No, I'm not. And even if I was, this isn't about me, it's about our baby's birth.'

'Look, darling, I'd never miss that. I'd cancel the stag do in a moment if you were going into labour. But those first couple of weeks... nothing happens. Look, I'll talk to Trotters. See if he can go the beginning of October. It's just a weekend. I'm sure we'll be able to work something out.'

And with that, Russ goes back to watching the TV, leaving me to sit with my disappointed rage and an awful sinking feeling that he's going to do everything in his power to get his own way.

Like mother like son, I guess.

THIRTEEN

I'm sure we'll be able to work something out. The clarion call of the selfish bastard.

The stairs feel particularly steep this evening, and by the time I reach the top I feel like I might have altitude sickness. I had been thinking about taking a bath, but now all I want to do is crawl beneath my covers and sleep.

I know he didn't mean it. To bring up my mum like that. And yes, it would be easier if she was still around. Much easier. But she isn't. And neither is my dad. None of my family are. The ones I have left all live up North, and over the years we've drifted apart, gone from living in each other's pockets, to going on family vacations, to only seeing them at Christmas, to sending birthday cards, to a name on a Facebook page I abandoned five years ago. It's not Russ's fault that he doesn't understand how sensitive I am to it all, even years later, but I do wish he'd sometimes try, just a little bit.

Before I head to our bedroom, I poke my head around Olivia's door. Now she has her Big Girl Bed she looks particularly tiny and even more doll-like. I tiptoe over to her and take a long moment, just gazing at her. She's laying on her side with her thumb half in her mouth, one of her froggies firmly clamped under one arm. Petunia says we should try to discourage her from sucking her thumb, that it's a filthy habit and we need to nip it in the bud. I reach out to smooth down her silky, slightly sweaty curls. I trace my fingertips around the curve of her skull, still able to see the tiny baby she once was not so long ago. An unexpected lump forms in my throat, one that has nothing to do with my sickness or how careless my stupid husband can be with my feelings sometimes, and everything to do with overwhelming wonder and fear and how we could have created something so beautiful and so fierce yet so, so fragile.

Olivia stirs in her sleep, muttering something under her breath. She smiles and jams her thumb firmly back into her mouth.

I hope whatever she is dreaming about is as wonderful as she is.

I tiptoe back out before I wake her up. She might be fast asleep now, but she's still only three, meaning I'm still up at night with her sometimes. At least that's something Jasmine and Petunia haven't robbed me of. It's still my job to do the night shift, the difficult shift, but also the loveliest shift, where I get to sit in my feeding chair, wrapped in a blanket, cooing at my baby as she dozes against my chest.

It takes me a while to undress. Every movement makes my head spin and my throat twist, the ever-present nausea determined to weigh me down. I open the walk-in closet and dump my clothes into the laundry hamper, pointedly ignoring the dresses that lurk there; dresses I love but can no longer fit into. I was hoping to be able to wear them at some point in the near future, but instead fell pregnant again, making my body pile yet more baby weight onto my already bloated frame. It takes everything I have to trudge into our en suite and brush my teeth with a special soft brush and enamel-saving toothpaste. Once upon a time, I had a great skincare routine: cleanse, tone, moisturise, three different serums plus gel eyepatches; now I use a face wipe to get the worst of the day off my face, smear on the only moisturiser that doesn't make me break out, then trudge back and collapse into bed.

But despite being exhausted, I'm still curiously wired.

There's a creak from above my head, a constant reminder that Jasmine's there, in my safe space. Someone I don't really know, not yet, but who's still managed to squirm her way into the very bosom of my family. When they came home from their afternoon tea, Olivia didn't run to me. Usually it's the first thing she does, to tell me what she's been up to. But today she came in, hand in hand with Jasmine, chattering about how fast Froggy went down the slide at the park and how yummy the cake was; completely absorbed in her own little world. One that, it seems, doesn't feature me.

The swelling sensation in my chest is back, but this time it has nothing to do with illness nor wonder, and everything to do with jealousy. It's hard to admit, even within the confines of my own mind. I keep reminding myself that this is normal. Of course Olivia is a little bit obsessed with Jasmine. She's new and exciting, a Disney princess made real, literally there for her entertainment.

I shift around, trying to find a comfortable position. This is something they don't really tell you – that it's almost impossible to get comfortable at bedtime, especially if you're usually a stomach sleeper, like me. But finally I begin to drift off, finding that lovely floaty space that occurs between sleep and wakefulness.

It doesn't last long.

I hear the soft creak of feet on the stairs. That usually doesn't rouse me, as Russ comes to bed later than me so often these days. No, what wakes me is that they're coming from the wrong place. The wrong stairs.

Jasmine's stairs.

I'm instantly alert. What is she doing? Her room has its own en suite, and she has a kettle and a microwave if she gets thirsty or peckish. It's like a little hotel room in our house. She's not on the clock – this is her own time, and so for her to be wandering the house doesn't feel right.

Then I hear voices.

They aren't loud. No more than a murmur. I sit up and strain my hearing, but I can't make out any actual words. Then there's a laugh. A light, tinkling, female laugh, followed by a deeper voice.

Russ.

My heart jolts. What are they talking about? Russ must have been on his way up to bed, and they just happened to meet on the landing. That must be it, nothing but a coincidence. I hardly think they'd arrange an illicit tryst a few metres away from my bedroom door. Nothing to worry about. Everything's fine. Right?

The soft-talk continues, and my patience thins.

I extricate myself from my nest of pillows and struggle up. When I open the door, sure enough, there's Russ and Jasmine at the top of the stairs, talking. Russ is smiling. Jasmine is wearing a tiny pair of pyjama shorts and a spaghetti-strapped pyjama top, her long blonde hair piled up into a messy bun. She doesn't have a scrap of make-up on her, and she looks absolutely radiant for it.

A plume of unease ripples through me.

'Is everything all right?'

I'm amazed at how reasonable I sound. Light, almost. Like I haven't just caught my scantily clad, very attractive live-in nanny chatting to my husband at the top of my stairs, just outside my bedroom door.

They both whip their heads in my direction.

Jasmine smiles at me, narrowing her eyes and tilting her

head a little, leaving me with the distinct feeling that she is challenging me somehow.

'Oh, Frankie!' she says. I can't help but notice the undercurrent of breathlessness. 'I'm so sorry if I woke you. I left my charger in the kitchen and didn't realise until my phone started complaining, so I was going down to get it.'

Sounds plausible. But her cheery tone doesn't carry to her eyes, leaving me to wonder if it's all a lie.

I shift my attention to Russ. He grins, unbalancing me. Surely he realises how this might come across? How this isn't okay? There's something going on here, something I find unnerving, from Jasmine's easy coldness to his seeming delight at bumping into someone who lives under our roof.

'It's okay... a happy coincidence,' Russ says. 'Just making my way up to bed. Goodnight, Jasmine.'

She turns her smile towards Russ. I can't help but notice the way she tilts her chin, narrows her eyes just enough, the slight lift of her eyebrows. I don't think she's even realised she's doing it, but I can see it. Is she flirting? The way she's standing, the way she giggles – is she trying to gain my husband's attention? If she is, judging from the way he's fixated on her, it's working.

She bids us both goodnight, then saunters past Russ, just close enough to allow her arm to brush against his.

I don't say anything until we get into our bedroom.

'What was all that about?' I hiss.

Russ has the gall to look confused.

'What was what about?'

'Uh, I don't know, just our nanny in her underwear making puppy eyes at you.'

Russ's confusion is replaced by something I think he thinks might be sympathy, but is actually stuck on 'condescending bastard'.

'Oh Frankie,' he says. 'It's hardly the middle of the night, and pyjamas aren't underwear. It's like she said: she forgot her charger. We've all done it. Totally innocent.' He stretches his arm out and worms it under my shoulders, forcing me to cuddle up against him. 'This isn't about Jasmine, is it? This is about Dubai. Honestly, you don't have to worry. It'll be totally above board. You're not allowed to drink or do anything unseemly there. It's a very strict country.'

I lay there, stunned. Is he that oblivious that he thinks I'm still upset about that blasted stag weekend? I mean, I am, but that's not what *this* is about, in this moment. I glance up at him, but his eyes are already closed, a wistful smile twisting the corners of his mouth.

'No,' I say, a little colder than I intended. 'It's not about Dubai.'

He opens one eye and peers down at me.

'It's not? Oh, fab. Does that mean I can—'

'No, Russ, it doesn't. That's another matter entirely.'

'Then what's wrong? You... you don't think...' He turns his head, towards our bedroom door. 'Oh Frankie, don't be silly. You have nothing to worry about. Nothing at all.'

I don't reply. Instead, I listen to his heart beating steadily in his chest. Either he's telling the truth or he's a stone-cold psychopath. But like a bad tooth, I can't help but prod him.

'Russ, how well do you really know Jasmine?'

He doesn't answer me immediately, but his heart remains steady. But, then again, he's a surgeon. He's the king of remaining cool and collected under pressure.

'I mean, I know who she is, of course. And I know her mother well enough; she's probably the closest thing I'll ever have to a sister-in-law, after all. As for Jasmine, I saw her at family gatherings and the like. Since she's been at uni she's not really been around much. If I'm honest, I'd kind of forgotten about her. Sure, I'd put her name in the Christmas card, but apart from that, I didn't really pay that much attention to her.'

'And now?'

'And now what?'

'What about now? She's... older now.'

He withdraws his arm and sits up, forcing me away from him.

'I'm not sure I like what you're implying, Frankie.'

'And what do you think I'm implying?'

He rubs at his face.

'I knew it. I knew you were lying about being okay with it. You're never going to forgive me, are you?'

No.

'No, Russ, it's not like that—'

'Then what is it like? If you were worried, why didn't you say something?'

'I did! But you made the decision to hire her *without me*, and then you waived the week's trial *without me*, and then—'

'For fuck's sake,' he mutters into his hands. 'I did that for you. Because I am fed up of coming home and finding you in a state—'

'Oh, so I'm a state now, am I? I'm sorry I'm not perfect. I'm sorry we had to cancel the surgery, that your baby is making me ill and I can't cater to your every whim—'

'That is totally unfair,' Russ snaps. 'And not what I meant, and you know it. I'm sorry you don't feel well. I'm sorry I found someone to help you. And I'm sorry I'm trying to make the best of what is, let's be honest, a shitty situation.' He jumps up out of bed, clutching one of his pillows to his chest. 'I'm going to sleep in the spare room.'

'Russ—'

'No, Frankie, I'm not going through this now. You're not thinking straight. You're tired, you're sick and you're looking for problems where there aren't any. Get some sleep.'

And with that, he stalks out of the room.

I sit there, clutching my own pillow. I'm not going to cry. I'm not, because I'm not wrong. Although maybe I'm not entirely right, either. Maybe I did make some mountains out of molehills this time. Is that what I did?

I lay back, allowing the tears that collect in the corners of my eyes to roll down my cheeks. It wasn't like this last time I was pregnant. Last time was a fairy tale. We found out, we told everyone, I glowed, we celebrated. It was all about as close to perfect as it could get. We went to the NCT classes. He massaged my feet. Sure, Olivia was ten days overdue and ended up as an emergency C-section, but the actual pregnancy was textbook.

But then I didn't lose the baby weight. The dark circles around my eyes became a permanent feature. All those expensive dresses Russ bought me... none of them fit now. No wonder he's looking at Jasmine. She must remind him of me, before I had Olivia. Young. Slim. Beautiful.

The complete opposite of what I am now.

I don't even know who I am anymore. I look in the mirror and a haggard stranger stares back.

I think about getting up. Going to see him. Not to apologise, but to... I don't know. Even now, I don't feel I did anything wrong.

This is the problem with trust. It's broken once, and no matter how many years ago it happened, or what life changes you make afterwards, there's always that little worm of doubt.

Will he do it again?

I found out by total accident. About the affair, that is. That's why we split up. We'd been together for five years at that point. It was serious. We were talking about getting engaged. I was twenty-three, he was thirty-three.

She was nineteen.

I'm still glad we got over it. Glad that we managed to work it out.

Although... am I? If Russ had stayed away, my parents would still be alive. But I can't think like that. It wasn't his fault.

My dad decided to drink and drive. It wasn't the first time he did it, either. Sure, this time it was because he heard me and Russ got back together... but that's not Russ's fault.

Maybe this isn't Russ's fault, either.

God, I'm tired.

Maybe everything will be better in the morning.

Clean slate and all that.

FOURTEEN

TWENTY WEEKS AND THREE DAYS
PREGNANT

'Good morning, Frances. And how are we today?'

The midwife is a short Black woman. She is wearing over-sized glasses and has an oversized smile to match. She oozes the warm confidence of someone who has been doing this job for years, and despite Russ asking if there was an obstetrician around, I'm glad we have her for this appointment.

'I'm fine,' I say. 'And you can call me Frankie.'

'Frankie it is, then. And you can call me Elsie. So you're here for your twenty-week scan?'

'Yes,' Russ says, before I can. 'And before you can ask, things haven't been fine. Frankie's still really sick. Throwing up multiple times a day, totally exhausted. We had to employ a nanny to take care of our daughter.'

'I see.' Elsie scrolls through my case notes. 'Yes, it's been noted. Potential hyperemesis. You've been signed off work.'

'She has,' Russ says.

'Frankie?'

'Yes, I have been. I was finding it impossible to do anything.'

'And now you have a nanny?'

'Yes, we do,' Russ says. 'She's a family friend.'

'Well, that must be nice, being able to entrust your daughter's care to someone you know.'

'I'd never met her before,' I say.

The midwife shares a look with me before exchanging one with Russ.

'She's my sister's partner's daughter. My family have known her for years.'

'But not Frankie's?'

The urge to tell her that my parents are dead and my brother lives abroad raises its monstrous head, but I manage to force it back down.

'My family aren't local.'

'I see.' She goes back to my notes. 'I can see here that you've been monitored quite closely and that while your sickness isn't ideal, you're not in the danger zone so you've avoided hospitalisation. That's good.' She smiles at me again, and I smile back, grateful for her warmth after a chilly morning with Russ. 'So what we will do today is check your blood pressure and do a urine sample. Did you bring one, or do you need to go and do one now?'

I dip into my handbag and wave a specimen jar at her.

'All done.'

She beams.

'Ahh, A plus, lovey, I do like it when my mummies come prepared. I'll just go and do the dippy thing to make sure everything's okay, then it's on to your blood pressure, and then the sonographer. Is this okay?'

I nod. Russ does too, but I can tell it's only out of politeness.

A few awkward minutes tick by as she sorts out my sample. This part is always a bit fraught. What if they find something? I won't lie, I live in fear of pre-eclampsia or gestational diabetes or—

'Right.' The midwife comes back to us. 'Things don't look too bad. You're a bit more dehydrated than I'm comfortable with, but it's not enough to admit you. Still, you'll want to keep an eye on your fluid intake, okay? I know it's hard when you have extreme morning sickness, but if you can't keep those fluid levels up, then I'm afraid we'll be getting you in to help rehydrate you.' She must have seen my look of horror, because she pats my arm in a reassuring manner. 'Don't worry, we'll just pop you on a drip for a bit. You're not in any real danger, but we do need to monitor you. Hyperemesis is no joke, so I think we'll have to get you in soon to assess that.'

'What, today?' I say.

'Oh, love, no, not today. We'll give you a testing kit and ask you to test your urine every day for a week and then take it from there.'

'I can do that,' Russ says. 'I'm a doctor.'

'That's nice for you,' Elsie says, offering him a smile that tells me all I need to know about her opinion of doctors in general. 'But it's important we keep on top of this. Your proteins are a little high,' she continues, ignoring the glare Russ is giving her. 'But, like your dehydration levels, nothing to be concerned about. Just another thing to keep an eye on.'

'Protein? That's pre-eclampsia, isn't it?'

She's back to patting my arm. 'It can be, but not at your levels. It's more likely down to your hyperemesis than anything else. I'm going to book you in for a blood test, too, just in case. Now it's blood pressure time.'

She wraps the cuff around my arm and starts to squeeze the little ball to inflate it. I don't know why, but I really hate this part, that painful feeling of constriction, the way I can feel my pulse beat in my hand. She spends a good long time letting the air out, which in turn makes my anxiety spike. What has she found? Oh my God, this can't be good. Protein and high blood pressure? Shit, it's pre-eclampsia, isn't it? I knew it. I just bloody well knew it.

'Okay, you're a little low, but that can happen around this time.'

'Low?' I wasn't expecting that.

'Again, possibly linked to dehydration, but it's a common thing a lot of pregnant mummies have.'

'Your circulatory system is changing to compensate for the growing foetus,' Russ says.

'Thank you, Dr Daddy. Yes, that's exactly it.' She gives Russ a long-suffering smile, and I have to squash my desire to smirk down deep. 'Anyway, that might also explain why you're so tired all the time.'

'What can I do to help it?'

'Getting your fluid intake up will help.'

Great. That's the one thing I can't really do.

'Well, that's me done,' Elsie says. 'I'll just go and check to see if the sonographer's ready for you now. If you just want to wait outside for a bit, I'll be back soon.'

My heart jolts. This is it. The real reason we are here.

When I had my twenty-week scan with Olivia, I was surprised at how stressful it was. The moment you realise they're not scanning your baby so you can see how wonderful they are, but rather the medical staff are looking for abnormalities, your perspective shifts.

And, I am discovering, it doesn't get any easier the second time around.

Russ squeezes my hand. We've agreed that we're not going to ask the sex of the baby this time. I didn't want to for Olivia, but Russ argued that we couldn't plan if we didn't know. I thought that was a ridiculous thing to worry about, but he always has struggled with control issues. He likes to be 'on top of everything', as he puts it. But this time, I argued that we had everything we needed for this baby, so there's really nothing to plan. If Sprout is a boy, who cares if we haven't got a blue Babygro to put him in? Caring about such things is just not on my list of priorities. Russ had pouted a little, but in the end, relented. He got his way last time. Now it's my way. It's only fair.

'Mrs Minetti?' A young woman in blue scrubs clutching a clipboard smiles at me.

'Yes,' I say, gathering up my bag.

'Excellent. We're ready for you now.'

'So... what, do I just stay out here?' Russ asks.

The sonographer looks confused.

'No, you are more than welcome to come too. In fact, we encourage it—'

'It's only, you didn't mention me.'

I glance at him coldly.

Flustered, the sonographer apologises, and had I been feeling any better, I would have told her not to worry.

The sonographer's suite is always a little intimidating. The room is dimly lit, and the machine they use is much bigger than the little doppler ultrasound they use at regular check-ups. I guess it's because they need more power to find the anomalies.

Please don't let there be any anomalies.

'Right, you make yourself comfortable... that's right, lift your top. I'm just going to tuck some paper around you so I don't smear gel all over your clothes.' The sonographer speaks quietly, soothingly. She then presses a few buttons on the screen next to her, settles herself on her chair and warns me the gel might be a bit cold.

The sensation of her pressing down on my swollen tummy feels curiously wrong. Not painful, just... wrong. We spend so much of our pregnancies being told to be careful not to put pressure on the bump that having someone do this feels out of place.

'Right, so here we go...' She drags the wand across my belly. 'Here we have a spine... and a little head...' She moves the wand again, and any discomfort I had been experiencing simply evaporates.

Because there's Sprout.

They're really real.

I look over to Russ and smile, but he doesn't notice. He's captivated by the screen, drinking in all the details of our baby.

Our little life.

'Okay, just going to ask you to shift onto your left a bit... yep, that's good, stay there.'

She continues to move the wand around, digging it in under my ribs. Not that she notices; her attention is on the screen.

She's frowning.

A pit opens in my chest.

'Is everything all right?'

The sonographer turns her attention back to me.

'Yes, it's fine, it's just babies often don't get the message and lie in weird positions, making it hard to see everything. Your little one is lying so I can't quite get a good look at their heart... I'm ninety-five per cent certain everything is absolutely fine, but I just want to make sure.'

Ninety-five per cent? That's not good. That's not perfect. That's not—

'Ah, there we go. Lovely.' She smiles at me. 'It's as I thought, everything's fine.'

The pit crashes closed, and tears spring to my eyes.

'I'm so sorry, I just—'

'It's fine,' she says in that soothing way, and hands me a tissue. 'I think everyone does it. The relief. I know it can be stressful.'

I take the tissue and smile gratefully. Just as I blow my nose, she asks, 'Do you want to know what you're having?'

I go to shake my head, but before I can find my voice again, Russ pipes up.

'Yes.'

I whip my head in his direction, momentarily stunned.

'But—' I say.

'Yes, we do want to know. We've got to plan, after all.'

'Aw, that's nice.' Before I can gather myself and stop her, the words are already out of her mouth. 'It's a little girl.'

'A girl? Are you sure?' To an outsider, this might seem like a reasonable question, but I can't help but catch the note of disbelief in Russ's voice.

My heart sinks.

'Well, I can't give you a one hundred per cent perfect guarantee, but yeah. You're having a little girl. Congratulations.'

A little girl. A little sister for Olivia.

I don't know whether to laugh or cry, so I do both. Thankfully, the sonographer thinks my tears are joyful. And they are. Despite all I've been through, I've still managed to grow a healthy baby girl.

But they're also tears of crushing disappointment and anger, because the last thing I needed was for my husband to undermine me.

I thank the sonographer, because none of this is her fault. If she's noticed my distress, she's not letting on. Elsie the midwife, with her soft, pillowy cheeks and motherly eyes gives me a hearty congratulations. The dreaded lump in my throat returns, and it takes all I have not to just stand there and bawl, even though they'd probably just take it as mother-to-be overwhelm.

Russ places his hand on the small of my back and ushers me out.

I shoot Elsie the midwife one last look, but she's chatting to the sonographer. I've already been forgotten; just another face, another bump, another appointment closer to the end of their shift.

FIFTEEN

'Why did you do that?'

It's taken me nearly twenty minutes to ask Russ this. We've been driving in heavy silence. He knows I'm angry, and he's angry because I'm angry with him. There's no way this won't escalate into an argument, so we may as well get it over with.

'Russ,' I say. 'Why did you do that?'

He lets out a tight sigh, his knuckles blanching white against the steering wheel.

'I asked because it was the sensible thing to do. It's ridiculous, not knowing. No, not ridiculous. Irresponsible. In this day and age especially. If you have data available, you use it. Simple as that.'

I stare at him open-mouthed for nearly a full minute. He keeps his attention fixed firmly on the road ahead, his mouth set in a grim line.

'Irresponsible?' I manage to say.

'Yes,' he snaps back. 'Irresponsible and stupid.'

'I don't think I like what you're implying,' I say, my temper reaching heights I haven't felt since I was a teenager. 'And I cannot see how knowing the baby's gender makes any difference to anything.'

Russ says nothing, but shakes his head, a sure sign that he's as angry as I am, even though I'm not the one who broke our agreement.

'We agreed we were going to leave it. You got your way last time, this time it was my choice—'

Russ lets out a bark of bitter laughter.

'What?' I'm snapping now, being drawn into this argument as a wasp is to ripe fruit. He laughs again, and if it wasn't for the fact that I'd be in just as much danger as him, I'd have yanked the steering wheel and forced him to crash into a tree. 'That's how things work. We're supposed to be a partnership—'

'Partnerships only work when both parties are equal in their cognitive abilities,' he says, through gritted teeth.

'Pardon?'

'You're not exactly the most rational of people at the moment, Frankie. It's a lot to deal with.'

'And what the hell is that supposed to mean?'

He screws his face up and blasts out another sigh.

'I come home. It's a mess. You're a mess. I ask my mother to help, but you don't like her, so not only do I get it in the neck from you, I get it in the neck from her. So I think, how can I help? I know, let's see if I can get you some support. I even manage to get someone my family trusts. But no, that's not good enough, either. All you want to do is wallow and whine and complain about everything—'

'I'm bloody well pregnant!' I know I shouldn't shout. I know I'm sounding shrill. But I don't care. 'You did this to me!'

'Only because you said you wanted it! Said it would make things better, make *us* better—'

'Oh no, you don't get to pin this on me. I said that Olivia was enough. It's not my fault you chickened out of getting a vasectomy.'

'I did not chicken out,' Russ hisses. 'I made a decision about my own body—'

'Really? You made a "decision" about your own body? I wonder what that feels like. Must be nice.'

'You were the one who came off the pill and didn't tell me—'

'Of course I did! I believed you when you said you were getting the vasectomy—'

'So one mistake and I have to pay for it forever? Remember, I offered you the chance to get rid of it, but you were the one to say no—'

'I can't believe you. I just... are you seriously telling me, just after we've seen our new baby growing inside my womb, that you would have preferred me to have an abortion?'

'No, of course not! You're twisting my words.'

But I don't think I am. And my stomach sinks at that realisation. His face is now red, his hands shaking on the steering wheel.

'All I'm saying is that the option was there. No one forced you into this, Frankie.'

'Oh, shut up, Russ. You know that isn't the issue here, so stop trying to turn it on me. I just want to know why you did it. Why you disrespected my wishes like that, when I respected yours last time. That's all.'

He takes in a deep breath. Everything about him is sharp; the angle of his mouth, the tension in his arms, the way his chin is jutting out. It's been a long time since I last saw this version of him. Last time was when I confronted him about his affair with that nurse. He tried to turn that on me then, too. As I've said before, he always did have a problem with being in the wrong.

'I asked, so I could plan. You know I like to be organised. Secure. And life hasn't been very organised or secure recently. In knowing what we're expecting, I can take a little bit of control back. Make life seem a little steadier. That's all.'

'Okay, so you did it to make yourself feel better. What about what I wanted? I wanted to experience the "it's a girl!" or "it's a boy!" from the obstetrician just once – what's wrong now?'

As soon as I say 'it's a boy', I notice his jaw clench.

Oh no. Not this again.

'You wanted a boy, didn't you? That's really what this is about, isn't it? So you can get over your disappointment before we get into the delivery room—'

'It's not that.'

But it is. I know it is. When I was pregnant with Olivia, the first names he came up with were boys' names. When I told him he needed to suggest some girl ones, too, he just laughed. Only after the scan that confirmed I was carrying a girl did he start suggesting female names, and even then he only chose feminine versions of masculine names. His top boy name was Oliver, after his maternal grandfather, so we chose Olivia as a female alternative.

But I never thought his disappointment at not having a boy ran this deep. He's been a good dad to Olivia. He takes her out. Plays froggies with her. Plants vegetables and reads her bedtime stories. I'd hoped that, in having a daughter, he'd realised that having a son wasn't the be-all and end-all.

I guess I was wrong.

The silence fills the room like smoke, threatening to choke us both.

'You don't know what it's like,' Russ says quietly.

I can't even bring myself to look at him.

'I don't know what what's like?' I say.

'To... to know that your name, your *legacy* will end with you.'

I can't help but laugh.

'What in the Henry the VIII nonsense are you on about, Russ?'

'I knew you wouldn't understand.' He says this with such

resignation that I find myself feeling sorry for him, even if it is for only a few seconds. 'I don't think women can.'

'What do you mean, women don't understand? And anyway, things don't work like that anymore,' I say.

'I know. I get it, but even so...' He swallows.

Is he going to cry? I wait for him to compose himself.

'I won't lie to you, Frankie. Yes, I was hoping for a son. And yes, I have to work through the fact that we're having another girl.' I'm not sure I like the emphasis on 'another', but I let it slide. 'I suppose I just... I just thought I'd have a boy to share stuff with, show him how to fix things, what tools you need, go on hikes with him, like I used to with my Papa. The bond between a father and his son... it's special, Frankie. I know you always go on about my mother, but my Papa... he's my rock. He just... gets me, you know? I guess I wanted a little bit of that for myself and my own son.'

In a way, I do feel sorry for him. But at the same time, I can't help but think that he really needs to get a grip.

'Russ, just because we have girls doesn't mean they can't use hammers or build a wall or go camping for a bit. The world has changed. The whole "I need a male heir to continue my legacy" thing doesn't even apply to the royals these days. No one cares.'

'I guess you're right.' He offers me a watery smile. 'I will get used to it, I promise. And I'll love our new little pumpkin just as much as I love our older little pumpkin.'

I smile back.

I mean, what else can I do?

SIXTEEN

I will admit, the one thing I can't accuse Jasmine of doing is a bad job, because when we arrive home, Olivia runs over to us wearing her little apron covered in flour, a broad grin on her face.

'I makes you 'nana bread!' she announces. Jasmine follows her, also in an apron but covered in a lot less flour.

'Yes, we did! And you don't need to worry, I reduced the sugar and added some apple to raise the nutrients. It's something I used to make when I was at uni and wanted a treat that wasn't going to make me go up a dress size when I ate it.' She gives us both a goofy, disarming smile, like she's sharing something a little embarrassing rather than a sad story of the pressures young women are subjected to in order to stay a socially acceptable, tiny size, so they don't take up any room.

'Oh, I don't think you have anything to worry about on that front,' Russ says, and I can't help but notice how her goofy smile subtly changes into something a little more... knowing, but it's gone within an instant.

'So how did it go?'

We both smile and Russ places a protective hand on my bump.

'Another girl,' Russ says. To an outsider, he might sound a little choked with emotion, but I know it's just boring old disappointment.

'Oh, that's amazing, congratulations!' She's saying all the right words, but she can't hide the confusion that flits across her face. Because she remembered it right, I did tell her earlier that we didn't want to know when she'd asked. But she wisely keeps her mouth shut.

The news shared, Russ wanders off. Olivia takes my hand and drags me into the kitchen to show me her 'nana bread in the oven. I really want to be able to enjoy her enthusiasm, but the smell of it baking is really quite overwhelming. At first the sweet cinnamon scent seemed pleasant enough, but after a few minutes I have to seek the refuge of the garden, gulping down great lungfuls of air, hoping that might help settle my rebellious stomach.

Russ pokes his head out and says he's going back to work.

'Have you called your parents to let them know how everything went?'

He rolls his eyes like a moody teenager.

'Yeah, because I haven't got enough on my plate already. I don't know when I'll be back. I'll have a lot to catch up on from this morning.'

And then he's gone. No kiss, no wave, not even a grumpy goodbye. I guess it's up to me to call his parents and tell them that everything is fine. I don't think he appreciates how hard this is for me, and not just because his mother is an absolute nightmare. I'd do anything to be making this call to my own mum and dad. I wrap my arms around myself. I should be feeling on top of the world. Despite all of my issues, I'm having a healthy baby girl. But I can't feel the joy. And it isn't just because my husband is being an ass, and my in-laws are insufferable. It's simply because my parents aren't here, and if there was any justice in this world, they should be. And what makes it harder, is that it's my fault. Maybe I didn't force my dad to drink too much and then get behind the wheel. All I did was get back together with Russ, but that was enough. That was the catalyst. I wasn't even going to tell them because it was early days for us. I still wasn't really sure if I could trust Russ again, and was keeping my options open. So when he turned up, and my dad saw him, forcing me to explain why the man who hurt his little girl was at the door... let's just say he didn't take it too well.

My dad never liked Russ. He said he was too old for me. That he was a cradle-snatcher. And yeah, in a way, that's true. But it's not like he used me then left me. Sure, there was the affair, but things like that happen, right? Even the most perfect of couples can have bumps in the road. We got over it. That's the important bit.

We're a family now.

I scroll through my contacts until I find Petunia and press call. I could call Filippo – he is, after all, the more approachable of the two, but I know all too well that if I ring him first, Petunia will complain that I was trying to find ways to cut her out of things, and I simply don't have the energy for it these days. So I swallow my pride and wait for her to pick up. Just as I think it's going to go to voicemail, Petunia deigns to answer.

'Frances.'

'Petunia.'

'Well, how did it go?'

There is no warmth to her words. She may as well be enquiring about a missed delivery she's a bit miffed about.

'It was fine. Baby is perfectly healthy.'

'Oh, thank God. I was worried all of that throwing up you're doing might harm them. And what are you having?'

I grit my teeth. I *knew* she was part of why Russ asked.

'A girl.'

'Another girl?' She sounds disappointed. Someone says something indistinct nearby, and judging by the way she all but yells, 'A girl,' I'm guessing it's Filippo, listening in. 'Well, congratulations.'

'Thank you.'

'I'll be over tomorrow to take Olivia and Jasmine out to Bledwin Gardens.'

'Oh, I didn't know that.'

'Why would you need to? Jasmine's the one looking after her. Goodbye.'

And with that, Petunia hangs up.

I'd like to say that this was an anomaly; that I'd caught her at a bad time. But nope, this is pretty much how all our phone calls go these days. She's given up pretending to like me, and I've given up caring. I'm still irritated that she's bypassed me to arrange something with Jasmine yet again, though. Sure, she's technically right – Jasmine is the one being employed to look after Olivia and so she is the one who needs to arrange her schedule – but it still rankles me.

Come on, Sprout. You've got to stop making me feel so ill. I need to take my life back.

I close my eyes and count back from ten before wandering into the nook. It's taken me a while to feel comfortable in here since Olivia's accident, but now it feels as cosy as ever. I like the nook. It's a small room, the only room in the house that doesn't need to be 'perfect' at all times. I sometimes wonder if Russ might be happier living in a showroom, but he says it's because I don't know the meaning of the word 'tidy'.

The world is a little swimmy, so I adjust the cushions and lean back. I've left the TV off, so I can hear Olivia chattering to Jasmine in the kitchen. A pang of jealousy twinges in my chest.

I really have to at least try to get over this, because I can't really fault Jasmine. I hardly ever catch her on her phone or watching TV when she is with Olivia, something I know I'm very guilty of at times. She helps with the household chores, too, even though I've told her she doesn't need to. Then she tells me it's fine, she likes looking after people, and I feel bad for ever doubting her. She's like a real life Mary bloody Poppins. And I hate her for it. She makes me look bad. Even before the morning sickness. She's just... better at this than I am, despite not having children of her own.

... Oh God, this is a 'me' thing, isn't it? I'm the problem, aren't I?

'Mama, Mama, look, for you!' Olivia bursts into the nook carrying a plate. Upon it is a brown slab I'm guessing is banana bread. She watches me closely as I take the plate from her, and as I try to set it down on the small side table, she shakes her head.

'No, Mama, you must eat it. I made it with Ja'min.'

'It's all right, Olivia,' Jasmine says. 'Mummy will eat it when she's hungry.'

'But... but is for Mama!' Olivia insists, and I know that if I don't at least try it, I'm in for the high jump.

I break a piece of the cake off. The smell of banana is so strong, my stomach heaves a little.

This is a bad idea.

But Olivia is looking at me with something that borders on wonder, so I don't have a choice. I have to eat it.

I swallow hard and pop the chunk in my mouth, give it enough of a chew so I won't immediately choke, then force it down. My throat rebels, but I'm determined to win this one.

'Hmm, that's delicious,' I say.

'It delushis!' She beams with pride as she tries to repeat the word. But then her expression changes to something more stern. 'But no more than that or you will get all big and fat.'

I blink, unable to parse what I've just heard.

Did she... just insinuate that I'm fat?

I glance up at Jasmine, who is watching me carefully,

gauging my response. Because if there's one thing I'm sure of: there's no way Olivia got that from me. Or did she? I was planning on having a tummy tuck before I fell pregnant again. I did lament not being able to fit into my old clothes. Maybe that's it? Children are like sponges, after all.

Although it is telling that she's never said anything like this before. Or, at least, I don't think she has.

Before I can comment, my stomach twists again, forcing me to fight down a retch. Jasmine frowns.

'Okay, Olliebean, we have to go and finish tidying up the froggies' tea party upstairs,' she says, strategically giving me the chance to bolt for the bathroom; a chance I immediately take advantage of.

Thankfully Olivia has been sufficiently distracted by the thought of her froggies not to notice me throwing up her hard work.

SEVENTEEN

Olliebean.

That's another thing that bothers me.

I know it shouldn't, but it does.

Olivia has always been Pumpkin to Russ and me. One thing I wasn't expecting was the nanny to give her her own affectionate little nickname. And while I can't tell her not to do it, mainly because I'd come across as a control freak, that doesn't stop the name from dragging its nails across the blackboard of my soul every time I hear it.

They're out. Jasmine and Olivia. Out with Petunia at Bledwin Gardens. Russ is out, too. He's playing squash with Rav. He could have stayed home with me, but he still wants to punish me for making him feel bad yesterday, so I'm here, at home, on my own. It's times like this when I wish we still had a cat, but Russ re-homed Biggles the moment we found out I was pregnant. Said the risk of toxoplasmosis was too high. Cat poop and cat saliva, he said, were dangerous for pregnant women. And so Biggles had to go.

I miss Biggles. He was an enormous neutered ginger tom that I rescued after Russ and I broke up. All he wanted to do was laze in sunpuddles and have his ears fussed with. He had a low, drawling meow that never failed to delight me. I often joked that, if Biggles had been human, he'd probably be my perfect man.

Russ didn't like Biggles. He doesn't like cats in general, but Biggles seemed to really get on his nerves. At first, he suggested we put Biggles down, because he was an older cat and no one would want to re-home him. Thankfully, Russ was wrong, and Biggles ended up going to a care home for the elderly, where I expect he gets all the fuss he could ever dream of, and more.

Still... I miss him.

Maybe we can get the girls a pair of kittens once Sprout is old enough.

I sip at the smoothie Jasmine made me this morning. According to her, it is stuffed full of good things: blueberries, organic spinach, lemongrass, turmeric, coconut milk, half an avocado, spirulina powder and just a dash of maple syrup to bring it all together. She even apologised for using store-bought spinach, but qualified it with 'our home-grown stuff should be ready in about a week'.

It's a foul concoction, as all smoothies are. But, much to my chagrin, they do appear to be helping. I've been drinking these for three days now, and this morning my sickness has, touch wood, seemed better. Sure, it hasn't gone, but the mere whiff of cooking didn't have me dashing for the bathroom, and I've been able to get up the stairs without feeling like I went on a massive vodka bender the night before. You never know, I might not need Jasmine much longer if this carries on.

I turn the TV on. There's nothing specific I want to watch, so I end up surfing until something catches my eye, like a good little consumer.

Next thing I know, the sound of someone opening the front door wakes me. I wipe my mouth, momentarily disorientated, before I realise it must be Jasmine and Olivia coming home. I really hope Petunia doesn't come in – with any luck she'll just—

'Hey, how are you feeling?'

It's... Russ?

'Hi,' I say. 'You're home early.'

He wanders over and kisses me on the top of my head. Jasmine, Olivia and Petunia stroll in after him.

'Yeah,' Russ says. 'Mum said she was going out with the girls and asked if I had time to join them, and my list is pretty light today, so I thought "screw it" and bunked off for a bit.'

'Oh. That must have been... nice.'

'It was. Really nice to catch up, you know? No drama, just good coffee and good company. You have fun?'

No, I didn't. I had bad telly, a horrible smoothie and backache. You can now add a huge sense of missing out and a nagging feeling that I'm being sidelined by my own family. And that's not to mention the sense of betrayal that Russ would sack the day off for his mother and the nanny, but not for his sick pregnant wife.

But I don't say that. I want to, but I don't. The last thing I need is yet another argument.

'Not really. I just watched some TV and had a bit of a nap.'

He smiles indulgently at me.

'That sounds great. Just what you need, right? Rest and relaxation. Might end up asking Jaz to stay on to help once the baby is born at this rate!'

My heart drops. No. No, no, no. I was hoping with my sickness wearing off, I'd be able to get rid of her sooner – but there's my husband planning on extending her contract.

'Maybe,' Jasmine says, flicking her eyes over at Russ and offering him a coy smile. 'I'd have to try and fit everything around my studies.'

'You hear that, Frankie? Built in babysitter. Wonderful.'

They share another look, and something I want to pretend I don't understand, but can't quite deny, passes between them.

Petunia snorts and mutters something. I think it's along the lines of 'we wish'.

'Right,' Petunia says, 'I'm off. It's been lovely to see you all, but I have to bake something for the local homeowners' association meeting this evening, so I must dash. Olivia, come give Gramma a kiss.'

But Olivia doesn't want to give her Gramma a kiss. Olivia has gathered up her froggies and is currently trying to put some dolls' clothes on them. Judging by the way her little face is scrunched up, she's finding it a challenge.

'Olivia?' Petunia says as she stalks over to her granddaughter. 'Come here and give your Gramma a kiss.'

When Olivia ignores her again, Petunia reaches down and snatches the half-dressed frog from her.

I freeze, holding my breath. Olivia looks up, her eyes wide, like she can't quite believe what just happened.

'Olivi—'

But Petunia doesn't get anything else out before Olivia lets out a high-pitched wail of sheer fury.

'No, Gwamma! No! My froggy!'

Petunia rears back, and for a split second, the whole room goes pin-drop silent as we all process our collective shock. Then, before any of us can even think about how we are going to deal with this, Olivia reaches for her froggy.

'No!' Petunia snaps. 'Rude little girls do not get their toys back.' And with that, she straightens up and thrusts the frog at Russ, who all but fumbles it as Olivia erupts into a temper tantrum so ferocious I find myself covering my ears with my hands. I've never seen Olivia like this as she throws herself back and howls about her froggy and Gwamma and no, no, naughty, and I'm left completely helpless at what to do next. Petunia, however, knows exactly how she's going to handle this: blame everyone but herself, the person who started this.

'I have never seen such insolence,' she hisses as she rounds on me. 'What are you letting her get away with these days?'

'W-what?' I manage to say. 'This isn't my fault—'

'Then whose fault is it? You're her mother, more's the pity.'

And, to my utter shock and fury, she glances over at Jasmine, who is standing next to Russ.

And Jasmine *smiles*. She actually *smiles*.

'Mum—' Russ begins, but Petunia has swept out of the room. A second later, Russ drops the stuffed frog and runs out after her. I hear heated whispers: Russ, apologising. Petunia, indignant, like I'd actually planned for this to happen.

Jasmine scoops up the frog and holds it out to Olivia, who has now stopped screaming and is instead sniffling and hiccuping. She reaches out and takes her toy, even managing a small 't'ank you, Ja'min'.

I can do nothing but sit, paralysed by how quickly everything went to hell.

After a long moment, Russ returns. He shoots me a look, then focuses on Jasmine.

'Jasmine? Mum would like a word.'

'What? Why?'

Russ says nothing as Jasmine nods and trots out like an obedient dog. He then turns his attention to me, whispering viciously as he demands to know why I have to be like this with her, why I have to escalate things, until I'm left with a lump in my throat, because I have absolutely no idea how any of this is my fault and he isn't giving me a chance to figure out exactly what just happened.

Finally, I'm allowed to speak.

'Russ, how is any of this my fault? I had nothing to do with it!'

'Yeah, you say that, but Mum's been saying for a while that

Olivia's being very wilful, bordering on downright insolent with her.'

'And? She's three. That's what three-year-olds do.'

'You have to get over this,' Russ says, a warning look in his eyes as he jabs a finger in my direction. 'You can't say these things and expect there not to be any fallout.'

'Say what things? I don't know what you're talking about!'

'Right. You don't know. Of course. You have to stop this, Frankie.'

'Stop *what*?' I say, totally confused. I'm replaying all my recent interactions with Petunia in my head, trying to puzzle out what I might have said or done that she could misconstrue as rude, but I'm coming up empty. 'I don't understand.'

Russ says nothing, just shakes his head and stalks out of the room. My head is pounding, my stomach churning, and by the time I hear a crash from the kitchen, I'm just about ready to scream.

Olivia is still whimpering. I heave myself up off the sofa, pausing for a second as my vision swims before I can ask her if she's okay. Everything about her radiates stress, from the way she is clutching her frog to the way she's pulling in her head.

'Pumpkin, Mama isn't mad,' I say, as gently as I can. Because I'm not mad. I don't care what Petunia says, I don't think Olivia did anything wrong. Sure, shouting at her grand-mother for taking her frog isn't great, but then again neither is snatching a toy off a child because they won't show you the deference you think is your right.

Olivia sniffles and looks up at me. Her eyes are ringed red and a little puffy.

'Gwamma,' is all she can manage to say.

'Don't worry about Gramma,' I say. I ease myself onto the floor and rub her back as she climbs into my lap. 'What did you do on your visit?'

'We see'd all the aminals,' she says. I don't correct her

mispronunciation. 'There was sheeps and I feeds then. And little bouncy ones. They jump all over the others.'

'Were they goats?' I lean over to grab my iPad and search up an image. Olivia nods, already looking happier.

'Yeah! And they jump and jump and jump!' She gets up off my lap and starts showing me by jumping on the spot.

'Like froggies,' I say.

'Yah! Like froggies!' She holds out her frog and starts jumping again, and as if by magic, she's back to her normal self, the previous scene now forgotten.

I wish I could do that, sometimes.

I hear low voices in the kitchen. I close my eyes, take in a deep breath and struggle back up to my feet. Now Olivia is calm and playing, I can tackle what is undoubtedly going to be an even bigger meltdown if I'm not careful.

The mutterings stop when I enter the kitchen. Russ and Jasmine glance over at me, like I'm an intruder. This instantly gets my hackles up, along with no small measure of worry.

'That wasn't Olivia's fault,' I say. 'And wasn't mine, either.'

Russ shakes his head and mutters something. Then, to my utter disbelief, Jasmine lays a hand on his forearm, like she's the only one who can calm him down.

'Jasmine,' I say, possibly a little more forcefully than I should, 'can you please leave? I need to speak to my husband and Olivia is on her own in the other room.'

Jasmine glances at Russ. I don't know if she's seeking his permission or is silently asking him if he'll be okay with me on his own, but whatever it is, it bothers me. Russ gives her a little nod, and she leaves without a word, but as she passes me, there it is again. That little smirk.

I don't even know if she realises she's doing it.

EIGHTEEN

Things remain tense between Russ and me for a few days after Petunia's tantrum. He's been giving me the silent treatment, mainly because he knows his mother was in the wrong on this one, but doesn't want to admit it.

He doesn't have any such issues when it comes to talking to Jasmine, though. And she doesn't seem to mind this at all.

I keep trying to convince myself that I'm seeing things that aren't there. That I'm only noticing it because we're not speaking. That of course he has to speak to the nanny – she's looking after his daughter. That it's just my hormones and lack of sleep that's driving me nuts. That I'm being unfair, and that none of this is her fault. That she isn't trying to steal my husband, or indeed, my entire life.

That is until I notice the bracelet she's wearing.

At first, I try to wave it away. It's nothing. Just jewellery. But the more I see it, the more uneasy I feel. Short of demanding Jasmine's wrist so I can inspect it, it's hard to get a good look at it, to confirm my suspicion. It's only when I catch her showing it off to Olivia that I feel I can say something.

'Pretty!' Olivia coos as she turns it around in her pudgy

little hands. 'Look, Mama, Ja'min has pretty flower!' She runs over to me and holds it up so I can see it. It's gold, the body of it twisted to look like branches, or maybe long flower stems. There's a flower, a forget-me-not, where the branches meet. It's not exactly pretty – it's too indelicate for that – and looks wrong on her; she's too young to carry off such a statement piece. I know this, because I felt too young when I was given a similar trinket. It hung on my arm like a manacle, and I only ever wore it to make Russ happy, because he bought it for me.

'Oh, that's very pretty,' I say, trying to sound enthusiastic as I pluck it from Olivia's grasp. I turn it over in my hands, my stomach knotting as I finally get to study it. I look over to Jasmine, who is watching me intently, that same small smirk, the one I'm not sure she even knows she's giving me, playing on her lips. It feels like she's challenging me, daring me to say something. But that's ridiculous. How would she know?

Unless...

'Where did you get it?' I address Jasmine directly, trying to sound light but landing on accusatory instead. I can't help it.

Because the closer I look, the more I'm convinced it *is* my bracelet.

Jasmine holds her hand out, waiting for me to hand it back to her. When I don't, she lifts an eyebrow, like I'm the one in the wrong.

'That? It was a present. From an... admirer.'

'An... admirer?'

'Yeah,' Jasmine says. Her voice sounds as smooth as silk. 'He said it looked pretty on me.'

My mouth feels suddenly claggy, like I've been eating peanut butter straight out of the jar.

'Who was that? If it's not too intrusive.'

'Like I said, an admirer. Is everything okay, Frankie? You look a little peaky. Do you want me to go and get you a drink, or something?'

'A glass of water would be nice,' I say, mostly to give me time to think about how I'm going to deal with this. Because make no mistake, I am absolutely positive this is my bracelet. Russ had it made especially for me; he said it was a one-off that he commissioned after we got back together. To prove he was serious this time, he said.

Either she stole it from me, or...

Jasmine returns, a glass of water in one hand. I take a moment to sip at it, my mind racing. I have to say something. I have to challenge her. 'Look, I'm sorry Jasmine, but are you sure? Because I have a bracelet just like that, and it was made especially for me, so...'

'Excuse me?' Jasmine straightens up, affronted. 'What are you implying?'

What am I implying? That she stole it? That my husband lied to me about it being unique?

Or maybe that my husband is the mysterious 'admirer' and gave it to her. But then why would she wear it in the house, let alone show it to my daughter?

But then again... maybe that's exactly why she's wearing it. She wants me to see it. Wants me to know. I can't help but feel like she is in the process of setting a very elaborate trap, and I've just set off the first part of it.

'I'm sorry, Jasmine, but I'm going to have to go up to my bedroom and check my jewellery box. I'm not accusing you of anything, just... I have to make sure.'

'Okay. I understand.' Jasmine sounds maddeningly calm, like I didn't just accuse her of stealing an expensive piece of jewellery. 'In fact, I'll go with you. I'm intrigued to see your "one of a kind" bracelet that I also somehow seem to have.'

And just like that, all of her faux-sweetness drops away. She's no longer an awkward kid; now she's assertive, with a steely glint in her eye.

I gulp down the surge of acute uncertainty that engulfs me.

She is being far too reasonable, like she already knows exactly how all of this ends. 'Oh, well, maybe we'll leave it—'

'No,' she says. 'Let's go. I want you to be sure that I'm not stealing from you. Because that's what you were implying, right? That I stole it?'

The urge to snap back that the bracelet isn't the only thing she's at least attempting to steal is strong, but I manage to hold it in. She's staring at me now, those clear blue eyes of hers boring into me. My heart pounds, beating against the inside of my skull, and I take another sip of water in the hope of clearing my head, but instead it makes me cough as my unease tips over into anxiety.

But it's too late to back out now. I struggle up off the couch and make my way to the stairs. With every step, the doubts grow clearer.

I hardly ever wear my bracelet because, if I'm totally honest, I think it's a bit of a carbuncle. I've never been one for statement jewellery. In fact, I was a bit miffed when Russ presented it to me. Of all the things he thought might win me back, he chose gold? I've never worn gold! I'm a silver girl or nothing. But when he said he'd had it made for me, showed me the design depicting branches intertwined, representing how our lives were intertwined and growing together, and the forget-me-not, which he said represented a fresh start and the blossoming of our love again, I couldn't tell him I didn't actually like it. Especially since he was taking me to hospital to see my dying mother. He even helped me organise my parents' funerals and ended up paid for a large chunk of them. The truth was, Russ was no longer the playboy he had been. He'd said that I was the only thing he ever regretted losing, and he was never going to make that mistake again. And I believed him.

Am I ready to face the fact that maybe that belief was ill-placed?

We arrive at our bedroom door. I push it open. A waft of

scent envelops us: a hint of Russ's aftershave with a dash of my favourite perfume. Underpinning it all, however, is the animal smell of adults who sleep together: the sweat, the tears, the passion. Although maybe not so much passion these days.

My jewellery box is on my dressing table. I glance over at Jasmine; she looks suspiciously calm, like she knows exactly what's going to happen.

I open the box. Dig through the smaller containers until I find the bracelet box. I gingerly lift it out. It's heavy. Like there's a gold bracelet I never wear inside.

'I think you might owe me an apology,' Jasmine says. Her voice is thick with righteousness; it's all I can do not to run out of the room in shame.

'I don't understand...' My voice is as small as I feel. 'He said he had it made for me.'

'The evidence points to the contrary,' Jasmine says, lifting her wrist so I have to compare the two bracelets.

They are identical, right down to the choice of flower.

'But he said he had it made especially for *me*. That there wasn't another one like it. It was unique, because our relationship was unique.'

'I don't know what to say other than that clearly isn't the case. I got mine for my eighteenth birthday.'

She's looking intently at me now, studying me, drinking in my reaction. If I didn't know any better, I'd say she was enjoying this. It's almost like she knew. She knew about my bracelet and has gone out of her way to either find another one or... have one made with the specific goal of upsetting me. But that's insane. Who would do that?

And why?

But then again, she's only started wearing it recently. Why would she start wearing it now?

A nasty little thought pops up in my mind. *It's the kind of thing you might do if you're trying to stir trouble.*

'Look, I'm really sorry about all of this,' I say. 'I... I didn't...'

'It's okay,' she says, but I'm not quite sure what is 'okay' about any of this. 'Honest mistake. We all make them.'

'Yeah. We do. I'm just... I'm going to be having words with Russ tonight.' I try to smile and keep my tone light, so she thinks I'm joking.

'That's up to you,' Jasmine says. 'You know he'll try to deny it, right?'

'Pardon?'

She smiles at me, but there is no warmth there. Just triumph.

'So are we good?'

Not a chance.

'Yeah,' I say. 'We're good.'

'I'd better go and see what Olivia's up to,' Jasmine says. 'Can't take your eye off her for a second.'

And with that, she smiles at me and leaves as if nothing ever happened. Life, continuing as normal.

I sink down onto the bed, totally confused. I turn my bracelet over in my hands. I can't deny it. It's here. Jasmine didn't steal it. And she said she got it for her eighteenth birthday. That means she got it five years ago.

The same time Russ gave me mine.

I have absolutely no idea what any of this means.

NINETEEN

I think Jasmine's doing it on purpose. She's doing it because she knows it upsets me. A constant reminder of how she humiliated me. She keeps wearing that bracelet, even around Russ. *Especially* around Russ. It's like she's taunting me. Whether it isn't the unique piece Russ said it was, or she had her own version made just to mess with me, it doesn't matter: every single time I see her near him she now has that bracelet on show. Every time I expect him to say something, but he doesn't. And it's not because he hasn't noticed it. I know he has. I've caught him staring at it more than once. But he never says anything.

It takes a couple of days before I feel ready to confront him about it. I know it sounds silly, but it bothers me. Jasmine is playing a game with me, and I want it to stop.

Because I'm feeling better I tell Jasmine she can have the afternoon off. Russ will be home around two, and I thought it might be nice for us to go out as a family, just the three of us. We haven't done so in such a long time.

Jasmine is surprised, but seems happy with this arrangement, saying she's been meaning to catch up with one of her friends. She's gone before Russ gets home, so Olivia and I play with Duplo in the garden to pass the time.

'Where Ja'min?' Olivia asks as she builds a wonky tower.

'She's gone to see her friend for the afternoon.'

'Me not go with her?'

'No, baby, I thought we could do something. Papa'll be home soon.'

'Out with Papa? Is Ja'min out with Papa?'

My stomach drops.

'What do you mean, is Jasmine out with Papa?'

Olivia focuses on her tower like a true architect.

'Livvy?'

'Me and Ja'min go to the coffee and Papa was there too.'

'He was?'

'Yes.'

'When was this?'

'It was at coffee.'

Damn. It could have been yesterday, it could have been weeks ago. I forgot toddlers have literally no sense of time.

'Was it last time you went for coffee?'

Olivia doesn't answer me. Her face is a picture of fierce concentration as she places another Duplo brick atop her tower.

'Olivia? Can you answer Mama, please?'

But she's not listening to me. The brick is giving her trouble. It won't lay flat. I reach over to help her, but as soon as I touch it, her face screws up in an angry frown and she balls her hand up into a pudgy fist and hammers down on it. The tower collapses under the force of the blow. Olivia, now furious, screams.

'No, Mama, no, no, no!' This is all I can make out before her howls turn into an incoherent tantrum, something I hadn't really dealt with very often, until recently at least. I sit back, stunned.

'Pumpkin, Livvy, calm down, we can build it again.' I try to keep my voice smooth, my posture calm, but rather than help

Olivia regulate herself, my reaction seems to enrage her more. Quick as a little snake, she grabs up some bricks and throws them at me.

'No, Olivia!' I shout, more out of shock than anything else. 'You mustn't throw Duplo at Mama!'

She can't hear me. She's now on the ground, kicking her legs, screeching. My heart pounds as I try to get near her, try to soothe her, but she's feral. As I lean over her, she kicks out, catching me in the stomach.

I sit back, cradling my bump, devastated.

What has got into my little girl?

'Hey, what's going on?' I jump at the sound of another voice. It's Russ, home for the afternoon. He is looking at both of us in disbelief. 'Frankie? What happened?'

Upon hearing her father, Olivia stops howling, picks herself up off the floor and runs towards him. Her face is red, her nose snotty, and she's hiccuping as she tries to speak. Russ's expression has shifted from disbelief to accusation.

He's waiting for me to explain myself.

'We were building a tower and the brick wouldn't go on, so she lost it.'

'Bad brick,' Olivia says. 'Mama do it.'

'Mama did what?'

'I tried to help her and she got frustrated,' I say. 'It was just one of those things.'

'Where's Jasmine?'

A weight in my chest drops.

'I gave her the afternoon off. She's gone out to catch up with a friend.'

'And why did you think that would be a good idea?'

'Because I'm feeling better.'

'Are you, though?' Russ says, his tone sharp. 'I come home from a hard shift, and I find you and Olivia screaming at each other—'

'I wasn't screaming at her, I was trying to calm her down.'

'Of course. And you did an absolutely fantastic job.' He gestures to Olivia, who is clinging to his legs, whimpering. 'I don't need this.'

'I didn't do it on purpose. I thought it might be nice to, I don't know, do something as a family for a change? It feels like ages since we did anything together—'

'Go out? You know I've been up since five. I'm absolutely bushed. I was hoping for an easy afternoon.'

'Yeah, me too. I just thought we could go into town, grab a drink, maybe something light to eat? There's that new Greek place, they're supposed to do a cracking calamari—'

'Do you really think you should be eating calamari?' Russ says. 'And isn't feta sheep's cheese?'

'Uh, yes, I think so?'

'Is that safe for you to eat?'

'Papa, Mama sick, Mama shout.'

'Mama was sick?' Russ raises his eyebrows at me.

'No, I wasn't, I haven't been, I'm fine—'

I can tell he doesn't believe me. Olivia continues to chatter, saying 'Mama sick' and then, to my utter horror, 'Mama confoos again'.

'Olivia!' I say, far more harshly than I intended. 'Honestly, Russ, I have no idea what she's on about, I'm absolutely fine—'

'Really? Out of the mouth of babes,' Russ says as he bends down to pick his daughter up. 'She wouldn't make that stuff up.'

'Yes, but, she doesn't even know what that word means. I've never heard her use it before. She can't even say it right! No, someone has implanted that idea in her head—'

'Implanted?' Russ scoffs. 'You make it sound like a grand conspiracy.'

'No, I didn't mean it like that, I meant that she must be hearing it, other people say it, enough for her to pick the phrase up and when to use it—'

'Darling, I think you're blowing this all out of proportion. She's just saying what she sees. Nothing else.'

I sigh heavily and struggle up to my feet. There's no point arguing with him.

'Look... forget it. I'll go and make some coffee.'

'Coffee? Really? I know you said you were feeling better, but it's not advised—'

'Oh my God, I've got decaf for me. I'm not a total idiot—'

'For the love of... I'm not saying that. I'm just concerned, that's all.'

'Is Mama confoos?'

'Yes, Pumpkin. Mama's confused again.'

'Poor Mama.'

'I know. Poor Mama.'

TWENTY

'Taa daa!'

Jasmine beams at me as she hands over a tall glass of thick, green sludge with a metal straw sticking out of it.

'Yay,' I say, taking it from her. 'Today's glass of squashed up fruit and veg.' I smile so I don't sound quite so bitchy.

'Oh, but it's more than that,' Jasmine says. 'This is the first time I've made you a smoothie using your own homegrown microgreens!'

'Really? That was quick.'

'Yeah, they don't take long to grow at all. The baby kale was ready, too, so I added some of that as well. All totally organic, no pesticides or chemicals have ever been near them, grown with love by your very own green-fingered daughter.'

'By me!!' Olivia throws her arms up into the air, like she's just won a race.

'Well, that makes it amazing, then,' I say. 'Thank you, Olivia, for growing me these lovely vegetables.'

'Is leaves,' she says. 'The little seeds go into the mud and then we water them with special water, and then they grow!'

'Special water?' I say.

'Rainwater,' Jasmine says. 'I take it from the rainwater butt. It's better than tap water. Although it did take me a while to stop a certain little person from trying to drink it all the time!' She bends down and tickles Olivia, who shrieks in delight.

I leave them to their little wrestling match and take a sip of the smoothie. Yep, still disgusting. Turns out, it doesn't matter if you grew the veg yourself or not, it's all vile. But I can't complain. Smoothies or not, I'm feeling much better now.

'So, what are your plans for today?' I ask Jasmine, who is now sat on the floor helping Olivia to set up a froggies' tea party.

'Well, first we're going to Little Wrigglers at the community centre, then we'll probably go to the café with the other mums, then we might hop on the bus and go to the library as our books need to go back. We don't want to get a fine, do we, Olliebean?'

'No, we do not.' Olivia punctuates every word with a firm shake of her head, making her curls bounce.

'Okay, sounds like you guys have a busy day planned out,' I say, as lightly as I can.

'Right, that'll be me off, then.' Russ bustles into the kitchen and dives into the fridge for his lunch. 'I don't know what time I'll be back.'

'I thought you said you had another half day?' I say.

'No, Jacqui isn't coming in, so I have to cover her.'

'So we're not meeting for coffee?'

Russ all but runs over to me and kisses me on the forehead.

'Sorry, no. See you whenever.'

And with that, he's gone.

See you whenever? What does that even mean? I sip at my smoothie while Jasmine helps Olivia put on her coat. Then, just like that, they're gone too, and I'm on my own.

Again.

. . .

I'm lost.

What did I do before I had kids? Before Olivia's schedule dominated my life? Before everything had to be arranged around hospital visits? Before the world went sideways and my own body became my biggest enemy?

I log into Instagram. It's been a while. I'm not much of a social media person. Not because I think I'm above it or anything like that; back in the days when Facebook was everywhere, you'd find me with the best of them, cataloguing my life, selling my soul for the thrill of any kind of recognition. No, I was just as bad as everyone else, until it backfired on me in the most spectacular fashion.

All those posts where I bragged about my 'perfect surgeon fiancé'. Russ had just passed his last residency with flying colours. I was *so* proud. And I was – I'll admit it now, even if I didn't want to then – *so* smug. I thought I had it all.

Until I found her page.

It's funny. I can't even remember her name. She was always That Bitch to me. That Bitch who seduced my fiancé. She was a nurse. She might still be. I haven't looked her up in years. Part of my promise to Russ. That our second chance meant a clean slate, for both of us.

My notifications are slim pickings. No one has sent me anything specifically. Sadly, if you turn down one too many invitations to soft play, you'll be cut out of the conversation. And forget about work friends. They're spending their time pretending you don't exist, especially when you were medically signed off work suddenly, forcing them to find cover quickly which isn't easy when you work in HR. You're supposed to be the one preventing people from taking too much time off, not dropping off the face of the earth yourself.

I click on a few of my mummy friends and am greeted with

the sight of artfully taken photos of almost ethereal-looking children doing wholesome activities: winsome cherubs finger painting in the garden and little angels decorating home-made cupcakes with all manner of incredibly healthy berries. I feel weirdly alienated by it all, as if the life I once led was no more than a strange dream.

Then something... odd happens.

Olivia is in some of these pictures. I'm not sure how I feel about that. I should have at least been tagged so I knew they were up.

That's when I notice it.

I may not have been tagged in the photos, but Jasmine has.

Now I have my eye in, I can see she's in the pictures. Holding Olivia. Olivia sitting in her lap. Doing circle time at the library. And in every one, my mummy friends – women I went to NCT classes, breastfeeding groups and so many toddler activities with – are tagging her. Not me. *Jasmine*. Over and over again. Like she's Olivia's mother and not just an employee.

Of course I then go and look at Jasmine's Insta. It's a small account, perfectly managed. It's all smiles and nail appointments, healthy food and hair care.

And, most recently, pictures of her with my daughter.

Just as I'm about ready to rain down the wrath of God onto her in the comment section, something else catches my eye.

The last picture of Olivia she posted, only a couple of hours ago. The selfie where she's sitting in Jasmine's lap, showing everyone her painty hands. There, in the background.

A man.

This in itself isn't an issue. Dads are more than welcome to join these groups. But this man shouldn't be there.

I know this, because the guy in the background is my husband.

I sit back on the sofa, my heart a lead weight in my chest. What the hell is Russ doing at one of the baby groups? I double-check the timestamp on the picture. It's from three hours ago.

So I guess Jacqui did come in. That he didn't have to cover her.

Or maybe Jacqui was just a decent excuse.

All I can do for a good while is just sit there and stare, absolutely dumbfounded.

Of course I had my suspicions. Deep down I'd hoped I was just being paranoid and that Russ wouldn't do anything so stupid again.

But there he is, bold as brass. He's not even hiding it.

What I can't get my head around is why Jasmine would post this so publicly. Of course, we aren't Insta friends, so maybe she felt safe and decided the risk was worth it. Or maybe she just didn't realise Russ was in the background.

Or maybe she did. Maybe she suspects I am monitoring her via her IG account. Maybe that's the message.

I'm out with your husband and your daughter. Not you. Me.

They're mine now.

My stomach heaves, but this time it has nothing to do with morning sickness. I chuck my iPad onto the sofa and bolt for the bathroom, where I throw everything up, including that terrible smoothie.

It's a threat. It has to be.

Even I thought that my worries about Jasmine trying to worm her way into my family were probably down to me feeling sidelined. But now?

Now, I'm not so sure.

TWENTY-ONE

Even though I have every right to scream blue murder at Jasmine, something holds me back. Olivia runs into the living room and throws herself at me, screeching 'Mama!' as she lands in my lap. I have to tell her to be careful, that she doesn't want to hurt Sprout, and then hug her tighter than I think I have ever done.

My poor baby girl. An unwitting pawn in this mess.

Jasmine smiles when she tells me what they've been up to. Naturally, there is no mention of Russ at all. At first I'm not entirely sure why I don't call her out. Demand to know what she is playing at. For some reason, the thought of saying it out loud makes me feel nervous, like I'm the one in the wrong.

Even though I'm not.

And then it strikes me.

I'm afraid of Jasmine. Afraid of her influence on my family.

Mama confoos indeed.

'Wow, sounds like you've been busy!' I say, with forced enthusiasm.

'Yeah, yeah, yeah, see my picture, Ja'min, has you gots my picture?'

My heart skips painfully in my chest as Jasmine's eyes briefly meet mine. There's a strange twinkle in them.

She's enjoying this.

Jasmine turns her attention to a rolled-up piece of sugar paper pulled from the tote bag she was carrying. She passes it to me.

I unfurl it. It's painted in the same colours that Olivia had on her hands in the photo.

'Oh, baby, this is so good!' I say to Olivia. 'What is it?'

'It's us!' she says, pointing a pudgy finger at each blob. 'That Mama, that Ja'min, that Papa and that me!'

'Oh, right, yes, I can see.' And I can. It's clear that I'm the sick-green blob on the edge of the page, separate from the other blobs. The other three blobs are all close together: a brownish-orange blob next to a much younger, much prettier bright-pink blob, and a red blob in front of both of them.

I take in a deep breath, disguising it as a yawn.

'Well, it's very good,' I say. 'All of us together.'

'It go on the wall?'

No. I am not having that woman on my wall, even if she is just a pink blob.

'Of course, Pumpkin. We'll put it up later. Did you do anything else?'

'We gots books.'

These are also produced from the tote bag by Jasmine.

'Oh, I see. *Meg and Mog* and *The Frog and the Caterpillar*. That looks like a good one.'

Olivia nods enthusiastically.

'It has froggies in it.'

'I can see. Did you do anything else?'

It might be a trick of the light, but I'm sure I see Jasmine give me a sly glance, and that sneaky little smile is back playing at her lips. But Olivia isn't paying attention. She's too busy climbing off me and looking for her various frogs.

'Everything was fine,' Jasmine says, straight-faced. 'She played well, had a good dance, did some painting – she even asked to go to the bathroom, despite being completely absorbed in what she was doing.'

'That's good,' I say.

'Yeah, she's really coming along in leaps and bounds with regards to the potty training. No accidents at all today. It might be time to try her with proper underwear rather than toddler pants. I might do that tomorrow, maybe. See how she goes for the rest of the afternoon.'

'That's good news,' I say. 'And that's it? Nothing else to report?'

'No… I think that's it. She's going to sleep like a log later. Always on the go, that one.'

'Indeed. I wonder who she gets it from.'

Jasmine smiles sweetly.

'I think she takes after her Mama.'

'Hmm. So there's nothing else? You didn't bump into anyone?'

Jasmine continues to smile, but there's an edge to it now.

'I'm not sure what you're getting at.'

I leave her hanging, hoping to make her feel uncomfortable, but it turns out she could outstare Death itself. In the end, I'm the one who wants this to finish.

'Oh, nothing. It's okay. I wondered if maybe Petunia turned up. She mentioned she might see you today.'

'No, that's tomorrow. Today's Tuesday, not Wednesday.'

'Oh, of course. Getting my days mixed up.'

Then Jasmine does something that makes me want to claw her face off.

She smiles. Not a smile of happiness, or recognition. No, this is pure duper's delight, sly and secret. She must think I'm stupid, or something.

But I'm not.
I know her game.

TWENTY-TWO

The sickness is back.

I can't believe it. I had a whole week, one whole glorious week, where everything felt fine. Okay, so, not *fine*, because last week was horrible, but... settled? Clear? Whatever it was, I was able to think straight, to see life as it really was.

Now I'm back in that prism of sickness, I'm beginning to doubt myself again. If only I had the photo. They couldn't deny that. But when I logged back in to Jasmine's Instagram to take a screenshot, it was gone. Had she realised her mistake, or had Russ seen it and told her to take it down?

Or maybe it wasn't there in the first place. Maybe I'd imagined it.

Mama confoos again.

I have no idea why the sickness has come back. The midwife says it's probably hormonal – that the lack of sickness last week was simply a blip. That this is the true state of affairs. That I was given a slight reprieve, only for it all to come rocketing back at me.

So here I am, once again, back in bed, back to doing nothing but trying to keep something – anything – down so I don't end up hospitalised. So I drink the smoothies. I take the rest. I do whatever I can to ensure that I remain here, in the heart of my family, bucket by my side, a packet of gingernuts and a flask of ginger tea beside me at all times.

Because sick or not, I am not going down without a fight.

My opportunity arises three days later.

Jasmine is with me in the nook, watching Olivia play while I lay on the couch with my eyes closed. I can hear every word she says, but I'm pretending to be asleep, hoping she might let something slip, but of course, she doesn't.

She's too wily for that.

Eventually I grow uncomfortable and have to move. I huff and puff as I try to sit up, my eyes bleary and my head pounding. No matter what the midwife said, this time the sickness feels different. Less nausea, more like I have the flu.

'You need a hand?'

Not from you.

'No, I'll be fine... phew.' I flop back, my head spinning. 'I don't know what's worse. The puking or the dizziness and fatigue.'

'You're throwing up less, so at least your body is retaining more nutrients. That has to be a good thing, right?'

'I suppose so.'

Olivia is watching *The Little Mermaid*, so I don't say anything when Jasmine's phone buzzes. She picks it up, reads whatever has been sent to her, then sets it back down on the coffee table.

'If you're okay, can I just nip to the loo for a sec?' Jasmine asks.

'Yeah, of course, that's no problem at all,' I say, trying to keep my voice steady.

Because I've noticed her phone hasn't locked itself yet.

She grins and trots off.

'Won't be long!' she calls over her shoulder.

'Take your time,' I mutter as I lean over and grab her phone.

I know it's wrong. No matter what, you shouldn't snoop on someone's phone. But sometimes, you have no choice but to break the rules.

It doesn't take me long to find what I'm looking for.

Texts between Jasmine and my husband.

On the surface, they don't look too incriminating. They often start with innocuous things, like asking what he might like for dinner, or telling him we're out of milk and can he grab some on the way home. They still get my back up, though; the subject matter is too domestic for my liking, the tone far too familiar.

I glance over at the door to the nook. How much longer have I got?

I scroll down.

More texts, mostly to and from people I don't know. It's going to take forever to sift through these, even with a filter on.

I go to her photo library. Maybe there's something in there?

Lots of selfies, some with Olivia, some without. Nothing too scandalous in terms of attire. In fact, the whole library seems strangely sanitised.

I wonder if she has any other folders hidden away.

I glance up at Olivia to ensure she's still transfixed by the TV as I continue searching, waiting to hear the loo flush at any point. I open up her WhatsApp, her Snapchat, but there's nothing there. Until...

A hidden folder, in her Notes app. And in there, a photo of a naked man.

Even though I only have to glimpse the preview before a gurgling from the water pipes tells me Jasmine has probably finished, I still feel all strength leave my body.

It may not be him. It might be someone else. An ex-boyfriend, maybe. That's probably why it's in the hidden folder.

But every part of me knows that that's not the case. That the nude has been sent to her by my husband.

I know, because he used to send them to me, once upon a time. I used to reciprocate – not entirely willingly, but I was naive and desperate for approval.

Now he's sending them to our nanny, and she's saving them.

I wonder how many she's sent back.

Gulping back tears of righteous fury, I carefully close everything and place the phone exactly where I found it, then lay back down.

When Jasmine returns, she settles herself back down on the other end of the couch, picks the phone back up and starts to scroll again, like everything is totally normal.

It takes everything I have not to kick her in the face.

TWENTY-THREE

I have to pick my moment carefully. I want it to be just her and me. No Russ, no Olivia, just the victim and perpetrator.

I'm not sure who is who in this situation.

It comes late that afternoon. Olivia is tired, so Jasmine puts her down for a nap. She doesn't really have a nap schedule these days but she's been a bit whiny lately, making me wonder if she's coming down with something.

I know Jasmine will go up to her room after Olivia is settled, so I'm planning to meet her in the stairwell.

It's time, as they say, for a reckoning.

I try to make it look like I'm just bumping into her at the top of the stairs, so I take an armful of clean laundry with me. I don't know why I care, but I do. Even though it's my house and she's the one in the wrong, I guess old habits die hard.

I watch her as she slips out of Olivia's room. When she sees me, she smiles and whispers something along the lines of 'She went down easy.'

But I'm not here for that. I'm here for her.

'I'd like a word,' I say in my coldest tone.

Jasmine's smile falters as she straightens up and looks down her nose at me, her eyes narrow.

I don't say anything. I simply stare. This is a technique my old boss taught me. Silence is your best friend. People don't like silence. They try to fill it up, chatter their way out of it, and that's when they make mistakes. They reveal too much. Implicate themselves, often in ways they don't even realise.

And that's exactly what I'm hoping Jasmine is going to do.

'Is everything okay?' she asks. Her tone is level, bordering on harsh; nothing like the bubbly front she usually puts on.

'No,' I say. 'Everything is not okay. I know exactly what you've been up to. I know exactly what you're planning. And you're not going to succeed. Because it stops now. You are going to pack your things, and you are going to leave. And then we never, ever see you again. Do I make myself clear?'

Rather than look shocked, Jasmine simply cocks her head to one side, gives me a long look, then chuckles.

'Oh, Frankie, you really don't have a clue, do you—'

And with that, my cold and calculated routine burns away.

'I don't have a clue? How dare you!' I drop the laundry at my feet and take a step closer to Jasmine. She doesn't step back. 'You come into my house. I pay you to look after my kid, and what do I find? You texting my husband. Oh yes, I've seen them. I also saw that photo on Instagram, the one from last week, the one with him in the background? Was that a mistake, or did you mean to do it? Does everyone know you're screwing my husband, or do they just assume that?'

'Frankie, you—'

'*Don't you fucking DARE interrupt me!*' I scream. I can't help it. 'So when did it start? Last week? Last month? The night you went out for that meal with his parents? Jesus Christ, I'm such an idiot. All of you must find it so funny, yeah, let's drive Frankie mad, let's gaslight her until she goes round the twist, no one could contest custody for the kids then, she's obviously not capable of looking after them—'

'Oh, Frankie. You really don't get it, do you?' She raises her hand and takes a step closer to me. Now I've discovered her real intentions, she'll do anything to cover them up. But before she can reach me, I manage to jerk back. For one confusing moment, there is an odd sense of something not being right. Space, right behind me. A swooping sensation, both in my chest and stomach, like I'm on a fairground rollercoaster. Jasmine's eyes widen almost comically, and she lunges forward, but it's all at once too fast and too slow.

Then I realise that my foot isn't finding the floor. It isn't finding anything. Because there isn't any floor there.

My leg crumples under me, and I go down hard. Time comes crashing back in a breathless tangle of searing pain and screaming. I tumble over and over until I finally strike something solid and the momentum of my fall comes to an abrupt end. I try to raise my head, but I can't. Everything feels both too dim and too bright as I hear a thundering and someone gasping, 'Ambulance, ambulance, please, a pregnant woman has fallen down the stairs and I think she's really hurt—'

And then everything fades to black.

TWENTY-FOUR

The doctor says I'm lucky. I don't have any lasting injuries, just a sprained ankle and a bruised shoulder. They're more worried about concussion, which is why they're keeping me in for a couple of nights, but the medical team thinks I probably fainted from the shock of the fall rather than having been knocked out.

It doesn't stop every part of me from aching, though.

Thankfully, Sprout is fine. The little monkey is made of stern stuff, because her heartbeat is as strong as ever and she's passed all the tests they've done on her with flying colours. There were tears in Russ's eyes when they told him, so maybe all is not lost between us.

Jasmine came with me in the ambulance. The crew said she did a great job. Calmed Olivia down, helped them get me out, locked up, got in contact with Russ, the whole shebang. I'd be grateful, if she wasn't the reason I'm here in the first place.

I keep trying to play that moment over and over in my head, but it's fuzzy. Sometimes I'm positive she pushed me. Other times I'm not so sure. All I know for certain is that she got closer, and the next thing I know, I'm flying through the air.

She says I slipped on the laundry I'd dropped at the top of

the stairs. That I was upset about 'something'. Ha. Something. Of course she doesn't want anyone to know the truth. That wouldn't look very good, would it?

But at the same time, I haven't said anything, either. Because now, in the cold light of day, I'm not sure I come out of it any better. I still don't have any tangible evidence, so if I say anything now, all Russ has to do is play the 'hysterical pregnant woman' card, and we all know how that ends.

So I spend my time in hospital being good. I let the staff do their tests. I eat the food they bring me. I banter with the orderlies and nurses. I look forward to visiting times. I try not to think about what is going on at home. How they're alone now. How Jasmine can play the wife to her heart's content. How she's probably already moved herself into my bedroom. Into my bed. I can picture it all with far too much clarity. The expensive wine. The steak she cooks him for dinner. Reading Olivia her favourite story before bed. Cuddling up on the sofa to watch a movie until they're sure she's asleep, then unbridled passion, first on the sofa, then upstairs. I know, because at one point, that was us. That was our life.

But not now.

Now, things are... strained. We don't really feel like a married couple anymore, more like roommates who just happen to share a bed. Whatever connection there was between us has been stretched thin, to the point where it is almost transparent.

And now Sprout has come along.

We didn't plan her. If I'm honest, the last thing I wanted was another baby ruining my already ravaged figure. I used to be slim. I used to turn heads. Now all I get is sympathetic smiles.

I went from being someone to being yet another nobody.

I was trying to do something about it. I was going to the gym, had my surgery booked. Nothing drastic: a tummy tuck and breast lift. Maybe some liposuction to help contour my hips and thighs. We even got a discount because Russ works at the hospital. Obviously he wouldn't be operating on me, but he knew exactly what I needed to make me feel better about myself. Once I could fit back into my old clothes, I'd feel better. I'd *be* better.

But that all changed when those little lines turned blue.

I lie in my hospital bed, the curtain drawn tightly around me giving me the illusion of privacy, but I can still hear the woman in the bed next to mine snoring softly. I'm not even sure what's real and what isn't. What if I have it all wrong? What if everything is in my head, age-old paranoias colliding with brand-new ones I'm not even sure I'm ready to face?

And I'm left with the classic dilemma: what if, rather than bringing us together, this baby rips us apart?

I'm given the all-clear on day four. They kept me in another night because they were a little concerned about my blood pressure. I decided to keep quiet about the weird tingling feeling I keep getting in my hands and feet. I have a feeling that if I let that one slip, I won't be going anywhere.

Russ comes to pick me up with Olivia. She runs to me, her arms open wide, shouting 'Mama!' so loudly it echoes around the ward. Russ is grinning and holding a huge bouquet of flowers, which he gives me with a warm peck on the cheek. To an outsider, all of this must look like the perfect reunion. And it is. Or it would be, if I could let go of my nagging doubts.

'Where's Jasmine?' I ask.

'I gave her the afternoon off,' Russ says. There is no edge to his voice, no sense of tension or frustration, just warmth and relief. 'I thought it would be nice to be just the four of us for a bit.' He slips one arm around my shoulder and places his free hand on my bump. 'Now, you listen here, Sprout. Time to stop giving Mama such a hard time, y'hear? Not today, at least. We're going to have a nice, relaxing afternoon.'

'I makes cake!' Olivia says, jumping up and down and tugging at my arm.

'You did? How wonderful!' I say.

'Yup, it a lemony cake.'

I look over at Russ and then back to Olivia.

'That's my favourite,' I say.

'I know,' Russ says.

'Did Jasmine help you?' I ask Olivia.

'No, Papa did!'

'Papa... did?'

'Yep.' Russ's grin widens, making him look absurdly proud. 'I did. I found a recipe and it didn't sink or anything.'

I can't help but laugh.

'Good thing my favourite isn't a Sachertorte, then.'

His grin falters a little.

'What's a Sachertorte?'

'It's a posh chocolate cake,' I say. 'Quite delicious, but I bet not a patch on your lemon cake.'

'Well, we'll see,' Russ says. 'You got everything?'

And that's it. Back home, with my family.

Back to normality.

At least, I hope so.

TWENTY-FIVE

I don't notice anything out of the ordinary at first. At the very least, I was expecting to come home to loads of laundry and maybe a dishwasher disaster, but everything seems to be under control. Maybe Jasmine has earned the afternoon off after all.

I can see the cake Olivia and Russ made under the netted cake stand. It looks a little rough around the edges, but no less delicious for it. There's even a vase out ready for my flowers. The kitchen floor has been swept and the bin has been emptied. It's almost as if life can carry on without me being there to pick everything up after everyone.

It's only when I go out into the garden that I notice something is not quite right.

'Uh, Russ? Why is the dining room furniture by the summer house?'

Russ strolls out and hands me a glass of elderflower cordial, another of my favourites. Lemon cake. Flowers. The nanny isn't around. The house is immaculate. Now chilled elderflower cordial? Complete with a little sprig of home-grown mint in it?

It's almost like he's buttering me up or something.

'Ah, yes, well, I'm moving the table and chairs into the summer house.'

'Why?'

'To make room.' Gone is the easy confidence of before, replaced by something a little shadier. I give him time to expand on this, but when he doesn't offer any details, I have to prod.

'To make room for what? Oh God, you didn't buy a pool table or something stupid—'

'No, no, nothing like that.'

'So what did you get?'

'I didn't buy anything, silly.'

'So, why?' I gesture at the inside furniture that is currently very much outside.

'Okay, I wasn't sure how to approach you about this, but I guess now is as good as ever, so... and before I say anything, it's done, you can't argue, I've spoken to your medical team and they think it's for the best, and Papa came over and spent the morning with me getting all of this ready for you, and so while I know you're not going to like it, you can't take any more risks—'

'Oh, for pity's sake, just spit it out.'

'I've turned the dining room into a bedroom. For you.'

I know I should say something, but I can't speak. In the end, I just stand there, gaping at him, unsure if I actually heard him correctly.

'Don't look like that,' he says. 'It's for the best. I've made you a bedroom in the dining room. So you'll be safe. Well, safer.'

I can't say anything. All I can do is stand and stare at him. Because I'm not sure I heard him correctly.

'It's okay,' he says. 'Papa and I went up to Ikea and got you a lovely little daybed, very comfortable, plus it doubles up as a couch, should you need it. I've put in the telly from the nook, plus one of the Alexas, and... look, I know it's not ideal, but I can't have you tromping up and down the stairs all the time.

What if Jasmine hadn't been there? What if it had just been you and Olivia? I can't even bear thinking about it.'

I take a sip of my cordial, then immediately wish I hadn't. It has a strange, almost metallic back-taste, but I think that's probably just fury rather than there being anything actually wrong with it.

'So you decided to relegate me to the dining room without asking me first,' I say, as quietly and as steadily as I can.

'Oh, come on, Frankie, it's not relegating you—'

'Then what is it?'

'It's... keeping you safe.'

'Without asking me.'

'I'm sorry, I didn't realise that taking precautions to protect the physical health of my pregnant wife was something I needed to ask permission for.'

'I'm not saying you need to ask permission, but—'

'Frankie, please. What else was I supposed to do? You're pregnant and you fell down the stairs!'

But I didn't fall down the stairs, I think. *I was pushed.*

... wasn't I?

'I know, but I just don't want to sleep downstairs.'

'Why not? It's not as if it's forever.'

'I know, but, I... I just...'

'Frankie? Is there something you're not telling me?' Russ tilts his head to one side, as if he's sizing me up, the way a teacher might a naughty student. My chest caves, because I know I should tell him. We're supposed to be equals. Partners. But I can't. Because, according to him and everyone else, Jasmine is the heroine. She got me to safety. If it hadn't been for her, my tumble would have been a lot more serious.

How on earth am I going to tell them that if it hadn't been for her, I wouldn't be in this mess in the first place?

'It doesn't matter,' I mumble into my glass.

'Oh no, you're not going to brush me off like that. Spit it out.'

He's staring at me. I can see his impatience in the way the muscle in his cheek twitches. I can't tell him. He'd call me crazy. But I also can't stay quiet. Because what if I am right and Jasmine escalates? First she's pushing me down the stairs – what's next? If she really wants rid of me, how far will she go?

'I just... don't feel safe. Being downstairs. I wouldn't be able to hear Olivia, if anything happened in the night.'

Russ barks a disbelieving laugh.

'Olivia is fine. She hardly ever wakes in the night now, and I'm more than capable of dealing with her. If you're that worried, we can sort out a baby monitor for you.' He narrows his eyes. 'But that's not what's really bothering you, is it? This isn't about Olivia at all.'

I wrap my arms around myself and shrug, wishing I could sink into the ground and disappear. I feel a searing pain in my mouth followed by a coppery taste. It's been a long time since I nervously chewed up the inside of my mouth; I thought I'd conquered that habit, but I guess a leopard doesn't change its spots after all. I silently beg Russ to change the subject, but he seems quite happy to see me squirm until I can't help but blurt it out.

'I didn't fall down the stairs. I was pushed.'

'You were... pushed?'

'Yes.' I stare at the grass, unable to meet Russ's eye.

'And who pushed you?'

'Look, let's leave it—'

'Frances.' Russ's eyes are as black and as flat as a shark's. 'Who pushed you?'

I drop my head and whisper, 'Jasmine.'

He stares at me for what is probably only a second, but it feels like a soul-sucking age before he shakes his head and lets out a hollow laugh.

'Oh, Frankie, that's a new low, even for you. I mean, I know you have jealousy issues, and I've largely come to terms with that—'

'This isn't about jealousy.'

'Isn't it? Why else would you accuse *our nanny* of pushing you? My God, I love you, Frankie, but you are *delusional*. I'm trying so hard to hold everything together, to keep us afloat, and you're there making up grand fantasies in your head... like, I don't even know what to do anymore. I know you had to come off the meds for your pregnancy. It was rough last time, but this time, you're unhinged. Every day adds yet more insanity.'

'I'm not unhinged!' I say, blinded by unexpected tears. 'I caught you! I wasn't going to say anything, but I saw that you've been texting her behind my back—'

He starts laughing again.

'By "her", I assume you mean Jasmine again? Yes. I have been texting her. I've been texting her to keep an eye on you. To make sure you're okay. To ensure that nothing terrible has happened while I'm at work.'

'Oh, right, and you just so happened to be in the background of a photo she posted on her Instagram too, then?'

'What photo? What are you on about?'

'Jasmine took Olivia to Little Wrigglers the other day, the day you said you couldn't come home in the afternoon because you had to cover Jacqui, but later I looked at Jasmine's Instagram and there was a photo of her and Olivia and you were in the background.'

'Really? You sure about that?' He pulls out his phone, unlocks it and holds it out to me. He's already opened the Instagram app. 'Do you want to show me?'

'I can't,' I whisper.

'Why not?' Russ snaps.

'Because it was deleted.'

'It was deleted. Right.'

'Yes, it was, because I went back to take a screenshot later and it was gone.'

Russ puts his phone away and presses the heels of his hands into his eyes.

'Frankie, it wasn't deleted. It wasn't there because it doesn't exist! I don't know what else to tell you. I'm going to call the doctor again. I think you might need more help than I can give you. This has gone too far now.'

'No, I... I... but I saw... I...'

The garden spins around me. What was once warm and pleasant becomes oppressive, suffocating. I hear the distant crash of glass breaking, then the pungent odour of something sweet. Russ is saying something, but he sounds like he's underwater. Flurries of pins and needles race up and down my limbs, forcing me to the ground. I lie there, gasping like a fish, trying to drag oxygen from air the consistency of syrup.

The sensation of movement makes my stomach roll. I groan as I'm placed on something soft. It's darker now, but no cooler. Russ is still talking. I try to focus on his words, but I feel so tired.

So very, very tired.

TWENTY-SIX

I don't recognise my surroundings when I come to. For a moment, panic seizes me. Am I back in the hospital? But then little things begin to make sense. The clock. The pictures on the wall. The carpet.

This is my dining room, without the usual furniture.

To give him some credit, Russ has done his best. The daybed is comfortable. My flowers are in a vase on the table next to me. A small media centre has been set up in the corner. There's even a remote control within arm's reach. A jug of water with some half-melted ice cubes sits on the sideboard, the only thing that has survived the Furniture Purge. It has a generous sprig of garden mint bobbing in it. A packet of ginger biscuits stands guard next to it.

To all intents and purposes, this looks very thoughtful. If I was a guest here, I'd be absolutely stoked. But I'm not a guest here. This is my own house, my own home.

I don't know what to do about it.

On the surface, what Russ is saying makes sense. Him not wanting me to be using the stairs after everything that's happened? I get it. If our roles were reversed, I'd probably suggest the same thing. Anything to keep my spouse and baby safe. But that doesn't stop the nasty, crawling sensation from skittering around my chest.

Something is wrong.

Is it me?

I haven't wanted to think about this. Russ has always protested his innocence, even when the evidence mounted up against him. He said it was a conspiracy against him. Against *us*. Even when I showed him everything I'd uncovered, he said it wasn't true. That I was believing other people over him. That he couldn't believe I'd do that to him.

At first I swore I'd never have anything to do with him again. But time makes fools of us all, and I did. A coffee here. A drink there.

A night spent together, reminiscing.

Why? Because deep down, I wanted to believe him. I wanted him to be right.

Again he swore they had it in for him. That the girl, the nurse, was angry because he'd turned her down. She was crazy; a stalker; a dangerous fantasist. That he'd never cheat on me. I was too precious for that.

When we first split up, I was so proud that I hadn't fallen for it. That I'd kicked him to the kerb for daring to disrespect me. But as time went on, I began to wonder. The people who said they were only looking out for me, who said Russ was using me, were the same people who flirted shamelessly with him on nights out. I often had to hold onto him for dear life, not because I didn't trust him, but because I couldn't trust *them*. And then when he passed all of his medical exams and started working towards becoming a surgeon... that's when everything changed. My friends, even my family, found it hard to accept. People say they only want the best for you, but when 'the best' comes in a form that is so far above what they're used to? They get scared. Defensive. They feel inadequate.

Dad was like that. He said Russ looked down on him. That he'd never done an honest day's work in his life, despite him training to be a doctor. I think Dad would have been happier if I'd ended up with a mechanic, or someone who worked in construction. Those were the kind of men Dad understood. The graft they undertook was obvious; the work, honest. You want a wall? Build it. Your car fixed? Get under the bonnet. But Russ confused him. Everything from his accent to his manners, to the easy way he offered to pay for everything; to Dad it felt false. Mum was enamoured – she called Russ a 'real gentleman', but Dad... Dad only saw the threat. That this suave Southerner could offer his little girl a life he could barely imagine. To Dad, stocks and shares were just posh gambling, and if you didn't come home with dirt under your fingernails, you weren't really trying.

He told me 'that man is going to break your heart one of these days'.

Tears gather and my vision turns blurry. I don't know why I'm thinking of these things. It doesn't help. No matter what, the only family I have left is currently under this roof. Olivia and Sprout will never know their maternal grandparents. And, with any luck, they'll never know why that is, either.

That it's all their mother's fault.

I scrub at my eyes and grit my teeth. No. Now is not the time for maudlin nonsense. Because Russ isn't the issue here. Just like before, my issue isn't with him.

It's with *her*.

I have no doubt Jasmine's the one who planted this particular seed, most likely with help from Petunia. Under usual circumstances, I'd have brushed her off like a gnat. Unfortunately, she's come into our lives at a time of vulnerability. But that only makes her agenda even more evil. And the fact that it's probably being if not orchestrated, then at least sponsored by Russ's mother makes it even worse.

I have to be careful. I have to be prepared. There's no point confronting Russ with baseless accusations.

It all comes down to proof. Proper hard evidence that no one can wriggle out of.

I go to sit up. The room spins. My stomach turns in response, but a few deep, gulping breaths seem to have it under control.

This would be so much easier if I wasn't so sick.

The thundering of small feet on the floor of the room above my head tells me Olivia is up from her nap. I hear her come running down the stairs and I wait for her to burst into the dining room, full of smiles and demands for cuddles. But the footsteps continue past the dining room.

Ahh, she probably hasn't been told I'm in here. She probably went to the nook to look for me.

So I wait.

And wait.

A delighted shriek rings out from the garden. Olivia, clearly enjoying herself.

I stagger up from the daybed and pad over to the window.

There she is, being spun in a circle by Jasmine, as happy as can be.

They slow down, and both collapse into a giggling pile on the floor. Olivia is the first up, demanding, 'More! More!' Jasmine laughs a little breathlessly and tells her she needs a little break.

Then she stands up, and looks towards my window.

We lock eyes. She smiles.

Russ then comes out with two long-stem flutes. Probably a nicely chilled Prosecco of a decent vintage, because Filippo taught his son well when it comes to such things. Russ smiles as he hands her a glass. Jasmine smiles back as they chink the glasses together, then slides her gaze back to me. Olivia plays at their feet. They would be the perfect family, if it wasn't for the fact that his wife was the one watching them.

I ball my hands up into fists. She's not even hiding it now.

I'm going to put a stop to this, right now.

I march over to the door, grasp the handle and pull.

The door gives for a fraction of a centimetre, but refuses to budge any further.

I frown, some of my fury leaching away, only to be replaced with uncertainty.

With fear.

I pull the door again. Again, it refuses to open.

I don't understand. I can't be locked in. This door doesn't even have a lock.

Third time's the charm. Except, in this case, it isn't.

I pull the door again, this time using my body weight to try and dislodge whatever it is that's blocking it. But no matter how hard I pull, it won't budge. I jiggle the handle, and finally give the door a kick.

There's a shriek from outside. I waddle back over to the window.

Olivia has her Super Soaker out. She's chasing Russ and Jasmine with it. Everyone is laughing.

Everyone, except me.

I bang on the glass, hoping to catch their attention, but they're too far up the garden, engrossed in their game. Or, at least, Olivia is.

Jasmine is once again looking over at the house. At me.

Still smiling.

TWENTY-SEVEN

'Come on, Frankie. It was clearly an accident.'

It took them another ten minutes before they noticed me. Or, more accurately, it took Russ ten minutes. Ten minutes of me rapping on the glass. Ten minutes of me yelling. I tried to open the windows, but they were all locked. For 'safety reasons', allegedly.

By the time Olivia tugged on Russ's shirt and pointed towards me, I was on the verge of breaking the glass.

'An accident? I was locked in!' I'm still a little breathless from my ordeal. Jasmine comes into the room with a cup of tea and sets it down next to me. It takes all I have not to hurl the lot back at her.

'Honey, the mop fell and jammed itself under the handle. I'd been using it to get your room ready and hadn't put it away. It was just one of those things.'

It was just one of those things. Like this happens all the time.

Except it's never happened before.

. . .

After the locking-in incident, I can't help but feel a little paranoid. Every wet floor is now a trap, every stray toy strategically placed to trip me up. Given the staircase plot didn't work, it's clear she's trying again.

And again.

And again.

It's getting to the point where I'm not sure I feel safe leaving my room, but because I have no doubt that's her entire plan, I ensure I'm always around. I can't let her out of my sight. It's bad enough that she sees my mother-in-law alone. Who knows what they're plotting.

I'm so tired.

This morning she's ironing, something I've never asked her to do. Olivia is playing with her Duplo. I'm watching TV. I'm also desperate for the loo, but don't dare pass by her. All it would take is for me to 'nudge her'. For her hand to 'slip'. A third degree burn. A story about how it was all an accident.

Me, back in the hospital.

Her, alone in my house with my husband again.

She finishes the last shirt and puts it on a hanger, then unplugs the iron and takes it back into the kitchen.

At last. I rush to the bathroom.

By the time I'm out, Jasmine is in the garden. I can hear Olivia chattering away to her. I watch them from the kitchen as they water the tomatoes and strawberry plants, then move on to the sprouting greens.

While Jasmine harvests, Olivia plays. She picks up the watering can and sprinkles water over the grass, before lifting it over her head and watering herself.

'No, Olivia, you mustn't do that!'

Jasmine's reaction is swift – and over the top. Olivia drops the watering can, pauses for a second, then wails, clearly not understanding what she has done wrong. I don't, either. She's in her messy clothes. Playing with water on a warm day is fine. I consider intervening, but Olivia is now in full swing and I'm secretly enjoying the hard time she's giving Jasmine. That's my girl: scream, kick, throw yourself to the floor. Be difficult. Be challenging. Don't let the bitch grind you down.

Although... there's a twinge of worry mixed in with the triumph. I won't say Olivia is the perfect child. She has her moments; like all toddlers, she is no stranger to the tantrum. But recently... recently they have become more of a feature, and I can't help but be concerned that whatever games Jasmine is playing, they're having an effect on my precious daughter.

My stomach growls. I'm not sure if it's the sickness or hunger. Apart from the smoothie Jasmine made me this morning, I haven't eaten much today. Maybe a ginger biscuit might help settle me.

I keep an eye on Olivia's antics in the garden as I wander over to the pantry. She has seemingly calmed down, her screeches now whimpers as she counts the tomatoes on the vines with Jasmine. If they all ripen we should have a good haul—

At first, I can't work out what happened. I opened the pantry door, then... a crash, followed by searing pain. I gasp and clutch at my head, momentarily dazed. I back away from the pantry, then stumble over something heavy and warm.

It's the iron.

Something warm trickles down the side of my face. I take my hand off my head and stare at it.

Blood.

It takes me a moment to piece everything together. The iron. The pantry door.

Up on a shelf.

'What the... what happened?'

I have no idea how long Jasmine has been there. I wipe away at the blood rolling down the side of my head.

'The iron... it fell out. On me.'

'Oh no,' Jasmine says. She looks the very picture of concern. 'Here, let me look at that.'

I take a step back.

'Why did you put the iron on that shelf?'

'Um, because that's where I thought it lived.'

I eye her warily.

'No, Jasmine, that is not where the iron lives. Who would put an iron up on a top shelf like that? And in a pantry?'

'Yeah, I did think it was a bit odd, but you know, it's not my house so...' She trails off with a nonchalant shrug.

'I'd never put the iron up there,' I say.

'It's okay.' Her tone has shifted again, this time towards calm and soothing. 'You've been through a lot recently. Maybe you didn't realise—'

'I didn't put the iron up there!'

'Is Mama right?' Olivia has wandered in from the garden. She's undoubtedly heard me and wants to know what is going on. 'Is Mama confoos again?'

'No, it's okay, Olliebean. She's just had a little accident.'

'A accident? Oh no, Mama! Mama is bleeding!' Olivia's face crumples and I crouch down far too quickly to comfort her, causing my head to swim.

'Mama's fine,' I say, stroking her hair. 'I just bashed my head. That's all.'

'Mama... okay?' Olivia's bottom lip wobbles.

'Yes, Pumpkin, Mama's okay. Just an accident.'

Jasmine frowns as she peers at my head.

'I don't know... maybe you should go to minor injuries. Get that checked out.'

'No, it'll be fine,' I say, a little too quickly. Because there's no way I'm going back to any kind of hospital. At some point they're going to start asking questions, questions I'm not sure I can properly answer. Not yet, anyway.

'At least let me clean it. See how bad it is.'

I nod, because what else am I going to do?

I sit on one of the high stools that are tucked under the breakfast bar while Jasmine fetches the first aid kit. She cleans the cut with an antiseptic wipe; I wince as the astringent stings.

'It's not deep,' Jasmine says, peering at my scalp. 'I'll pop a plaster on, that should be enough. You're going to have an interesting bruise. There's already a lump forming.' She finishes the job and then rummages in the freezer for a cold pack, which she holds out to me. 'For the swelling.'

I take the pad and hold it gently to my head. Now the adrenaline has settled, I'm feeling tired and shaken.

'Poor Mama,' Olivia says, and pats my knee. 'Head all broken.'

As she says this, I can see Jasmine's lips twist out of the corner of my eye.

Because she knows this is true, in more ways than one.

TWENTY-EIGHT

I wake to the sound of whimpering. It takes me a moment to orientate myself; the door is in the wrong place, as is the window, but finally I manage to piece together where I am: the dining room. My own little slice of purgatory.

The whimpering is coming from the baby monitor. Russ tried to reassure me that I shouldn't worry about it, that he'd deal with Olivia if she woke in the night, but I insisted. And not just because Russ has never been one for dealing with Olivia at night. It would also be a way for me to keep an ear out on what was going on upstairs.

I have a horrible suspicion that's why he didn't want me to have it.

I struggle to sit up, my head swooning. I can't believe how dizzy I'm feeling these days. The midwife said it was probably down to being chronically dehydrated, so I take a few sips of water before I risk standing up.

Olivia is still whimpering, and there's no sign of movement, meaning I doubt Russ has even noticed. Quite how he sleeps so deeply when he knows he might be needed, I don't know, but I can't lie, I'm kind of jealous of him.

Every step is torture as I climb the stairs. I take in deep breaths, hoping that will be enough to ease my dizziness and bubbling stomach. Maybe Russ was onto something and sleeping downstairs isn't such a bad idea after all. By the time I reach the top of the stairs I'm sweating so much I feel a trickle down the side of my face. At first I wonder if it's my cut, but when I check, my fingertips come back clear. I guess I'm just unfit these days.

Olivia is waiting for me in the hallway. She has a froggy under one arm and is rubbing at her eyes with her fists. She looks dopey, and when I approach her, she lets out another whimpered 'Mama', which breaks my heart. I should be up here, ready to soothe her when needed, not relegated to the dining room, leaving her to suffer on her own.

'It's okay, baby,' I say, keeping my voice low and smooth. 'Mama's here.'

Olivia raises her arms. I try to pick her up, but something twinges deep within me, so instead I crouch down and let her wrap her arms around my neck. Her hair is damp against my cheek, and she's running a little hot. I wonder if she's starting a fever. I hope not. That's the last thing we need.

'Mama,' Olivia says again.

'I know, Pumpkin. It's all right. Let's get you back to bed, hmm?'

'There was lady.'

I stop trying to figure out how I'm going to carry her.

'What was that?'

But Olivia is yawning, ready to go back to sleep.

'Pumpkin? What lady?' When she doesn't respond, I give her a little shake. 'Olivia? What do you mean, there was a lady?'

Olivia's whimpers metamorphose into more of a howl, but I don't care. I have to know what she means.

My stomach drops.

'Olivia, answer Mama. Who was it?'

Of course, I know the answer. Who else could it be?

'Hey, what's going on out here?' Russ has appeared behind us, his eyes bleary and his hair rumpled. 'What are you doing up here, Frankie?'

'I heard Olivia on the monitor,' I say, a little more coldly than I intended. 'She was out of bed.'

'Sorry, darling, I didn't hear her. Come on, Pumpkin, let's get you back to bed.'

'She said she saw a lady.'

Russ bends down and takes Olivia from me. She immediately nestles comfortably against his neck, her thumb jammed in her mouth.

'Probably a dream,' he says.

'I don't think so. She said there was a lady.'

Russ sighs heavily.

'Darling, I have to go to work early tomorrow. I really don't have time for your nonsense right now. Olivia clearly had a dream, was confused—'

But I'm not listening to him. I'm fed up of being told I'm mistaken.

'Olivia, Pumpkin, who was the lady? Who was it, sweetheart?'

But Olivia has already returned to the land of nod.

'Olivia,' I say, a little louder. 'Who was the lady?'

'Frankie, what is wrong with you?' Russ hisses.

'I need to know who it was.' Even though I think I already know.

'Oh, for the love of... go back downstairs,' Russ says, clearly exasperated. 'I'll put Olivia back to bed.'

'But—'

'No, Frankie. I'm not doing this. I know what you're insinuating, and it's ridiculous. Stop it.'

He turns away from me and stalks off into Olivia's room.

I make to go back downstairs, but as I pass our bedroom

door, I notice that it's closed. Why would Russ close the bedroom door?

Unless...

I go into our bedroom. *My* bedroom. But despite this, I feel strangely uncomfortable in here, like I'm not welcome. I pad over to the bed, looking for any tell-tale signs that someone else, someone *female*, has been in here recently. All I need is a blonde hair, a smear of make-up, a—

'Frances, what the hell are you doing now?'

Russ runs both his hands through his hair and looks beseechingly at the ceiling.

I pick up one of the pillows and sniff it, just in case there's a lingering scent of a strange perfume.

'Frankie... stop it. This is ridiculous. I don't know what you think you're looking for, but this has to stop.' He leans towards me, like he's going to tell me off.

'I'm not crazy!' I don't mean to yell. 'I know why you want me to sleep downstairs.'

Russ starts laughing, but there is no humour behind it.

'I think I'm going to call someone first thing in the morning,' he says. 'Because you need help. *Professional* help.'

'I don't—'

'Is everything okay?'

Both Russ and I jump at the question. There, in the doorway of our bedroom, stands Jasmine. She's in yet another skimpy set of pyjamas that show off her toned legs and slim arms.

'Sorry, Jasmine, didn't mean to wake you.' Russ forces a smile onto his face. 'Olivia had a bad dream and Frankie heard her – I think it spooked her a bit. Why don't you just go back to bed, huh? Frankie's just going back to her room.'

Jasmine nods and gives us both a little wave.

'Okay, cool, if you need me—'

'We won't,' Russ says. 'I'm sorry. You shouldn't have to deal with this at night.'

She lets out a little yawn and leaves.

Once she's gone, Russ turns his attention back to me.

'You need to go back to bed.'

'I could just sleep here—'

'No,' Russ snaps. 'You need to go back downstairs. I need to catch up on my sleep, and I don't need you waking me up, accusing me of stupid things again.' He points over at our bedroom door, and I'm left with no choice. I shuffle from our room like a chastened child and make my way over to the top of the stairs, taking a moment to glance up the set that lead to Jasmine's room.

The door is ajar. Not closed, like I would expect.

Open.

She's mocking me. I'm sure of it. For all her efforts to make sure she looks suitably sleepy, she forgot one thing:

No one wakes up with salon-fresh hair.

TWENTY-NINE

I stare at the envelope. It has my name in capital letters on it. I don't recognise the handwriting. It's been left under the windscreen wiper of my car. I noticed it when I went out to water the roses. There is no address, postmark or stamp on it, meaning it's definitely been delivered by hand. I glance up and down the street, but I don't see any evidence of anyone out here. I'm pretty sure it wasn't there earlier, or Russ would have seen it when he went to work.

The fact that whoever left it has gone to so much trouble to remain anonymous causes a little pit to open in my stomach.

It's a pit that only widens when I read the letter the envelope holds.

It's written on plain printer paper, folded into quarters. The writing is the same blocky capitals as my name. The message is short and to the point:

YOU NEED TO GET OUT. PACK A BAG AND LEAVE NOW. DON'T TELL ANYONE. YOU ARE IN DANGER.

I steady myself against the side of my car. I'm in danger? From whom? Again, I look up and down my road, wondering who might have written this note. What have they noticed? What have they seen? Why can't they just come and tell me? They must know that I have times when I'm alone. They left the note after Russ went to work, so whoever they are, they're watching me. Watching us.

I fold the letter up and manage to stagger back into the house. It's a good job everyone expects me to be a bit pale and wobbly, so when Jasmine sees me, she doesn't ask if I'm okay.

'Was that a parcel?' she says.

'Pardon?'

'A parcel? Is that why you went out the front?'

'No, no, I went out to water the roses and I saw something on my car. Just some rubbish. I was worried someone had vandalised it, but it was just a piece of paper.'

'Ah, right. Been windy recently.'

'It has.'

I study her face, but it remains neutral as she launches into her plans for the day. She's going to do some basic phonics with Olivia first, then they're going for a walk up to the stream to play pooh sticks as long as the weather holds, then lunch, then they'll go and get some groceries because she's noticed we're getting low on milk and onions, plus a few other staples, and maybe some yeast so she and Olivia can make bread. She makes no mention of last night whatsoever. Her voice is temporarily drowned out by the whirr of the smoothie maker. A couple of minutes later, she hands me the concoction.

'So today I've put in some home-grown baby kale, some blueberries, some raw cacao, a teaspoon of honey, some home-grown sprout tops and almond milk.'

She watches me until I feel I have no other choice but to take a sip. It's awful, but I smile anyway.

'Is it okay?'

'Yeah. Thank you.'

'You're welcome.' She turns away and I realise I've been dismissed.

After selecting something suitably innocent on TV, I make myself comfortable on the daybed and wait until I'm sure no one is going to barge in before reading the letter again.

It's only eighteen words long, but I don't think I've ever seen a more menacing eighteen words in my life.

I'm in danger? What kind of danger? Maybe whoever it is saw the blowout Russ and I had in the garden after I came out of hospital? If that's the case, then it has to be someone who can see into our property. I get up off the bed, grunting a little as I momentarily forget I'm literally lumping a whole other person around inside me.

Who can see into our garden?

Well, the Singh-Kohlis definitely can. They live over the back of us. They have three kids and are very nice. They invite us to their Diwali celebrations every year, and in turn, they come to ours for Christmas Eve drinks. But I don't think it would be them. I'm pretty sure if either Gurpreet or Dhruv were worried, one or both of them would at least come over to check and see if things were okay. We'd do the same for them, after all.

Then there's our next-door neighbours. The Hendersons are an older couple, both retired. A bit prickly, both sensitive to noise and what they consider mess. They don't like confrontation, but are not above pushing passive-aggressive notes through our door if Olivia is too loud outside, or they think our lawns or shrubs are looking too unruly. On the face of it, they might be good candidates, except I know both of their handwriting really well, and this just doesn't match.

Surely, anyone with my number would text me, even call me. Ask to see me. Tell me in person if they were that concerned. I flick through my contacts, seeing if I can spot any likely candidates. Fiona? Jo? Zillah? Lauren? But I haven't spoken to any of them in such a long time. I've withdrawn from so many people, I think the first thing they'd do would be to contact Russ and ask if everything was all right. And I don't want them to do that. Because that would tip off whoever the threat is. They'd know I was on to them. And that would only make things even more dangerous.

Maybe I'm looking at this the wrong way. Does it really matter who sent me the note? What really matters is, what is the actual danger?

There's a tap at the door. My heart jolts. I stuff the letter under my pillow and let out a 'hmmm?', because I'm not sure if I can trust myself to speak.

'Oh, you are awake,' Jasmine says. 'I thought you might be taking a nap.'

'No, I'm fine, I was just doomscrolling, you know...' I try to smile, but it feels so false on my face.

'Do I ever. Anyway, I'm just going to take Olliebean up to the stream for a bit. Not sure when we'll be back, but we're meeting Petunia, so it'll probably be after lunch. It's eleven now, so probably around two-ish?' She looks so earnest, so innocent. She has absolutely no idea that I'm on to her, that I know exactly why she keeps meeting up with my mother-in-law, that I've figured out their schemes and plots. I'd consider it almost Shakespearean if it wasn't actually happening to me right now.

'Okay, that's fine,' I say, trying to keep the mood light. 'As you've probably guessed, I don't really have any plans, so I might just catch up on *Bake Off*. Russ hates it and complains like hell if I watch it when he's home. He doesn't like Noel. Says he's too silly.'

Jasmine lets out one of her fake Cinderella laughs. 'Ahh, I think he's funny. Anyway, you have fun.' She cocks her head to one side and gives me a look that I can only describe as 'motherly'. 'Are you sure you're going to be okay on your own? You're looking a little peaky.'

'Really? I hadn't noticed.' I smile weakly so she knows I'm joking. Kind of.

'You poor thing. I'll try and find something nice for dinner. Maybe that will make you feel better.' She doesn't wait for me to reply as she leans out of the doorway. 'Olliebean! Come and say bye bye to Mama!'

I shudder at the use of that nickname, hating that Olivia responds so readily to it as I hear the familiar sound of my daughter thundering up the hallway. She ducks under Jasmine's arm and runs into my makeshift bedroom, collapsing in my arms.

'Bye bye, Mama,' she says. I can't help but notice the two high spots of colour on her cheeks. I reach over and feel her forehead; she's not fever-hot, but she is still warmer than I'd like.

'Pumpkin, are you feeling okay?'

Olivia doesn't say anything, just buries her head into my chest.

'She's been a bit hot,' Jasmine says. 'She might be coming down with something.'

'I had a ice-lolly,' Olivia says.

'You did? What flavour?'

'Swabewy!'

I can't help but smile. We've been working on helping Olivia say her 'r' sounds correctly, but she still can't say strawberry for the life of her.

'That must have been nice.'

Olivia nods with her whole upper body, and my heart melts. I'm seized by a sudden desire to scoop her up and never let her go, to take her away, away from all of this insanity, where it's just the two of us, no deranged mother-in-laws, no scheming nannies, no hopeless husbands, just a mother and a daughter, pootling along, living their best lives.

But that's not how it works, and when Olivia tells me they're going to meet 'Gwamma', I let her clamber up off me. I stagger after them so I can wave them off at the front door with tears in my eyes.

Once Jasmine's little car turns the corner, I dash them away and set my jaw.

I now have a good couple of hours on my own.

I have work to do.

THIRTY

Motherhood makes you paranoid. Even though you had blithely declared you'd never need one of '*insert baby safety item for paranoid mums here*', you end up with seven of the blasted things anyway. 'Throw as much cash at the problem as you can' seems like a solid plan when you're sleep-deprived and scared.

This is why we have more baby monitors than we can shake a stick at. I don't think we're alone in this.

Even though I've only been sleeping downstairs for a couple of nights, the stairs feel so steep. It's amazing how out of shape I am, and by the time I reach the landing, I have to take a little break to catch my breath before near-hobbling into Olivia's bedroom. I don't know why my joints ache so much. The midwife said it happens sometimes, something to do with hormones softening ligaments, and it can be more prevalent in second pregnancies, but I'm not so sure. This feels more fizzy, like extreme pins and needles. I get it in my arms, too, and I wince as I reach up into the wardrobe to bring down a box filled with old baby monitors.

I dither over which one to pick, but end up going for the travel one. While it's sound-only and it would be useful to have visuals, it would also be harder to hide. The travel one is literally a clip, is totally wireless, but crucially isn't Bluetooth – you have to use it with the device it comes with rather than your phone, which is useful because it means if anyone looks, they won't see any suspicious devices trying to pair willy-nilly with everyone's phones. Much to my dismay, I realise it needs to be charged and my laptop is in the living room, so I have no choice but to stagger back down again. At least I won't have to fake being absolutely knackered when everyone gets home.

While the monitor charges it strikes me how sad all of this is. This should be a happy time, preparing for a new baby, looking forward to the completion of our family, but instead I'm a stranger in my own house, being replaced by a woman who wants to live in my skin, a situation arranged by another woman who despises me.

I check on the baby monitor. A hundred per cent. Thank goodness for fast charge. So it's back up the stairs, pause to catch my breath, then time to tackle the attic stairs up to Jasmine's room.

The door is locked.

I rest my sweaty forehead against the cool door. Of course it is. I gave her a key. Because that's what you do. She's allowed privacy. Thankfully there is a spare. But it is back downstairs. By this point I'm near to tears and wondering if the universe is trying to tell me something, that whatever is going on in this house is something I don't want to know after all.

Nevertheless, I trudge back downstairs, back into the kitchen and the drawer where we keep the spare keys. I dig through half-spent batteries, long-paid bills that never made it to the shredder, a whole treasure trove of elastic bands and screws of all lengths, until I finally find the spare keys. Each one is labelled.

The one to the attic is missing.

I stare in disbelief and check again. And again, the attic key is missing.

We didn't give Jasmine this key. I know we didn't, because Russ had another one cut for her. Said it made sense. 'Just in case we need it.'

And now it's gone.

I could spend the next hour tearing the house apart, hunting for it. But a nasty suspicion twists in my stomach, a sneaky little feeling that has nothing to do with Sprout.

Because as much as I don't want to admit it, I think I know where that key might be.

This is definitely one of those cases where I dearly wish I'd been wrong.

The pit in my stomach hollows and I ready myself for an emergency dash to the loo, but thankfully I manage to gulp down a few breaths and steady myself.

The key to the attic room sits cold and hard in my hand.

It took me a little while to find. At first I'd felt a warm wave of relief when I couldn't find it in Russ's bedside table. He stuffs all kinds of things in there: bits of paper, expired credit cards, pens that don't work, plastic tat from Christmas crackers. Every pretence at being a neat freak is lost in that drawer; I can't even identify half the items, nor fathom the reason why he's kept them all.

At first I rummaged, then took a load of the contents out, but there was no key. Maybe he wasn't involved after all.

But as I began to shove it all back in, something slid out from between the sheets of an old notebook.

A key.

One that matches our attic key perfectly.

And so here I am, standing in front of the attic room door,

trying to find the courage to actually use the key that might blow my entire life to smithereens.

I guide the key into the lock and turn. There is a moment's resistance, and for a second I wonder if Jasmine has had the audacity to change it, but with a little more pressure it clicks and the door opens. The pleasant scent of a warm, floral perfume wafts out.

This is it. No going back now.

It's strange how wrong I feel, going into what is essentially my own room. This has always been a nice space; the windows were designed to capture the best of the light so it always feels airy. While Jasmine isn't untidy, she by no means keeps a pristine room. I feel a little smug when I notice she isn't averse to the utilisation of the 'floordrobe'. I used to do that, too. That's why we have built-in wardrobes with plenty of space. It always drove Russ mad before we moved in together. He said he was fed up of tripping over yesterday's jeans. Well, it looks like Little Miss Perfect isn't so perfect after all, judging by her pair of yesterday's jeans slung over the back of her desk chair, and the dress bundled up on the end of her bed—

I pause as a wave of recognition sweeps over me. I pick up the dress and shake it out.

It's an asymmetrical dress with ruffles at the neck and hem. It's also one of mine. One of the ones that doesn't fit me anymore. I know it's mine, because I adore it. It's an original Dior, from their 2016 Spring Collection. Jasmine didn't find this dress on the racks at Zara or LK Bennett. For her to have the same one, she'd have to have bought it in Paris, like I did. It's one of the reasons I agreed to the tummy tuck, so I'd have a chance of being able to wear it again.

And now it's nothing more than a scrunched up ball of fabric at the end of the nanny's bed.

Rage plumes within me. The bracelet was odd, but the

dress? The dress was at the back of my wardrobe. Either Jasmine has been snooping, or someone gave it to her.

Someone who thought she'd look lovely in it, just like his wife used to before she bore a child for him.

But I can't say anything. If I do, Jasmine will know I've been in her room. I could make up an excuse. Say I heard a tap running and went in to switch it off.

I give myself a little shake. No. I can't get sidetracked. She can't know I've been in here. She'll get suspicious and might discover the monitor. Plus, I don't have forever to get this done. I check my phone. It's already half twelve. Crap! They've been gone nearly an hour and a half! How on earth has this taken so long?

As much as it pains me, I screw the dress back up into a ball and place it back on the end of Jasmine's bed. I scan the room, looking for somewhere to hide the baby monitor. There are a few potted plants dotted around, and while they're in perfect positions, if they get watered the monitor runs a very real risk of getting wet. This is a lot harder than I thought it might be. Under the bed? But what if she makes the bed and spots it? Or... I could tape it to something. It's small enough. I have a quick rummage around in Jasmine's things and find two rolls of washi tape. I pinch off a length of both so I don't use too much of either. Then I take the monitor and carefully lower myself onto the floor. I switch it on and, feeling around the base of the bed, I manage to tease it under the headboard, where I stick it in place with the tape. I sit back up and wipe beads of sweat out of my eyes, then turn on the corresponding monitor.

A little green light blinks back at me, meaning it's connected. I make sure it's set to 'listening' only, so it should be silent from this end. Still, I turn down the volume, just in case. I peer back under the bed. The washi tape doesn't quite cover up the light entirely, but it's so faint that if you didn't know it was there, you definitely wouldn't see it.

Or, at least, I hope that's the case.

I chew at my fingernails. I can't leave anything to chance.

Leaning heavily on the bed, I struggle up to my feet. Sprout starts to kick, undoubtedly protesting at this sudden uptick in physical exertion. I rub at my belly as I reach for the window blinds and pull the string. The room plunges into darkness. Even though I know where the monitor is, I can't see any sign of a green glow.

Excellent.

I open the blind back up and let out a long breath. Almost done.

Next: evidence collection. There has to be something to go with the dress. The first thing I see is Jasmine's iPad. I know it's a long shot, but I try it anyway. Of course, it's fingerprint and passcode locked. In the movies, I would be some crack passcode-hacker or know how to make fake fingerprints from bits of Sellotape, but this isn't a movie and I know straight away it's basically useless to even try. If I mess around with it too much, she's potentially going to be asked awkward security questions, plus if it's linked to her iPhone... no. It's not worth the risk. Despite it likely being the best source of information, I put the iPad down.

Next to her bed is a Bullet Journal, because *of course* there's a Bullet Journal. It's all very feminine with a soft mint pastel cover, and the affirmation 'If Not Now, When?' in gold calligraphy on the front.

The first few pages are exactly what I'd expect from someone like Jasmine: wholesome doodles, a few choice words that sound profound but don't really mean that much, a to-do list that includes drinking more water and getting out into nature more, but after that, things get... weird. Gone are the affirmations and twee wholesomeness; now it's all random sentences, letters and numbers.

E? For the B net 5682. Gave him that one. No? JJ yes.

I flick through more pages, but it's all like this.

SQ D 44. Carpark. Where? 7&9. FD3. FU22SNU. 5.

I mean, that could be a number plate... but the rest of it? I don't have a clue.

It goes on for page after page, a strange code that only she understands. Letters, numbers, the odd word that I can read but only makes everything more confusing. Whatever all of this is, it makes me feel very uneasy, an unease that turns to dread and disgust when I turn one of the pages and find a photograph that has been stuck to the page using the same kind of washi tape I'd used to hide the baby monitor.

The photo is small and has been inexpertly printed on cheap photo paper, so the colours are a little gaudy, the subjects' features a little blurred. But that doesn't stop me from recognising who the people in the photo are.

Russ and Jasmine.

Together.

THIRTY-ONE

I sit on the floor before I can collapse.

The photo must be a few years old, because Russ is completely clean shaven and Jasmine looks disturbingly young. I spend a moment trying to convince myself that this is just evidence of a girl with a crush, that she's accepted this job because she has a crippling case of unrequited love, that this photo was probably taken at one of the countless family parties Petunia holds... but when was the last time you went to a family party and your friend's teen daughter sat on your knee and you nestled your head against her chest? Because that's what it depicts.

Russ and Jasmine, looking for all the world like a couple.

I take a moment to steady myself, because the last thing I need is to throw up all over Jasmine's bed. Forget the baby, all of this is making me feel sick to my stomach. Say she is eighteen in this photo, so technically an adult – that still makes Russ thirty-six. And if she is eighteen and Russ is thirty-six, that means this photo was taken five years ago.

We got back together five years ago.

I need to get on. Time is ticking. But I can't help staring. I can't help taking in all the horrible details. His hand on her thigh. His head, resting on her chest. Her arms around him.

The happy smiles on their faces.

The bracelet she is wearing.

The one that's the exact match for the bracelet Russ bought me when we rekindled our relationship.

He didn't... no... he couldn't have...

... could he?

My vision swims then tunnels, and for a moment I worry that I might pass out. Did he get them in a special BOGOF deal or something? One for me, one for his teenage squeeze? The desire to shred Jasmine's journal seizes me, but I know I can't surrender. If I do, I'll be giving the game away. So instead, I take out my phone and photograph every page from the photo of her and Russ onwards. I'm using that as a guide for when she first moved in here – why else would she have stuck the photo in it?

Outside, I hear the purr of an engine. I freeze, clutching the journal.

It could be anyone. One of my neighbours. A delivery driver.

But I know deep in my gut that it's Jasmine, returning from her lunch with Petunia.

I take a peek out of the window, praying for it to be anyone else.

Jasmine's little Kia is idling by the kerb. I can see her sat in it, fiddling with something. Olivia is in the back, still strapped into her car seat.

I don't have long.

My heart gallops in my chest as I place the journal where I found it. I don't have time to check the room over; all I can do is hope she won't notice if I have left something out of place.

A car door slams. I hear Olivia chattering away.

I literally have seconds to spare.

I run down the stairs, my chest swooping when I slip a little.

Thankfully, I don't fall. The front door opens as I'm returning the key to Russ's bedside table.

'We're home!' Jasmine announces in a sing-song voice.

'We home!' Olivia copies.

I'm stuck. I shouldn't be up here. I should be in the dining room. Why am I up here?

I know. The shower. I needed to take a shower.

I stuff the monitor under a pillow and bolt from the bed into our en suite. I turn on the shower and quickly strip off my clothes. The cascade of water muffles the sounds of movement downstairs. I just about hear Jasmine calling my name as I step inside the cubicle.

The water is still cold, but I don't care. I scrub at myself, as if that might help clean away the horrible crawling sensation under my skin.

All the while, I try to stop myself from crying.

I fail miserably.

THIRTY-TWO

By the time I've finished my shower, I've managed to compose myself. It's okay if I look a little red and puffy around the eyes. I have gel masks for that. Since my dressing gown is downstairs, I make use of Russ's and am forced to fight back more tears as his scent envelops me.

In a way, I should be feeling triumphant. I have what I was looking for. Confirmation, of a sort. At least confirmation that my husband has been lying to me. To what degree, I still don't know, but whatever is really going on, he can't get this particular picture deleted and try to gaslight me into believing it never existed in the first place.

And then there's my nanny, the woman to whom I've entrusted the most precious thing in my life, my daughter, clearly obsessed with my husband and writing all of her plans to get rid of me in an encoded journal.

Downstairs, I hear a sudden whine, followed by crying. Olivia. I straighten myself up. I can't wallow in this. Because it's going to affect more than just me. Olivia doesn't deserve any of it, either.

I have to be strong for her sake.

Olivia's sobs have quietened down to a grizzle by the time I make it into the nook. Jasmine is sat on the floor next to my daughter, who is laying on the couch looking red-faced. Neither of them notice me hovering by the door.

'Are we going to do that again?' Jasmine says in a stern voice.

Olivia continues whining.

'Olivia? I asked you a question.'

'What's going on?' I ask. I feel a little ripple of satisfaction when I see Jasmine jump.

'Oh, hello, Frankie. I didn't know if you were in or not,' she says, and I can't help but notice the undercurrent of what I'm sure is irritation in her voice.

'I took a shower,' I say, as if she couldn't have worked that out on her own. *Hold it together, Frankie.*

'Mama...' Olivia croaks, and holds her hands out for me to pick her up.

'She bit me,' Jasmine says, holding up her arm. There's a clear mark there, little red indentations that could very well be a bite.

'She did what? But Olivia's never been a biter.'

'Well, she decided she was going to be one today.'

I reach over and brush the sweaty hair from Olivia's brow. She feels warm, and the high spots of colour are still there on her cheeks.

'I don't think she's well,' I say.

Olivia grizzles at me in agreement.

Jasmine rubs at her arm and lets out a tight sigh.

'She still shouldn't bite people.'

I agree with her. She shouldn't. But I can't help but feel there is more to this than meets the eye.

'I'm sorry she did that. Let's just get her into bed. Hopefully she'll feel better after a nap.'

For a moment, I wonder if Jasmine is going to say no, maybe

demand an apology, but after she's allowed the moment to stretch into the realms of 'uncomfortable', she nods and stands up.

'Come on, Olliebean. Let's get you to bed.'

To my own dismay, Olivia doesn't make a fuss as Jasmine scoops her up.

I may as well not even be here.

The rest of the afternoon passes slowly. Jasmine retreats into her room while Olivia naps, and I feel a momentary twinge of dread and excitement, waiting for her to thunder downstairs with the baby monitor in hand, demanding to know what the hell I'm playing at. But she doesn't. Everything is quiet in the house.

I retreat into my room and dare to turn the corresponding monitor on.

At first, I'm not even sure if it's working, because I can't hear anything. But then there's an unmistakeable thud, and Jasmine starts muttering to herself. Not loud enough for me to make out every word, but enough to get the gist of her chosen topic.

Unsurprisingly, it's me.

'... such a nightmare. Can't even... why she does it... what is wrong with her?' I can tell she's pacing. Something I've done must be really bothering her.

Good.

She continues like this, complaining about how difficult I am, until she clearly runs out of steam and falls silent for a while.

Then:

'I'm going to have to do something... needs it... he's mine, she's not getting the whole...'

I hold my breath, clutching the monitor to my ear, straining my hearing as I try to pick out all the words, but I'm still only catching snippets. What is she going to have to do? What don't I get?

'Time to step things up.'

My heart judders, then races.

Time to step things up? What the hell does she mean by that?

The jumbled memory of me stepping back and being momentarily confused when my foot was met with fresh air slams into me, followed by a swooping feeling in my chest.

She *did* push me down the stairs. She must have.

It's then that I realise that just being angry at Jasmine isn't going to be enough. Because I don't think she's trying to simply steal my husband away.

I think she's going to make sure I'm not around to mess with her plan. I need to figure out exactly what 'stepping things up' involves. And fast.

THIRTY-THREE

'You all right, love?'

I stop gnawing on my nails and give Russ a distracted smile. It's a habit I fought long and hard to break. I glance down at my hand; I've absolutely ruined my manicure.

'Oh, yes, of course. Just... tired.'

Russ nods beatifically.

'Not long to go now,' he says. 'Nearly there.'

I smile and nod back, then stop myself from chewing on my nails again.

It's hard to sit here. Hard to be here, slam-dunk in the middle of a web of lies I hardly understand but nevertheless have to stop. We're watching some US crime drama, not sure which one, not sure it really matters, anything to distract me from my roiling thoughts and boiling stomach.

They had salmon tonight, with noodles and stir-fried veg. It smelled lovely. Of course, Jasmine asked if I wanted some, too, but I could see she'd only bought two fillets. Not that I could stomach it, even if I wasn't sick.

I left him and Jasmine to eat their salmon in peace.

Olivia is already in bed. Even after her nap, she was so tired. There's definitely something wrong with her.

Just like there's definitely something wrong with me.

It's not just the sickness. It's not just the fatigue. It's the sickness and the fatigue and the joint pain and the headaches. I've got to the point where I'm even losing my hair. I brushed it after the shower and it felt like half of it fell out.

I have no idea if it's the hyperemesis, or stress, or something even more worrying than that. I've made up my mind.

I'm taking the note seriously.

That doesn't mean I'm leaving immediately. But I am making preparations in case I need to leave in a hurry. So while Russ is watching his crime drama, I'm on my phone, making a coded to-do list.

How very Jasmine of me.

It might be seen as a risk, me sitting here, doing this. And it is. But it's also a test. To see if he notices. To see if he asks.

He doesn't.

His phone rings, and judging by the way he answers it, it's his father. They talk quickly in Italian, laughing every now and again. Russ looks at me a few times, leaving me in no doubt that I am at least a topic of their conversation. I wish I understood more Italian beyond the basics; I asked Russ to teach me, but he grew frustrated when I struggled with something that came so naturally to him, so in the end I gave up and resigned myself to relying on him when it came to communicating with the Minetti side of his family.

After a final round of *ciao*, Russ hangs up.

'Papa,' he says, like I'd never guess.

'Anything important?'

'Not really. Just wanted to catch up.'

He goes back to watching the TV.

So far, I only have a few things noted down. No matter what,

I'll need cash, because it's harder to trace. Enough to allow me to spend a few nights at a cheapo Travelodge or something, at least. I wish I'd listened to my mum. Even before I met Russ, she told me to never go all in with anyone, to keep a rainy day fund. I was shocked at first, finding out that she had two grand hidden away, just in case. She and my Dad were as happy as any couple who'd been together long-term, but she said that didn't matter. It wasn't a case of happiness, or love, or even trust. Because as much as we treasure those things and wish they'd stay with us forever, they can be ripped away in an instant. But I didn't listen. I thought there was no way I'd end up like those women. I'd see it all coming. I'm not stupid. I'd fight tooth and nail for what was mine. I realise now how naive I've been; how dismissive I was of women in situations like mine.

Although I'd be the first to admit that I don't know exactly what this situation is.

I glance over at Russ. I notice he's drinking again. Tonight he's on the scotch, and that's never good. I don't like scotch. It smells like petrol and burning pine cones and tastes even worse. I'd never ask him to give it up completely, but it always makes him so handsy after he's had a few drams, and the stench of his whisky breath always turns my stomach. In a way, I'm glad we'll be sleeping apart tonight.

He catches me looking at him and raises an eyebrow. Even with everything, my breath catches. He's still very handsome, and the eyebrow thing... I've always liked it. It makes him look rakish, kind of naughty, like he knows things he shouldn't. I can't help but smile, and he leans over and rubs at my foot.

Oh, God, what if I've got all of this wrong?

But the photo in Jasmine's journal. My dress in her room. 'Stepping things up'. Even if I don't know exactly what's going on, things have been kept from me. No matter the outcome, or the plan, or whatever the hell this is, that's still wrong. I'm still allowed to be aggrieved.

Right?

I shut down my Notes app. Maybe I should sleep on it all. I'm so tired and confused. I exaggerate a yawn and tell Russ I think I'm going to turn in. He smiles up at me as I struggle up off the sofa then bend down to kiss him goodnight. He stretches out a hand to touch my bump and says goodnight to Sprout, and then to me, which just deepens my confusion. Maybe I should just talk to him. Ask him about it all. There could be an innocent explanation, like he said in the garden the other day. It could all be a mixture of hormones and half-truths and old fears and crossed wires, whipped up into whatever mess is currently fermenting in my mind.

But I don't. Instead, I straighten up, puffing a little as my back twinges, and waddle out of the living room to take myself off to my own personal prison.

THIRTY-FOUR

I don't know what woke me. These days, sleep comes in extremes: it's either brain-shattering insomnia or I am one with the dead. I wasn't expecting to get much tonight, but I guess my body decided it was going to call time on my mind, so instead of lying there, ruminating on everything I found today, I was out like a light within moments of my head hitting the pillow.

I try to reposition myself. I'm finding it harder to get comfortable at night. Once you get over the twenty-week mark, your body isn't your own anymore, and everything you once took for granted has been hijacked by your new miniature boss.

Footsteps, slow and steady, above me. Probably Russ going to the bathroom.

Is that what woke me up?

Probably.

Except... I didn't hear the flush. Nor the taps.

And why would he go out into the main bathroom anyway? We have an en suite.

I ease myself up into a sitting position and take a good gulp from the glass of water on my makeshift bedside table. So thirsty these days.

The baby monitor I've hidden next to me crackles.

I freeze, the glass halfway to my mouth.

It could just be the connection.

Tap-tap-tap.

I put the glass down, pick up the monitor and stare at it, willing it to show me what's going on, lamenting that I didn't choose the one with a screen.

There's a pause. Then, again.

Tap-tap-tap.

If I didn't know better, I'd say someone was knocking on Jasmine's door.

I grip the monitor and bring it closer to my ear. I hear a sigh and a rustling sound, like someone turning over in bed.

Tap-TAP-tap.

It's louder now. More insistent. A hard fist of sick dread and fury clenches in my chest.

He's nothing if not persistent.

Next, I hear the soft creak of a door opening. My mind supplies what happens next. Coy smiles. Russ, his hand on the top of the door-frame, wearing only his pyjama bottoms. I think back to all the times I teased him, calling him my silver fox, despite him only going slightly grey at his temples. He gives her a wolfish smile. She bites her bottom lip and looks up at him through her lowered lashes—

An actual voice cuts through the imaginary scene I am torturing myself with. Same as before, it's hard to make out what's being said. All I do know is, Jasmine isn't asking him why he's there at two in the morning and demanding he leave her alone.

'... I see it, I know what you want...' That's Russ. The hairs on the back of my neck bristle as I hold the monitor as close as I can to my ear, afraid of missing a word, but equally terrified of what I might hear next.

I can't hear Jasmine's reply, as it is masked by a rustling sound. One of them has sat on the bed.

At least, I hope it's just one of them.

'... what you want?' Russ again, but this time is sounds like a question. I'm caught between hating him for being there and hoping beyond all hope that he is actually challenging her behaviour, asking her what she's playing at, something I know is unlikely given the time but I desperately want to believe nevertheless.

But then I think back to Olivia the other night. The lady outside her door. I suspected it then, but now I'm pretty sure I'm right. It was Jasmine, leaving our bedroom.

How long has this been going on? Since I was admitted to hospital?

Before that?

My heart is shattered. I don't want to listen anymore, but I also can't turn the monitor off. I clench it tightly as tears roll down my face. My stomach convulses, and I involuntarily tighten my grip even more. There's a crack, and it takes me a moment to realise that I've split the plastic back of the monitor. Pain flares, and I instinctively snatch my hand away; two thin red lines blossom on my fingertips where the plastic caught me. Too late, I realise that the monitor has slipped from my grip. It lands on the floor with a sad little *crunch*. Oh no. No, no, this can't be happening... Steadying myself against the frame, I lean over the bed and retrieve it, but the back has fallen off and half its wiry guts are hanging out. I suppress a screech as I scoop it up and try to listen, but there's nothing; no murmurs, no rustling, no half-caught sentences, just the damning silence of a broken machine. In a fit of sheer fury I throw the broken monitor at the wall, only realising the moment it leaves my hand that it's going to make a lot of noise in a silent house. I hold my breath as it smacks against the plaster, leaving a little dent, waiting for a flurry of footsteps down the stairs, but there's nothing. Russ isn't in the room above me, he's another floor up from that doing God knows what with the nanny, and I had the perfect opportunity to catch him at it but instead I ruined it—

Except, have I?

He thinks I'm downstairs, asleep and clueless. But I'm not.

I could go up there. Catch them in the act.

... or at least I would if I could get out of bed without wanting to throw up.

No. Not now! The sickness usually eases at night. But there's no mistaking it. Maybe it is stress after all.

It's all I can do to roll out of bed and near enough crawl out of the dining room, over to the downstairs toilet, where I slither over to the bowl and empty my stomach.

It's mainly water.

Water.

I don't remember taking a glass of water with me to bed.

But there was one by my bedside.

Someone must have left it there after I fell asleep.

My stomach drops, and this time it has nothing to do with sickness.

Was I sick when I was in hospital?

Initially, yes. But once I'd been in for twenty-four hours, I felt better. Tired, sure, but the nausea wasn't as bad.

Until I got back home. Then it started up again

Time to step things up.

Step things up from where?

Tears come in a rush, despair chasing away my anger as I realise the note-writer is right. I'm not safe.

Because the sickness returned as soon as I came back home.

Right after I had my first smoothie in four days.

THIRTY-FIVE

I don't come out of the dining room the next morning. Instead, I lay on my side, cradling my bump, too exhausted to even cry.

How did I let all of this get so out of hand?

No matter what, I can't give up. One way or another, this has to end. I can't live like this. I *refuse* to live like this.

There's a knock at my door. Jasmine doesn't wait for me to answer. She barges in, bringing me one of her vile concoctions. Needless to say, I don't have to fake my sallow expression.

'Oh my gosh, are you okay?' she asks. She looks genuinely concerned. I don't know how she does it. In another life, she's winning Oscars in those movies critics gush over but no one actually watches.

I don't even pretend to smile.

'No.' It's all I can manage. Even looking at her hurts. 'Where's Russ?'

'He went to work about an hour ago,' Jasmine says.

'I see.'

'He said he didn't want to wake you.'

'Of course he didn't.'

'Are you sure you're okay?'

No, you scheming little tramp, I am not okay.

'I'm just tired.'

She gives me one of those pity smiles I've grown so used to, and hate so much.

'Poor you. Would you like me to make you something else for breakfast?'

'No.'

'All right, well, when you're ready.' She sets the smoothie down on the bedside table. 'Try to drink this. It's strawberry, banana, spinach and coconut milk. I've put some cacao powder in it so it tastes extra yummy. I'm going to take Olivia out to Little Wrigglers in a bit, so you try and get rest.'

'Okay. Jasmine?'

'Yes?' The smile is still there, but there's now something in her eyes that I don't like. Not a twinkle, but rather its crueller, nastier cousin.

It takes me a moment, but I finally place it.

It's triumph.

I should say something. Despite what she thinks, I'm still in charge. I have every right to get rid of her. Hell, I could probably even go to the police.

But I won't. All they'd need to do is go through my medical history. I can hear them now. *A history of mental instability.* That's far more believable than a conspiracy to slowly kill a pregnant woman so you can steal her life.

'Nothing. Have fun at Little Wrigglers.'

Jasmine's smile widens into something I can only see as predatory. She just can't help herself.

'We will! See you later.'

I don't wait for her to leave the room. I turn over and face the wall.

I listen as she gives Olivia her breakfast. Brushes her hair. Smirk at the ensuing tantrum, because if there's one thing Olivia hates, it's having her hair brushed. Tells her to find her shoes. All of these tiny domestic pinpricks of motherly light that I used to take for granted, stolen from me.

But not for much longer.

When I hear the front door close without Olivia coming in to say goodbye to me, my heart both rips in two and boils with rage.

I throw the duvet off me and snatch up the smoothie. First things first – that's going down the toilet. Then I'm going to eat something simple out of a packet so I know it hasn't been messed with, and drink some water directly from the tap. I'm still feeling absolutely dreadful, but a powerful concoction of desperation and fury is propelling me this morning.

No matter the outcome, I am not just going to lay down and die so she can get what she wants.

I go up into my bedroom and retrieve the attic room key from Russ's bedside cabinet. Once I have that, I'm back up the stairs and into Jasmine's room.

It's stuffier in here than it was yesterday. That could be down to the window not being opened, but to me it feels more intimate than that. To me, it feels like the kind of fug you only get when two bodies have been in a small place, lathering up a sweat. The tang is still there. Poisoned or not, it's enough to have me leaning over the toilet bowl.

Thankfully, the nausea passes. I quickly retrieve the other baby monitor. Given I broke its twin, it's useless now, so why leave it in here? There's no point risking it being discovered if it doesn't even work anymore. I then move over to her desk and tap at her iPad screen. Still password locked.

Damn.

So what else is there? The journal. Maybe she's added a new entry? Even if it's in that stupid code, I might be able to glean something from it. But it's clear that she hasn't written anything since the last time I peeked inside it. Again, the seem- ingly random jumble of numbers and letters interspersed with the occasional legible word makes me uneasy. Is it an actual code? Or just a personal kind of shorthand? And why bother with it if you've got nothing to hide?

I flick back to the photo. Jasmine and Russ, the cosy couple.

If there's one thing I'm sure of, it's that she has plenty to hide. But none of this is going to help me. I need something tangible, something I can confront her with, something that won't backfire on me. If I confront her with the diary, I'm going to end up looking like the bad guy. She already knows I saw the texts and the deleted photo on Instagram, and the last time I checked, having a crush on your boss isn't a crime.

No, I need something else. Something damning. Something irrefutable. Something…

The wastepaper basket catches my eye.

Okay, this is a new low, but desperate times call for desperate measures.

There's not a lot in the bin. A few sweet wrappers. Some withered leaves taken off the houseplants. And some balled up tissues.

I gingerly pick up the tissues and begin the grim task of unfolding them, dreading what might fall out.

But nothing does. All of them, every single one, has either streaks of black mascara on them or has been used to blow her nose. After last night I was expecting to find at least one artfully swathed condom, but no. Not even a wrapper.

I dig further into the bin, but there's nothing. A Coke can. Some cotton balls.

What looks like a small medicine bottle.

Now that *is* weird. Not that Jasmine might be taking medication, more that anything you need to self-administer usually comes in the form of tablets or liquids that you drink. This bottle is more like the ones they use to draw injectable fluids out of. Frowning, I check the label. It's a little bit water-stained, possibly by the dregs of the Coke can.

What I can make out reads: *Thallium 201*. And in a smaller font: *Thallous chloride. Tl 201 Injection. Sterile, nonpyrogenic, diagnostic agent for intravenous injection.*

And, rather more alarmingly:

Caution. Radioactive material.

I almost drop the bottle. Radioactive. Why would Jasmine have this? What could be wrong with her that she'd need something like this as a treatment?

Then it strikes me. There's no prescription label. No directions for use.

My chest tightens.

'No...' The room tilts around me as blood rushes to my head, leaving me feeling hot and sweaty and freezing cold all at once.

I don't know what this stuff is. But that doesn't mean I can't take an educated guess at what she might have been using it for.

I take a photo of the bottle before carefully placing it back into the bin, rearranging the rubbish back on top of it so it looks like I was never here. Then I get up and carefully make my way over to the door, locking it behind me. To an onlooker, it might seem there is no urgency to my actions, that I'm perfectly calm, but believe me, they couldn't be further from the truth. Because inside I am screaming. The only thing holding me together is that if I lose my shit now, I might fall down the stairs again, and if I fall down the stairs again with the key to Jasmine's room in my hand, I may as well slit my own throat.

With exaggerated care, I replace the key. Then I space-walk down the main staircase, placing my feet with a precision I don't think I've used since I was a teenager trying to convince my parents that I was indeed perfectly sober after an illicit night out. Finally I'm in the living room with my phone, where I set Google to incognito mode and search for Thallium 201, because I don't want anyone tracking my movements, not even strangers.

Thallium 201 is used in medicine as a tracer element for

heart stress tests. A bit like a barium meal, they use it to test arterial function, or something like that. The websites are quite detailed, but I'm in no state to take in that amount of information. It is indeed radioactive.

Obviously, when it is carefully used in a medical setting, it's quite safe.

When it isn't, however...

It used to be known as 'The Poisoner's Poison' and 'Inheritance Powder', and was readily available as a rat poison and as a treatment for ringworm until they realised just how incredibly toxic it really is. It's colourless, odourless and tasteless, and you don't need a lot of it. It's highly regulated, but by the looks of it, not as hard to get hold of as it should be.

Symptoms of thallium poisoning include abdominal pain and 'mixed peripheral neuropathy'. Usually I'd ask Russ what medical terms mean, but I can't this time, so I spend a couple of minutes looking that up, too, and discover that it's a catch-all term for dizziness and issues with nerves in your arms and legs. I guess that might explain my pins and needles. Prolonged exposure can also make your hair fall out. I absent-mindedly run a hand through my hair is I read this, and gag when I realise just how much comes away from my scalp, caught up around my fingers.

As far as I can tell, the only good thing is that thallium poisoning is reversible if caught in time.

I have no idea if I've caught my case in time.

I slump back on the sofa, suddenly exhausted. I stare at my bump, at Sprout, too drained to even cry. What have I done to you? How is this going to affect you? I'm so sorry. My poor little baby. I couldn't protect you, even while you were inside me, where you should be the safest of all. I'm so, so sorry.

I know I should look up the impact of thallium poisoning on a growing foetus, but I just can't. It's bad enough that I have to face this myself, but to face my baby going through this too... here, in this moment, it's too much. All I can do is hope that the dose was low enough to keep me ill rather than kill me. Although why she'd want me alive, I don't know.

I take in a few deep breaths. As scared as I am, having pieced all of this together, I can't sit here and stew over it. I don't have time. I have to act. Today. I can't put it off, because God only knows how long I've got left before Jasmine's patience runs out.

I close the internet and bring up my list. It seems so frivolous now. I don't need a lot. Money might be an issue, but I can always skim some out of our bank account. Maybe I'll ask Russ if I can order something expensive, then take the money out for myself. He won't realise I haven't actually bought anything until it's too late. Then, if push comes to shove, I can take out a few grand in town just before I get on a train, any train, and then maybe use the cash to seek refuge with one of my cousins. I may not have seen them in years, but blood is blood. Someone, somewhere, will help me.

They have to.

Next: a new email account. That should be easy – a throwaway Gmail account. I might even be able to get one of those dodgy payday loans with one of those. I can worry about paying it off later. Now, it's all about survival.

I note down a few numbers for charities that might be able to put me in contact with women's shelters, although I have to be careful with these. My abuser is a woman I hardly know and I'm not sure how seriously they will take me when I try to explain my situation to them. They, like the various medical professionals around me, including my own husband, might think I'm stressed at best or going totally round the twist at worst. Stupid thing is, if it wasn't for Olivia, getting myself sectioned might have been an easy way out. At least it would have given me time to breathe. But I don't have that luxury. I'm not leaving my daughter behind.

No matter what happens, she's coming with me.

And yes, I know. Go to the police. Show them the bottle. Make a report. After all, that's what they're supposed to be there for. To protect us. But let's be real. To say that the statistics around domestic abuse are depressing is an understatement. And that's when it's an obvious case, and not whatever this mess is. If I go in with an empty bottle of thallium and tell them my nanny has been spiking my morning smoothies so she can steal my family, they'll be shipping me off to the mad house before they even speak to her.

No. This is the way. Whoever wrote the note is right.

I have to leave. Quietly.

And soon.

THIRTY-SIX

TWENTY-SIX WEEKS

It's hard. Pretending everything's perfectly normal. Most of the time I fake sleeping. No one questions it. I guess it's easier for them, too.

Every now and again, Olivia comes in and snuggles up next to me. She strokes my hair and calls me sleepy Mama. Asks if I'm 'confoos'. Tells me that 'Mama poorly, in her head'. I dread to think the lies Jasmine is telling her.

I think I'm almost there. Thankfully Jasmine takes Olivia out most days and Russ is always at work, so I'm able to sneak out to get the things I need. The few times Jasmine asks where I've been, or where I'm going, I tell her I have to go to the surgery to get my blood pressure checked, or I have to do a urine sample. She always believes me. Why shouldn't she? She has no idea that I'm on to her.

That I now know exactly what she's up to.

I park my car in the closest space I can find to the entrance of our local budget supermarket. I used to come here quite regularly, but Russ didn't like it. Said we didn't need to shop like poor people. Insisted that if I had to go to the supermarket, at least go to a decent one. This means I'm pretty sure

I'm safe here. There's no chance I'm going to bump into Russ here, and I can't imagine Petunia or any of her cronies would even deign to know Asda exists, let alone shop here. Despite this, I still feel like I'm wearing a massive sign over my head as I grab a trolley and walk into the shop. *This is Frankie. Frankie shouldn't be here. Please make sure you tell her psychopathic nanny. And then her mother-in-law, for good measure.*

I don't need much. Clothes, basically. Maybe a few snacks. I've left this bit until last because the longer I have to hide things, the more chance there is someone will discover them. My skin feels raw, my every nerve on fire when anyone so much as glances in my direction. It's okay. I'm just another pregnant woman out getting everyday essentials. They don't know me, I don't know them. All I have to do is not make a scene.

Unfortunately, that's a lot harder than it seems. Every time I try to pick something up I drop it and it isn't long before my nervous clumsiness has attracted the attention of one of the staff.

'Is everything all right, love?'

She's an older lady, probably in her late fifties, possibly early sixties. Her badge says her name is Paula. I try to widen my smile, make a joke about how I don't have butterfingers, I have baby-fingers, but instead I let out a short bark of a sob. Tears spring to my eyes.

'I'm okay,' I manage to croak out.

'Oh, love, first one?' I decide not to correct her. Her expression turns to pity, and I hate it. Why can't she just go back to doing her job and leave me alone? 'How far along are you?'

'Twenty-six weeks.' I whisper it, worried someone might recognise my voice.

'Aw, so you've got a way to go yet. People don't realise how draining it can be. But when they hand over that little bundle of joy... there's nothing like it. By the way, if you're looking for maternity clothes, they're over there.' She gestures with her head.

I thank Paula and trundle over to the section she pointed out. My heart is thrumming and my legs feel like they're made out of water as I pick up some cheap leggings and oversized tops. Nothing is particularly stylish, but that's good. I don't want to stand out. I want to look like just another stressed-out mum-to-be.

Next, I look at the children's clothes. Thankfully Paula doesn't follow me. At first I look in the girls' section, but then I turn my attention to the boys' section. Forget cheap jumper dresses – absolutely no one's going to recognise Olivia in a pair of joggers and a dinosaur T-shirt. I snatch a multipack of T-shirts and a tracksuit off the peg, not caring what colour I choose. I have a sinking feeling that I've been here too long already.

Next, I head off to the phone section to buy a burner phone. I never thought in a million years I might need one of these. You hear about them all the time on the TV, but I didn't have a clue how to go about getting one for myself. It isn't half as difficult to get one as you might think. It's just the name people use for a pre-paid phone. I was under the impression you had to go to someone shady to procure one, but no, you can literally pick one up in a supermarket.

Unlike the clothing section, the phone department is over-whelming. There are so many models here, ranging from cheap Nokias to expensive smartphones. I don't want anything fancy, so I pick out a dumb phone, complete with a brand-new sim card. Even though I know people do it all the time, I feel like a criminal as I go to the electronics desk. The shop assistant here is younger and clearly disinterested, something I'm grateful for. Still, I have to fight down the urge to flee when he goes to look for my requested model. By the time he returns, I'm almost in tears.

After I grab a few more essentials I'm finally able to slot myself into one of the checkout queues. I'm paying with cash. I got the money out after telling Russ I'd booked a tradesman to go up on the roof and see why the guttering near the garage was leaking. Russ often leaves these things to me, so it didn't raise any suspicions. Or, at least, I hope it didn't. If he changes his mind and decides to go and look at the roof himself, I'm screwed.

'Good morning!' the lady working the checkout says as she starts scanning my purchases. 'Oh look, how adorable! A little boy, huh?' she says as she scans Olivia's new clothes.

'Yes,' I say.

'Dinosaur mad? They all are at that age, bless 'em.'

She continues to chatter as I pack everything away. By the time she cheerfully tells me 'that comes to one hundred and fifty four pounds, fifty three pence', I all but throw a handful of twenties at her.

'Do you want a receipt?' she asks as she hands me my change.

'Um, no, I'll be fine.'

'Are you sure? Might want to take it in case you need to return anything that doesn't fit.'

I bully a wan smile onto my face and nod. She hands me my receipt.

I chuck it into the bin by the exit.

I manage to hold it together until I'm back at my car. I lay the bags as flat as I can in the boot and cover them up with my picnic blanket so if anyone glances inside, nothing will seem out of the ordinary. Finally, I slide into the driver's seat, but I'm not ready to go anywhere quite yet. The moment I sit down, I can't help the flood of tears that assails me. It's all I can do to hide my face to stop concerned shoppers from asking if I'm okay; one older lady comes over to me and the best I can do is tell her that I'm fine, that it's just my hormones. Almost as if on cue, she gives me that bloody smile they think is so understanding but is in fact as condescending as hell and leaves me alone. When I'm in enough control to drive off, I find somewhere more secluded to lose it for a bit before going home and pretending everything is fine, and that I haven't just bought an entire escape kit in a budget supermarket.

Back home, Jasmine is still out, thank God. I quickly stash my purchases in a cheap rucksack and shove that as far as I can under my bed. Then I go and fetch myself a cold glass of water straight from the tap and find a cereal bar. Should have had something to eat while I was out. Damn. Must bear that in mind if I need to do this again.

Will I need to do this again?

I run through my list in my head. I've deleted the one off my phone, because I've already decided I'm leaving that here, so there's no chance anyone can use it to track me. All I need to do now is figure out how I'm going to be able to take more cash out without Russ getting suspicious. I've already used the tradesman excuse. What can I do now?

I'm still ruminating when Jasmine and Olivia arrive home. Olivia is half-asleep, so Jasmine takes her straight up to her bedroom. An awful tension grips my body as I watch her cradling my daughter. She hasn't been right in a while. I'd been putting it down to catching something at one of the groups – they are germ factories after all – but this has been going on for days now. If it was something viral, surely she should have come down with it completely and be in some kind of recovery by now? The fact that she isn't, she's just hovering in this zone of 'not being quite right', floods me with suspicious dread.

Is she poisoning my baby, too?

'How did it go?'

Now Olivia's upstairs, Jasmine is with me in the kitchen, putting away some groceries.

'Uh, what? How did what go?'

Crap. Did she see me? How does she know—

She cocks her head to one side, studying me.

'The doctor's appointment?'

'Oh, that, yes, of course, sorry. I'm in and out of the place so often, I kind of forget it's not normal. Everything's fine.'

'Really? That's good.'

'Yeah, it is. I might feel like rubbish, but there's no harm being done.'

She continues to watch me, to the point where I'm wondering if there's something wrong with my face. I self-consciously touch my hair. What has she spotted? Oh God, no, I haven't managed to, I don't know, transfer some of the receipt ink onto my cheek or something.

'I'm glad to hear it.' She smiles, but again, it isn't one of understanding, or even commiseration.

No, she's smiling because she thinks her plan is still working. That she is able to spike my food and drink and for it to go undetected by the medical profession. I can only begin to imagine how smug she must be feeling right now. And as much as I hate it, I have to keep playing along. I can't let on that her plan is no longer working.

Because if I do, who knows what she'll do next?

THIRTY-SEVEN

While Olivia naps, I take myself off to my makeshift bedroom so I don't have to keep up any form of pretence. It's exhausting to constantly be on your guard, having to suspect everything and everyone. Hoping that it might help to soothe my fractured nerves, I surf Netflix. I find some trashy dating show, something I wouldn't normally entertain, but right now is exactly what I need. Mindless nonsense. Just the ticket.

I must have dozed off, because the next thing I know, there's a crash and an 'uh oh!' coming from the living room. Since I now have the TV from the nook in here, Jasmine and Olivia have been spending more time in there. I rub at my eyes and struggle up off the bed, scurrying out of the dining room to find Olivia sat on the sofa and Jasmine picking up shards of pottery off the floor.

'Careful!' Jasmine says when she sees I don't have any shoes on. 'The piggy bank got smashed.'

'I'm sowwy, Mama,' Olivia says, her eyes wide and wet with tears. 'The ball, it rolled and rolled and then I chased it and then piggy was there and it falled over and smashed...'

'It's okay, sweetie,' I say, as soothingly as I can. Olivia stands up on the sofa and half walks, half crawls over to the edge of it nearest to me, her arms outstretched. I ensure I give the smashed piggy bank a wide berth and scoop her up as she wraps her arms around my neck and buries her face against my shoulder.

'It was all an accident,' Jasmine says. 'No one's fault.'

Except yours, of course. But I don't say this. It isn't worth it.

Because it's all I can do to stop myself from staring at the pile of two-pound coins spilling out from the belly of the smashed pig.

'Wow, was this your rainy day fund?' Jasmine asks with a laugh. 'There's a fair bit in here.'

'Yeah,' I say, trying to keep the surprise out of my voice. 'When I first fell pregnant with Olivia we said we'd put our two-pound coins in it and then see how much was there when she was five, maybe put them into a savings bond or something. I'll be honest, I'd kind of forgotten it was there.'

'Really? There must be over a hundred pounds in there. I don't think I'd forget that.'

'Well, you have to remember, this was over a couple of years.'

Jasmine scoops up the larger pieces of pottery and gets to her feet.

'I'm just going to chuck this away and get the hoover. Why don't you fish the coins out and then I can finish clearing up the mess?'

I don't argue. Instead, I set Olivia back down on the sofa and carefully extricate the money, piling it up in columns of ten.

By the time I'm finished, Jasmine is back with the vacuum cleaner, and I've worked out that there's £212 in the smashed piggy bag.

It's almost as if someone's trying to tell me something.

· · ·

This feeling only continues as the next day dawns.

Now I'm free of Jasmine's poisonous food and drink, I'm beginning to feel a bit better. I'm drinking loads of water in the hope of flushing out my system, and so far all signs point to the positive – as long as I'm within brisk walking distance of a loo, because my bladder isn't what it used to be. I may need to ease up on the water over the next day or so, because I think it's very nearly time to put my plan into action.

'Frankie, just to let you know, Petunia wants to meet up with me and Olivia this Thursday at twelve. She wants to go out to Bramley House. They've got that royal exhibition and she's keen to go. They're doing an afternoon tea that she's booked for us.'

'And she wants to take Olivia to it?'

'She says it'll be educational.'

'Yeah, she's three. I'm not sure how much she's going to like looking at paintings and eating off fine china.'

'There might be horses there?'

'Let's hope so.'

'Allegedly Petunia's friend Ellen can't go and she's already bought the tickets. Amanda hates royalty and Russ is at work, so she's asked if I'll go with her – she says it's okay because under-fives get in for free, so it looks like I don't really have a choice.' She gives me a rueful smile. If it wasn't for the fact that she's trying to kill me and steal my family, I'd feel sorry for her.

Screw the money. I'll sort that out once I'm gone.

As long as nothing drastic happens, I'm going to be leaving in two days, on Thursday afternoon – and one way or another, I'm going to take Olivia with me.

Funny how far away Thursday can feel on a Tuesday, but how imminent it can then feel the very next day.

Tomorrow. That's it. Tomorrow is when it all happens.

I think I'm ready. I found some Benadryl left over from when Russ went to the US last year, the kind that makes you sleepy. You can't get it over here and it's not supposed to be used on children, but I'm sure it'll be fine if I crush up half a tablet in Olivia's juice before nap time. It feels a bit hypocritical, but I need to ensure there's no way Jasmine can take Olivia with her when she goes to meet Petunia for the afternoon. If I have to spike my daughter's drink to keep her safe, then so be it. Because make no mistake – I'll do whatever it takes to keep my daughter safe.

If anything, it's the waiting that's driving me up the wall. Russ is off this afternoon, which makes it even harder. He's currently sitting across from me in the garden, scrolling on his phone. Olivia and Jasmine are playing with the sand and water table on the patio. I'm sipping at a glass of iced water, trying to look content. Every now and again, Russ looks up and smiles at Olivia's antics, then at me. It's all very idyllic, and it's doing nothing for my nerves.

'You look better today,' he says.

'I do? Thank you.' I don't know what else to say. Russ leans over and rubs at my belly. I have to force myself not to physically recoil at his touch.

'How's Sprout doing these days? Feels like ages since we've connected.'

It feels like ages because you banished me to the dining room so you could screw the nanny.

'Fine. Wriggly. Good kicker.'

'That's my girl.' He winks at me. I make myself smile in return.

Just twenty-four hours and this charade is over.

Russ buries himself back into his phone. Usually he'd be reading out headlines that catch his eye, but today he's silent. I shift in my seat; sitting in these chairs isn't easy now my bump is bigger, and my back is starting to ache. Russ sighs as my chair squeaks.

'Honey, do you think you could give that a rest?'

'Sorry, I'm just uncomfortable.'

He gives a little snort that I might once have mistaken as affectionate but now feels more mean-spirited. I want to snap at him, to tell him I'm so very sorry for being pregnant, but instead I stand up – or, at least, I manage it after a few false starts – and stretch my back out.

'You don't have to get up, you know,' Russ says. 'It was only the squeaking,'

'It's okay,' I say. 'I was thinking about getting up and having a little wander anyway. Might go and fetch my ball. That's much more comfortable to sit on these days.'

'In that case, do you think you could fill me up?' He holds up his coffee mug. Coffee I can't have. It's like the wine scenario all over again.

I smile sweetly and take his mug from him.

'Sure.'

'That's my girl.'

I grit my teeth and turn away before he notices anything is wrong.

After the glare of the garden, the house feels unnaturally dark. I set Russ's mug down on the counter and select a coffee pod. I know I could have a decaf, but ugh, decaf. Instead, I have more water. Got to keep hydrated, keep flushing those toxins out. My heart thumps with worry. I try not to think about the damage the thallium might already have done to me, to Sprout. If I was a particularly vindictive person, I might have looked to see if I could find out where Jasmine kept her stash and used it against her. Hell, I could be putting some in Russ's coffee now if I wanted to be a complete psycho. But I'm not, and I won't. Because I'm better than them. Than her.

When the time comes, I don't want anyone to say that I was at fault.

I'm not ready to return to the garden just yet, so I wander through the house. It's hard to think that this could be my last day here. Will I ever return, or is this it? Everything I've built here, lost forever?

No. I won't let them do that to me. Once I'm stronger, once I know my rights, I will return like a whirlwind, and I will take what is mine. They won't get away with this. I just need time. When I'm ready, they won't know what's hit them.

I grab the little watering can I use for my roses and fill it, adding a few drops of Baby Bio. This might be the last time I get to do this. I open the front door and look out into the close. As usual, it's quiet. I've parked my car in the garage in preparation for tomorrow; I figure it'll be easier to pack it up without anyone watching me in there. Because while the close may be quiet, you better believe someone, somewhere is watching.

Beside the front door, my pride and joy, a potted pink rose bush, is flowering ferociously. I take a moment to inhale its heavenly scent. Tears prickle. I grew this from a cutting from my mum's garden. It was her favourite, too. I haven't got a clue what it's called. All I know is that I love the way it smells. Russ says it's tacky, that most roses are, and pink roses especially. I'm actually amazed that he's allowed me to have it for so long, let alone this close to the front door. I think the only reason he does is because it's the one thing of mine Petunia likes, too. She commented that the scent of roses as you approach our front door was inviting. I think she thought it was Russ's idea to put it there, but I don't mind, because it meant my rose bush stayed in its planter.

A flash of white catches my eye. Deep within the branches is something in a plastic bag.

Annoyance flares within me. Has someone been littering? And why would they push rubbish into my rose bush? I set down my watering can and carefully snake my hand towards it, hissing as the thorns catch my skin. Then I tweezer the bag out, tearing it a little as I go. Once I have it out, I realise the bag is just the container. Inside is an envelope. On the front, in horribly familiar capital letters:

TAKE INSIDE

I turn the little package in my hands. As before there is no postmark or address, confirming that this was hand-delivered. This time, though, the envelope is fat and heavy, indicating there's more than just a note inside. Again, I peer up and down the road, wondering who is doing this. Whoever it is, I wish they'd make themselves known. I appreciate them looking out for me, but if they're that worried for my safety, surely they could do more? Like, I don't know, call the police? Be an actual witness? I glance behind me. I can still hear Jasmine and Olivia chattering to each other in the garden, but I don't know where Russ is—

'Darling?'

As if called, he rounds the side of the house, looking concerned. I jump, quickly shoving the envelope behind my back, hoping he didn't see it.

'Russ, gosh, you made me jump.'

'Clearly. What's going on? I thought you were making me a coffee.'

'Oh, I was, I mean, I am, but I thought I heard the door go and so I came to see who was there, but it was just some junk mail and then I thought the roses were looking a little wilted, so I—'

'Junk mail?' My stomach sinks. I know that tone. 'For pity's sake, even with the sign... I swear to God I'm going to sue whoever is sending this nonsense. Where is it? They're going to get a nasty little surprise of their own in the mail—'

'No, Russ, darling, it's okay. It was just political bumpf, nothing to get riled up about. Just... go back to the garden. I'll bring you your coffee through.'

There's an awful moment where it looks like he might not back down, but finally he snorts, turns around and stalks back the way he came. It takes me a good minute to find my legs again, and another one before I can trust myself to even think about carrying a cup of hot coffee. I don't dare look inside the envelope – instead, I hide it inside my pillowcase, ready for when I need to take a nap.

When I finally feel I can say I need a lie down, I don't need to fake the tremor in my voice. Russ doesn't even look up from his phone. I have no idea who he's talking to, but he's been texting and chuckling at things for a while now. Good. I'll take any distractions at this point.

Olivia is napping, so Jasmine is up in her room doing God only knows what. Not that I care. Let her plot and scheme. None of it matters anymore. I'm ahead of her. At least, I think I am.

I hope I am.

I kick off my sandals and lay on the daybed, pulling a light blanket over myself. I don't really need it, but it's a good screen for when I retrieve the envelope from under my pillow. The paper rustles, and my heart shoots up into my mouth. Have to be careful. Can't let anyone hear. I gingerly tear at the envelope's seam until it reveals its contents.

My mouth hangs open.

Money.

And a lot of it.

Twenty pound notes, by the looks of it. Used. There has to be over a grand in there, alongside another note and a plastic key card from a Premier Inn.

The note is simple and to the point.

WESTON POINT. RM 402. LEAVE ASAP. 3 DAYS PAID.

Christ. This is serious. Who the hell is this? This isn't an insignificant amount of cash, and they've paid for three nights' accommodation in a place I only know as a train station.

What is clear is whoever left it is either really concerned for my safety... or they're really, really keen to see the back of me.

THIRTY-EIGHT

There is £1,750 in the envelope.

I know this, because I counted it twice.

Added to the money from the petty cash box, the leftovers from my roofer ruse and the two-pound coins from the piggy bank, I've managed to scrape just over two thousand pounds together. It's not much in the grand scheme of things, but it's definitely better than nothing.

I can't sleep. I know I should at least try, but I'm so wired. So much could go wrong tomorrow. Petunia could cancel. Jasmine could say they'll wait until Olivia wakes up. Jasmine could be ill. Petunia could decide she wants me to come and won't take no for an answer. Russ decides he's going to take another ad hoc day off. The Benadryl doesn't work and Olivia won't sleep.

So many, many points of potential failure.

I feel a fluttering in my belly and instinctively rub at it, to soothe myself as well as my baby. *I'm so sorry, Sprout. I never meant for any of this to happen to you. To any of us. It's so unfair. You don't deserve this. Neither does your sister. Hell, neither do*

I. I thought I was doing everything right, but I guess I should have known better. I promise to do better. I promise it won't be like this forever. I promise...

The floorboards creak above me. That'll be Russ, getting up. Once I would have said to use the bathroom, but who am I kidding? I don't want to listen, to see if I can hear the tell-tale flush of the toilet that will confirm that it's all as innocent as it seems, but I can't help it. Of course there is no toilet flush. Of course there are more footsteps. From our bedroom and across the landing. Over to the top of the stairs. They hesitate there. Do I hear whispers, or is that just a figment of my imagination? I pull my pillow over my head and clamp it over my ears.

It doesn't matter anymore.

None of it matters anymore.

I don't have to pretend I'm feeling awful today. Just one look and it's obvious. Lack of sleep has definitely caught up with me, as has my diet of what is basically high-quality junk food. As it turns out, woman cannot live on prenatal vitamins and granola bars alone.

Russ goes to work as usual. Jasmine potters around the house with Olivia as usual. I sit in my purgatorial room as usual. In fact, everything feels so normal that I have to keep checking the bundle of items I have stashed under my bed to reassure myself that everything I'm planning on doing isn't some kind of elaborate dream.

When it's about an hour before Petunia is due to pick Jasmine and Olivia up, I crush up half a Benadryl with the back of a teaspoon and dissolve it into Olivia's juice. I watch her drink it all up, then wait.

Half an hour later, she's on the sofa, laying on her front, her eyes drooping.

'Hey, Olliebean, can't go sleeps now, got to get ready to meet Gramma!' Jasmine says, her voice painfully bubbly.

Olivia doesn't say anything, just yawns.

'Pumpkin, are you okay?' I say, filling my voice with just the right level of concern. I reach over to stroke her hair, and she lets out a perfectly pathetic 'Mama'. I sit next to her and she crawls into my lap, resting her head on my bump. 'She feels a bit hot,' I say. 'I hope she's not coming down with something.'

Jasmine contrives to look suitably concerned.

'Yes, she does look a bit peaky, doesn't she? Poor little love.' She hunkers down in front of me so she can look directly at Olivia. 'Do you want to come out with me and Gramma?'

Olivia responds by burying her face into my bump and whimpering 'Mama' again.

Result.

'Okay, if that's what you want. I can text Gramma and tell her.'

... oh no. No, no, no!

But before I can come up with an excuse for her not to text Petunia and tell her that Olivia is ill so they can't go with her, the doorbell chimes. Jasmine straightens up and frowns.

'You expecting a delivery?'

'No.'

The doorbell chimes again.

'Must be Petunia. She's early.'

My whole body turns fluid in relief. This is the one and only time where Petunia's pathological need to wrong-foot me has worked in my favour. So when I hear her arch voice exclaim 'What do you mean, she's ill?' I have to seriously fight to stop myself from grinning.

'Oh, for heaven's sake, this is ridiculous.' Petunia storms into the room.

'Hello, Petunia,' I say, simply because I know it annoys her.

'Are you still malingering?'

'It's only malingering if you're faking it.'

Petunia snorts.

'Come on, Olivia, let's get you up.'

Olivia lets out a tiny squeal and tightens her arms around me.

'Mama,' she mutters sleepily.

'She's not well,' I say.

'She hasn't been quite right for a couple of days,' Jasmine says, and I have to stop myself looking at her in surprise, because I thought Jasmine was doing her best to keep reminding Petunia that she's much better at the parenting game than I am. Maybe I misjudged the situation, and Jasmine isn't as keen to go out with Petunia as I thought she might be. But then again, my mother-in-law is awful to literally everyone, so why would she be? 'But it's really hit her in the last hour.'

'So what are you saying? I have tickets. They weren't cheap.'

'You can still go,' I say, secretly enjoying every moment of this. 'If there's an issue I can call you, but she's my daughter and it's only an afternoon. She'll probably sleep through most of it.'

'I mean, I don't know—' Jasmine begins to say, before Petunia butts in.

'I suppose that might work. Under-fives are free to enter, but I would have to pay extra for her to eat with us, so I won't be out of pocket if she doesn't come. And who knows when this exhibition will be back. Jasmine, darling, honestly, it is one of those once-in-a-lifetime things, I tried telling Amanda, but that girl, for one so intelligent, she can be just so stubborn and quite frankly lacking in taste, and I know that you have a good eye, I think you'll love it...'

Petunia keeps talking as she shepherds Jasmine towards the front door. When Jasmine stops to put on her shoes, Petunia calls someone on her phone: Filippo or Amanda, I'm guessing, given she's complaining about me and how Olivia's not coming because she's unwell. Once Jasmine is ready, she doesn't even say goodbye, just ushers her outside. I wave to them as they leave. Jasmine waves back.

'See you later!' she calls before Petunia shuts the front door.

'Not if I can help it,' I mutter under my breath.

THIRTY-NINE

I watch as Petunia's car pulls away from the kerb. I give it a few minutes, just in case either of them have forgotten something. The seconds tick by, and my anxiety ramps up with it, until I can't take it anymore. That's it.

No more waiting.

It's now or never.

I lay Olivia down on the sofa. She fights a bit, refusing to let me go, but eventually I manage to convince her. I stroke her head, and promise that everything will be all right from now on.

It has to be.

The house feels eerily quiet as I scuttle into my makeshift bedroom and drag the rucksack out from under my bed. It's harder to get down on the floor now my bump is bigger, and by the time I've reached it and struggled back up to my feet, my head is spinning. I rub my belly as I feel a squirm, promising Sprout that it's okay, everything's going to be all right.

Mama will protect you.

I heave the rucksack over my shoulder. It doesn't contain much, but it still feels much heavier than I thought it would.

I've only packed the essentials: basic snacks, the burner phone. The clothes I bought us. I think about changing into those now, but I decide against it. The important thing is to get away from the house with as much time as possible to spare. I can worry about changing clothes later. Lastly, I check the little zip-up wallet. The cash my secret benefactor left me is still there. I keep being seized by this irrational fear that I hallucinated the package all along.

That I've made all of this up, and I'm actually going just a little bit mad.

Okay, that's part one of the plan done. Next, get Olivia in the car and drive to the train station – not the nearest one, that's too obvious, maybe Woolerton or Cheshaw, I haven't decided yet. Then catch the next train that gets me closer to Weston Point. Not that I know where Weston Point is. Along the coast somewhere, I guess?

But I'm not going to worry about that now. Once I'm far enough away, I can look it up. Right now, I have far too much on my plate to worry about anything other than simply escaping.

I glance out of the bedroom window. It's just before lunch, and as usual, our cul-de-sac is quiet. And even if someone was out there, why would they question me taking Olivia to the park on such a lovely day? Nonetheless, worry twists in my chest.

What if this doesn't work?

No. I can't think like that. It *has* to work. Because if it doesn't... I don't know how to finish that sentence.

It's too awful to contemplate.

Next comes the really hard part. Olivia is now asleep. I stroke her hair away from her face.

'Come on Pumpkin, wake up. It's time for us to go.'

I give her a little shake, but she doesn't stir. My heart, already pounding, leaps to my throat, a familiar dread that only parents of small children truly understand rising with my growing panic. I feel the all-too familiar sensation of my body preparing to purge as I try again to wake Olivia, now scared to death that I've given her too much Benadryl. Is she breathing? Oh my God, oh no...

Olivia mutters something in her sleep and twitches a little. I'm so relieved, I feel like crying. I lean over to pick her up, but I misjudge her weight. Something twinges in my belly, and I realise that I can't just scoop her up. Instead, I wrestle her up into a sitting position.

'Mama?'

She's very drowsy, but at least she's conscious.

'Hello, Pumpkin. Yes, it's Mama. We're going for a little drive, okay? Come on, up we go.'

This time, I manage to drape her sleep-heavy body over my shoulder and struggle up off the sofa. I take a peek at the clock on the wall.

It's already taken me twenty minutes to get this far.

If I'm not careful, I'm going to run out of time.

I decide shoes can wait. I'll put them on Olivia when we arrive at the station. Right now, I just need to get away from here. The destination can take care of itself.

I take a moment to shove my feet into my shoes and grab our coats. The realisation that I should have bought new ones along with our new clothes strikes me, but it's too late now. I can buy new coats later. Then we slip out of the door to the kitchen, go through the utility room and into the garage.

'Mama, what we doing?' She yawns and rubs at her eyes.

'Hey, Pumpkin, we're going for a little drive,' I say, as cheerfully as I can.

'Is Ja'min and Gwamma coming?'

'No, darling. They'll be home soon.'

She smiles sleepily at me as I finally snap the buckles in place.

I take in a deep breath, hoping to steady my nerves.

It doesn't work.

'Okay, Pumpkin, you ready? Everything's going to be fine. Mama's got this.'

I think.

I hope...

PART TWO

FORTY

EIGHT YEARS EARLIER

Jasmine

I hate these things.

Oh sure, these parties *look* like fun, all the pretty candles on the edges of the flower beds, and the gazebo is decorated with solar fairy lights and no one is really looking after the drinks so no one notices when I swipe the odd glass of Prosecco, but the thing is, with no one else my own age here, it's all just so boring. Like, *so* boring. I mean, yeah, I have my phone, but as soon as I get it out, Mum's there complaining, saying I'm always on it, and Auntie Amanda starts teasing me and honestly it's just embarrassing, so in the end I just have to sit there in the corner doing absolutely nothing but eating old-fashioned finger food and trying to pretend I haven't had anything to drink, promise, I wouldn't, I'm only fifteen, I don't even know what alcohol tastes like. Or that's what they think, at least.

I don't even know why I'm here. Okay, so I do, but I'm not sure if I'm meant to know, which is hilarious because I live with them, how can I not? Mum and 'Auntie' Amanda have been together since I was a little girl. I was even called the girl with two mums in the playground. It doesn't bother me, but I think it bothers the ancients, so they're pretending it's not happening, which is kind of sad. Like, who cares? But I suppose it's better than my mum and Amanda being completely ostracised, so yeah. Families are complicated. If the only way they can cope is by pretending that Mum and Amanda are 'best friends', then whatever.

Oh God, what now? They're all cooing and doing that stupid air-cheek kissing thing at some new people who have just arrived. Although... hang on. Who is that? He's fit as! Suit, no tie, dark hair, sunglasses, kind of looks a bit like that hot guy off *Gossip Girl*. Petunia is all over him, as is Amanda – oh, wait, someone is with him. A woman. She's wearing a black dress with ruffles at the neck and an asymmetrical hem. It looks expensive. If I ever get to wear a dress like that, I think I'd probably look a little happier about it, because she is clearly angry. Whoever she is, she keeps pursing her lips and glaring at Petunia. Is she his girlfriend?

Whoops. Hide the glass. Looks like they're coming over. Put the phone down. And smile. No, not like that. Don't look too keen. A bit of pout. Not a duck face.

Oh my God, he's even more gorgeous up close.

'Darling, you remember Jasmine?'

The man's eyes widen as I stand up. The smile he beams at me makes me stumble a bit, and my cheeks flush red.

'Jasmine? Look at you!' Initially I think the gorgeous man is going to shake my hand, but instead he leans over and hugs me. He smells amazing and I can feel how toned his chest is under his shirt. 'I think the last time I saw you, you were showing me your My Little Ponies. I think one was called Sparkle Dash or something?'

I giggle as he pulls away, a very hazy memory floating to the surface of my mind.

'It was Twilight Sparkle,' I say. 'And you're Amanda's brother, aren't you?'

'Guilty as charged.'

'You're a doctor, right?'

'Ah, two for two. Smart girl.' He grins at me, and my knees go weak. 'It's Russ,' he says. 'And you don't have to call me Uncle, unless you want to.' He leans in again, his voice lowering to a conspiratorial whisper. 'Just between you and me, it would be weird.'

'Yeah, it would be,' I whisper back.

'You want a drink?'

'I've got a Coke, thank you.' I point to the half-full decoy glass on the table.

'Oh, come on, Jasmine, no one's buying that. A family gathering where the lone teenager isn't sneaking drinks? Please. I was your age once, not too long ago. The secret is, don't go for the obvious. If you put it in Coke, the Coke doesn't have to be a decoy.'

'But there's nothing here that goes in Coke,' I say. 'I know, I looked.'

'Really? Where's your imagination? Everything goes in Coke if you need it to. Don't worry. I'm a doctor. You can trust me.'

Okay, so maybe I was being a little bit hasty earlier. Because he didn't come back. I waited for my drink, but he kept getting cornered by other people, which is understandable, I suppose... but it's still annoying.

I've been kind of lurking near the back of the garden, because all these creepy old dudes keep coming over to talk to me. The woman who arrived with Russ hasn't said much, though. I've been keeping an eye on her. She's kept herself to herself most of the night. I don't think she wants to be here, and judging by the looks Petunia is giving her, I don't think she's very welcome. She's also been knocking back drinks like they're going out of fashion. There's a tension to her, like she's going to snap at some point, and I'm not sure I want to be there when she does.

Russ isn't ignoring her, not exactly, but he isn't really paying her much attention, either. Every now and again he'll go over to her and she'll hiss something at him, he'll raise his hands like he's a lion tamer and back off, then she'll gulp down whatever drink she's holding and go and get another one. Everyone else is giving her some major side-eye, which doesn't surprise me. This kind of behaviour is very much Not Appropriate at these gatherings. It doesn't matter if half the attendees despise the other half, everyone remains polite no matter what. And this woman isn't being very polite to anyone.

Finally, Russ comes over with two drinks. He offers one to me.

'Sorry it's a bit late,' he says. 'Got waylaid.'

'I noticed,' I say as I flip my hair over my shoulder and try to play it cool, even though my heart is galloping in my chest. I take a sip of the drink. It kind of tastes like Dr Pepper, but there's definitely still a kick to it. 'What is this?'

'Well, you see, the thing is' – Russ leans in conspiratorially again, speaking out of the side of his mouth – 'when you've grown up in a house – and, more importantly, know exactly what and where all the drinks are – you can basically make whatever you like, as long as you're careful.'

'Careful?'

'Don't just top the bottles up with water. That never works. Some stuff goes cloudy, and when your dad goes to pour himself a nice scotch only to find out it's more like apple juice...' He exaggerates a wince, and I can't help but giggle again. He's so funny. And charming. And hot...

'Anyway, it's Disaronno and Coke. Some people optimistically call it a cocktail, but it's not really. I think you need more than two ingredients to make a drink a cocktail.'

'I had a cocktail once. On holiday last summer. With Mum and Amanda. They were drinking them, too, and I think they were a bit more drunk than they realised. I asked them if I could try one, too. I thought they'd say no, but they didn't. It was nice.'

'Oh?' Russ raises his eyebrows and takes a sip from his own drink. Oh my God, he's just so fit, he looks like he could be going to a Hollywood party or something. 'What was it?'

'Um, Sex On The Beach.' My cheeks flush as I mumble out the name, suddenly embarrassed to be saying such things out loud to a hot guy.

'What was that?' He leans closer, allowing me to catch a whiff of his aftershave. 'Didn't quite catch it.'

My cheeks are proper burning now, but I can't back down. Only kids get embarrassed saying these kinds of things, and I'm not a kid. I'm sixteen in two months.

'It was a Sex On The Beach.' This time, I say it loud and proud, and Russ rears back a little, giving me an impressed nod with it.

'Ooh, fancy. That's a good one to start with. A proper grown-up one, too. Did you like it?'

'Uh, yeah, it was good.'

'And the drink?'

I pause, confused. Russ holds my gaze, his dark eyes intense, to the point where I feel like I'm being hypnotised. My chest feels like it's filled with fluttering butterflies as he smiles, then lets out a laugh.

'I'm just teasing,' he says, his voice low. 'I can't make you a Sex On The Beach, but I can get you another one of those.' He inclines his glass towards mine. 'So—'

The rest of his sentence is cut off by a yell.

'No, don— don't you touch me! No— look! He's at it again!'

It's the woman, the one who arrived with Russ. And she is

capital D Drunk now. She's staggering around, yelling at Petunia, telling her to leave her alone. Petunia looks furiously mortified and I don't blame her. Getting drunk at a party is one thing. Getting drunk at a party and yelling at the host is something else. Even I know that.

'Oh God,' Russ mutters, then touches my arm. Goosebumps flurry up my skin. 'I'd better sort this out.'

'Who is that?' I ask.

'My girlfriend.' He sighs heavily, and I don't think I've ever felt more sorry for anyone, ever.

By now, Filippo has joined Petunia. He's always been the calmer one, and is trying to reason with Russ's girlfriend, but it's clear it's not working. The woman is getting shriller by the minute; it's hard to make out exactly what she's saying because she's drunk, but whatever it is, it's clearly something about Russ as she absolutely loses it with him as he approaches her. He tries everything he can to calm her down, but nothing works. In the end, Filippo calls a cab and then threatens to call the police if she won't leave. By now the woman is sobbing, everyone is staring and I kind of feel sorry for her.

Before the cab comes, she shoves Russ and storms off. He follows but comes back a few minutes later. People crowd around him, asking him if he's okay, giving him another drink – and just like that, things are back to normal again. It's almost like Russ's girlfriend was never there.

Feeling a little rattled, I take myself off to the bottom of the garden, to the little covered seat by the pond. I sip at my drink and watch fish that cost more than my shoes gulping at the surface, no doubt thinking I am there to feed them. Gosh, this drink is nice, but strong. A warm, fuzzy feeling has crept up the back of my neck and is now travelling along my jaw. If Mum came to speak to me now, I'm not sure I could pretend I was sober.

Still, I keep sipping.

There are no candles down here. No solar lights. All of those are around the patio, where the adults congregate, meaning this end of the garden is dark and secret. I kind of like it. I don't have to be on my best behaviour here. I pull out my phone and start to scroll. Shame the internet service out here is so crap, really—

The shrubbery near me rustles. I straighten up and peer into the shadows as my heart leaps in my chest.

'Hello?' I say. I'm not sure quite why I'm feeling so nervous. Probably because I know I'm going to be in loads of trouble if that's my mother.

But it isn't my mother. Or Auntie Amanda. Or anyone else I'd expect.

It's Russ.

'Hey,' he says, and holds up a full glass. 'I said I'd get you another, and I don't break my promises.'

I take the glass off him and take a sip. If anything, this one is even stronger than the last. I smile up at him.

'Thanks.'

'Can I join you?'

It takes me a moment to gather my thoughts. He wants to... join me?

Hell, yeah!

'Yeah, sure.' I shuffle over on the seat, making room for him, a little perplexed as to why he'd want to spend time down here with me but pleased he's here nonetheless.

He sits heavily and throws his head back. Then he fiddles in his pocket and pulls out what looks like a small tin. Inside are rolled cigarettes. Or, at least, that's what they look like. When he lights one up, the smell tells me my mistake immediately.

'You don't mind?'

'No, of course not.'

He takes a long drag then offers the joint to me.

'You want some?'

I could say no, but what would Russ think? That I was a stupid little girl. And I'm not a stupid little girl. So I smile and nod, and take the joint from him. I try not to inhale too deeply, but the smoke still burns. I attempt to suppress a cough, but can't help it. I pass the joint back to Russ, ready for him to tease me, but instead he just smiles, leans back and takes another long drag.

'It's nice out here, isn't it? I used to sit out here for ages when I lived at home. The fish are so peaceful. They don't care what grades you get, or what state your room is in.'

It takes me a moment to figure out what he's talking about, but then it strikes me – of course, this is his childhood home. I dare to settle myself next to him and take a long sip – more of a gulp, if I'm honest – from my drink. I know weed is supposed to calm you down but my heart is galloping in my chest, and I think I might actually be at risk of passing out when Russ offers me the joint again, like I'm one of his friends or something.

'I'm sorry you had to see all that earlier,' he says. 'It's just Frankie... she's... we're...' He lets out a long sigh, his expression pained. 'Things aren't great.'

I nip at the joint, not wanting to cough again.

'No?'

'No. Everything was great at first, I mean, it always is, isn't it? But recently... she's so paranoid, you know? Constantly accusing me of stuff, checking my phone, borderline stalking me at work – it's ridiculous.' He leans forward and puts his head in his hands. 'I just don't know what to do.'

I'm not sure what he wants me to say, but before the silence becomes uncomfortable, he continues.

'Ah, but look at me. I'm sorry. I shouldn't be unloading this on you. It's not fair. I guess you're just so mature for your age, I forgot you're what, sixteen?'

I offer him a small shrug. Close enough.

'What I'd give to be sixteen again.' He leans back and stretches his arms out, this time resting his hands behind his head. 'Life was so full of promise back then. I felt untouchable. There will be a lot of people out there trying to give you a lot of advice over the next couple of years, Jasmine, and most of it will be utter bullshit.'

Again, a giggle surges up within me, and I try to wrestle it down.

'Yeah, yeah, you can laugh, but it's true. They'll say you have to knuckle down and focus and do as you're told and that these years can't be wasted... but it's all Grade A, twenty-four carat bullshit. You know I failed my first year at uni? Don't look so shocked, I did. The way my parents behaved, you'd think I'd murdered someone. They told people I'd decided to take a gap year, to spare their shame. Not my shame, their shame. Did it ruin my life?' He holds out his arms, inviting me to study him in his entirety, an offer I don't refuse.

'I'm guessing... no?'

He grins at me devilishly.

'No, it did not. I like you, Jasmine. You're in charge of your own mind. You know what you want, and you're not afraid to go for it. I respect that.'

Actually, I am none of those things, but I'm not about to tell him that. I take a long swallow from my drink, and another giggle escapes me. My face feels numb, and as I try to adjust my seat, I lose my balance and fall towards Russ. My drink spills a little, splashing on his shirt. I go to gasp an apology, but instead he catches my wrist so I can't spill any more, then laughs with me.

'Young lady, I think you might be a little drunk.'

'I am not!' But even I can hear myself slurring.

'Like I'm going to tell anyone,' he says, with a sly look. 'I think I'd be in as much trouble as you if anyone found out.'

'Oh no!' I say, and put a finger to my lips. It takes a few attempts, but I finally get there. 'Then we'd better be quiet. Shhhh.'

'Indeed, shhhh.'

I shiver as he puts his arm around my shoulders.

'You smell nice.'

I don't know why I said that.

'So do you.' Russ hands me back my glass, and this time I drain it. The world spins around me as the alcohol surges into my bloodstream. Above me, the stars whirl as I'm lowered back until I'm lying down. I try to say something, but my mouth won't work. Then I try to shake my head, but I can't do that, either. All I want to do is sleep. But I can't sleep. Russ will be so disappointed. Already passing out after only a couple of drinks, such a lightweight.

'You're such a good girl...'

FORTY-ONE

Frankie

We're going to be all right, Pumpkin. Mama's going to get us to a safe place. Everything's going to be okay...

I thought morning sickness was brutal. Hell, I thought recovering from Olivia's C-section was hard. But this?

This is something else.

I think it's easier to say what doesn't hurt. My earlobes? That's probably about it. Everything else is agony, like my entire body is on fire.

Where the hell am I?

I want to open my eyes, but even that's too much. My nose feels like it's about three sizes too big, and I can taste blood at the back of my throat. I try to think back, but there's nothing but a big black hole where my memory should be. I was at home, then I was in the car, driving down the back roads, trees all around me. I was relieved. I'd... escaped? I rub at my eyes, wincing at even that small movement, the taste of blood in my mouth making me gag.

I was in the car. Driving. Then... behind me. I didn't see them. Didn't spot the car until it was too late...

(*... glass, breaking...*)

... smashed into the side of me...

(*... the world, spinning...*)

... they were going so fast, I couldn't see who was driving...

(*... the smell of blood, Olivia screaming...*)

... no, not now, I have to get away...

(*... a cold ball of dread beneath the agony as they stepped up to the broken window...*)

... I... something... something is... wrong. Very wrong.

Baby

Oh my God, my baby! It hits me like a lightning bolt. I curl up into a protective ball, wincing in pain, cocooning my bump, praying that she's all right. I squeeze my eyes shut, focusing, waiting to feel the flutters. Come on, baby. Just one. Just a little kick. It doesn't have to be much. Just enough to let me know you're there—

A faint sensation, like bubbles, grazes against my insides. Tears well in my eyes.

'Well done,' I whisper. 'Now let's try again, just to be sure.'

But before I can feel her again, I hear a soft whimper.

'Mama?'

A warm weight shifts against my side and another part of the puzzle of my life slots into place.

Olivia.

With new purpose, I bully my eyes open and manage to turn my aching body over. My sweet, beautiful daughter, barely three years old, is clinging to me; she's cold and has a large bruise on her cheek. The rest of her face is dead-white and her eyes are ringed red from crying.

'Mama, mama, mama.'

'It's okay, baby, it's okay,' I murmur, forcing myself to sit up. Every muscle I own shrieks, but I ignore them. Nothing, not even my own body, is going to keep me from my daughter. I wrap my arms around her little body and offer her as much comfort as I can. 'Mama's here.'

'No, no,' she says, in more of a moan.

'I know. I know. It hurts, but we'll be okay, I promise, Pumpkin.'

'Mama, no, no. Papa.' Olivia starts to cry again, and as I rock her, I join in.

Now I'm sitting up, I can see that we're in a dilapidated room. The brickwork is exposed, and the floor is just dirt. There are no windows – the only light comes from a little camping lantern stood on a crate in the corner. I have no idea what's powering it, but then again, that really is the least of my worries. Next to the lantern is a box of cereal bars and some bottles of water. In the other corner is a plastic bucket with a toilet roll on the ground next to it. The whole place stinks of damp and earth. The only word that comes to mind is *basement*.

With a growing sense of pure horror, I try to stand up. My aching body makes it hard enough – given the absolute agony in my shoulder, I think I might have dislocated something – but there's something else.

Something *wrong*.

At first, I can't work it out, like my brain literally can't comprehend it. The sensation of weight, the way it rubs against my ankle, the clinking sound it makes when I move. Even as I look down, it takes me a good minute to understand.

It's a chain. Around my ankle.

A length of chain, fixed to the back wall.

The cement looks horribly new.

I stagger sideways at the enormity of this.

I was right.

But even I didn't think I would be *this* right. I knew she wanted my family. Or, at least, she wanted Russ. But to kidnap me and Olivia and chain us up in a basement?

I have to sit back down before I fall.

Olivia squirms back into my lap. She's still whimpering, unable to say anything other than 'Mama', 'no' and 'Papa', over and over again until I want to scream at her to shut up, to please shut up, Mama has to think, Mama has to...

Mama has to...

... Mama has no idea.

Is it really this simple? Has Jasmine won? Surely she doesn't think she'll get away with this? Running me off the road and—

Running me off the road!

The memory surges, loud and painful. How I'd taken the back roads because it was quieter and didn't have any speed cameras. How I thought that would work in my favour, because it would make me harder to track, but instead it just made it easier for Jasmine to follow me and force me off the road.

Except...

... except, I don't remember seeing Jasmine's car. In fact, I don't think Jasmine's car would be able to do that. Sure, my car's small and pretty light, but hers is basically a roller-skate. If I'm remembering it correctly, the car that drove into mine wasn't even a car. It was one of those awful trucks, maybe a Range Rover or a Ford. That prick Toby got one not that long ago and it was all Russ would talk about for a while. I know he was planning on replacing his BMW with one until we found out I was pregnant again and I pointed out that trucks aren't exactly baby-seat friendly. Which means Jasmine must have either borrowed one, or she has an accomplice.

What if that accomplice is actually Petunia? God, that would actually make sense, because Filippo does have one of those big truck things. Petunia bought it for his sixtieth birthday, but he doesn't drive it much because it's too hard to park in town. But would she have convinced him to run me off the road? I don't think he would do it. Maybe she paid someone. Maybe this was a... a hit, or something? For the right price,

people will do anything, including deliberately driving a pregnant woman off the road, knocking her out and then chaining
her up in a basement with her toddler daughter.

And that sounds completely mental, even though it is
precisely what's happening to me right now.

I tug on the chain. It's securely bolted to the wall, but even
if it wasn't, I don't think I'd be able to pull it free, because I feel
horribly weak. I give Olivia a cuddle and try to gently explain
that Mama needs to put her down now, but she just climbs
higher and wraps her arms so tightly around my neck, it feels
like she's strangling me.

'Honey, darling, please, Mama has to—'

'No, Mama, no, no, Papa...'

I manage to disentangle her arms and finally stand up again,
swaying a little as the world spins around me. Given I was most
likely knocked out, I probably have some kind of concussion.
But I can't worry about that now. Olivia clings to my unchained
leg, and even though it takes me a while, I manage to work out
that the chain is long enough for me to reach the crate with the
snacks and lantern, and the bucket with the loo roll, but not
long enough to reach the door on the other side of the room.
The fact that it's only a couple of feet short leaves me
wondering if that's by design: long enough to get your hopes up,
but short enough to dash them.

Whoever set this room up, they're a real sadist.

Even though I know it's probably pointless, I try yelling
anyway. My voice sounds thin, deadened by the stone walls,
and as suspected, I don't hear anyone call back in return, nor do
I hear the distant wail of a police car siren.

In fact, I can't hear anything.

Where has she taken me?

I think back to the journal I found in her room. I never did
manage to crack its code. Not that I really tried. I guess, deep
down, I didn't really believe she was this serious. Not until I

found the thallium bottle, anyway. And by that point, it was too late. All my energy was in trying to escape. Something I thought I was managing.

Something I tried so hard to achieve, but only ended up failing anyway.

Desperation claws its way up through me again. No. This can't be it. There has to be a way out of this. She can't win. She just can't. I start yelling again: 'Help me, anyone, please, can anyone hear me, please, I need help!' Olivia joins me, sobbing 'No, no, Mama, Papa, Mama' but I can't stop to soothe her, to tell her it's going to be okay because that's a lie and I promised I'd never, ever lie to her, my beloved baby girl. What I need to do is get her out of here, get her to safety, but I don't know how, I don't know, I can't, I just can't...

I don't know how long it goes on for. When my voice cracks, my legs sag and I collapse in a crumpled heap on the floor. When Olivia says, in a small voice, 'Mama I go wees,' I look over to the bucket, but it's too late. Jasmine hasn't left me nappies, or even a spare pair of knickers.

And that's when it strikes me.

I thought she wanted to take over my family. Get rid of me.

But now I realise it was much more than that. It wasn't just me. She wanted to get rid of all of us. But she had to make it look believable. Make it look like she was helping, and that I was a crazy lady. I can see it now. *She was so ill... I have no idea where she's taken her. I hope she doesn't do anything silly.* And by silly, she, of course, means the inevitable murder-suicide perpetrated by a woman with pre-natal psychosis, a condition less well-known than post-natal depression, but just as deadly. More so, in my case, because it would involve three lives.

We sit in the gloom. I try to sing songs to help pass the time. We share a cereal bar and a bottle of water. Olivia curls up on my lap and naps for a bit, leaving me to contend with the cold reality of our situation alone. When she wakes up, she doesn't smile, or coo, or ask for her froggies. Instead, she gives me a fearful look and my heart breaks anew.

How could anyone do this to a child?

'Mama, I cold.' Olivia shivers next to me. The quality of the light has darkened further, so I guess it's now night-time. I have absolutely no idea how long we've been down here. Could be a few hours, could be a couple of days. Was Olivia also knocked out? If she wasn't, maybe she can tell me what happened?

'Livvy, darling,' I say in the gentlest way possible. 'Did you see who came with us down here?'

She buries her head against my side and whines.

'It's okay, Pumpkin, it's okay. All Mama wants to know is who was it?'

'Carry Mama down stairs,' Olivia says. 'Mama was sleeping.'

'Yes, Mama was, good girl. And who carried Mama down the stairs?'

'Mama, no, no, Papa, no, no!'

'I know, darling, I know you want Papa, but I have to know who did this to Mama. Can you tell me? Was it Jasmine?'

Olivia looks at me, confused.

I realise my mistake straight away. Of course it wasn't Jasmine. She was out with Petunia, and there's no way she could carry me in here. She must have hired someone, or, I don't know, seduced someone into doing her dirty work. That's why Olivia can't tell me who they are. She doesn't know them.

'Papa, no, no, Papa.'

'It's all right, sweetheart. I'm sure Papa will find us.'

Olivia shakes her head and plucks at her ears, something she only does when she's really upset. 'No, no! Papa!'

'All right, it's okay, it's all going to be fine,' I say, wrapping her back up into a hug. She's trembling. So am I. There isn't even a blanket in here for us to lie on. Surely Jasmine doesn't mean to keep us down here for long without basic amenities?

But, then again, if she intends to make us disappear, why would she care about our comfort?

Apart from Olivia's whimpers, the room is eerily quiet, making me wonder if it's sound-proofed. It would make sense. It also hints at a level of organisation I am uncomfortable with. Maybe this plan has been much longer in the making than I realised. Maybe Petunia is the one who arranged all of this, and Jasmine is simply the first acceptable compliant woman she's found to include in her scheming? But again, that doesn't explain Olivia, or the new baby. She's always seemed to love her grandchild.

How many red flags have I been ignoring over the years? But that's how it works, I suppose. They don't show up all at once. They get drip-fed over years; a word here, a look there, an action, a reaction... they all build up until everything is normalised, and behaviour that once would have had me fleeing to the hills now doesn't make me bat an eyelid.

A shower of dust patters down from the ceiling above. I jerk my head up as a floorboard creaks, followed by a scraping sound.

Someone is up there.

This could be it. Our salvation. If I shout now, this could all be over in a matter of minutes. Our story could be breaking news within the hour.

Olivia climbs up my body, her eyes wide. She is holding on to me limpet-tight, and I feel it too. That tight, squirming feeling in my chest that isn't elation, isn't even relief.

It's dread.

Because whoever is up there could be our salvation, but every cell in my body knows that it's anything but.

FORTY-TWO

Jasmine

June 14th 2016

It's my birthday! Finally. I'm sixteen now, it's just a shame that I'm in the middle of my exams so no party for me yet. The prom is next week, though, so that's fun. Not that I can go with who I want to. I did ask him. But he said it would be weird, and that people would talk. Even though I'm sixteen and so everything is totally legal now, he said people won't understand. They'll see me as a kid and not as the blossoming young woman I have become. Omg, how romantic is that? He said that he's got a surprise for me, too. He can't see me on my actual birthday 'cos he has to work, but he says he'll be down at the weekend, which is really cool 'cos Mum and Amanda are going out so I'll be home alone Saturday night – I was thinking of inviting Amber over, maybe having a sleepover, but when he found out he said he could come over to keep me company, and there's no way I was going to say no to that.

He's so dreamy, and such a gentleman. Always saying how

nice I look and how mature I am for my age. He says he knows there's a bit of an age gap, but age is just a number, and anyway, I'll be eighteen in two years and that's not that far away. He says we can do everything at my pace, too. He's so thoughtful. Last time, I wasn't feeling so great and he just held me until I fell asleep in his arms... it was so romantic...

I don't know why I've kept these. I used to write a Tumblr blog, a private one just for me. A place where I could write down my thoughts without worrying about my mum discovering them.

After I found out what was really going on, I downloaded all the entries and saved them to a private Google Docs file and deleted the blog, but you know what they say, the internet is forever, so there's always that worry that someone, somewhere will rediscover them at some point. I just hope I've been able to do what I need to do before that inevitably happens.

One thing I do know is that he groomed me. For a long time. But I'm older now. Older and much, much wiser, and once I've finished with this, I'm going to take him to the cleaners—

'Crap,' Russ growls.

I tense and look up from my iPad. He's pacing again.

He hasn't stopped since Frankie left.

'You okay?' I ask, a little warily. From the outside, it might look like he's worried. Some men are like that. They don't cry when something terrible happens. They rage. But I know Russ well enough to know that's not what this is about.

He's angry. And that worries me. I catch the occasional *bitch* among the nonsensical hisses, and it's all I can do to send up a little prayer to whoever might be listening that Frankie and Olivia actually made it out and are now well on their way.

I let him rant for a little longer, then check my phone. The AirTag I slipped into Olivia's coat pocket went out of range ages ago, but even so, I keep checking, just to make sure they're definitely not coming back.

Russ's temper tantrum is showing no sign of letting up. He's been like this since he realised Frankie was missing. It's been two days and he hasn't shown any fear, no worry, just anger. As far as I know, he hasn't even called the police yet. I said I'd do it, but the look he gave me told me that would be a very bad idea indeed. Because he knows. Deep down, he knows. All abusive assholes do. They all know what they're doing is wrong. The difference is, they don't feel bad about it. If anything, that's the draw. They don't care that they're hurting others, because the power and control their behaviour affords them is exactly what they want. It's a feature, not a bug. Russ knows his behaviour has been terrible, but that isn't what's bothering him. What he doesn't like is being foiled. And that's why he's so angry. This isn't about worry; this is about Frankie doing her own thing. About Frankie defying him, refusing to put up with his bullshit anymore. And that's the one thing men like Russell Minetti don't take too kindly to: women defying them. So in public he's going to be all *poor me, please come home safe, I love my wife so much...* but in private, he's a volcano due to blow, and I fully intend on not being anywhere near him when he does.

'Fuck this,' Russ spits. 'I can't do this.'

'Where are you going?' I say, more out of politeness than any real desire to stop him.

He half snorts, half growls as he stalks past me.

'To my parents'.'

I could just go home. I'm under no obligation to go to Petunia and Filippo's. In fact, that's the last place in the world I want to be. But there's something about Russ's anger that worries me. It's so extreme, so focused.

I don't know what it is, but I just can't shake the feeling there's more to all of this. That he's hiding something.

When he's out of the room I grab my handbag and rummage around in one of the pockets, looking for one of my AirTags. I have a bunch of these, mainly because I lose things all the time, but also because they're a handy way of keeping an eye on things that might need your scrutiny. I hear Russ go into the bathroom, and use that time to slip one into his jacket pocket.

You know.

Just in case.

The downstairs toilet flushes, and I run back to the sofa. He collects up his things, including his jacket.

'You stay here, just in case someone calls.'

It isn't a request.

I nod. He leaves. I wait until I hear him pull out of his driveway and disappear around the corner.

I check my phone, and smile. There he is, a dot on my screen.

Time to see where he's really going.

FORTY-THREE

Jasmine

I follow the dot on my screen easily. Not that I really have to follow it. I know this route well. The senior Minettis live in a very exclusive area near the coast, not quite rural enough to worry about being able to smell livestock, but rural enough not to have to worry about your neighbours looking in over your garden.

As I turn down the lane that leads to the Minettis' house, my phone pings. It's probably a text, maybe from Mum or Auntie Amanda. But when I slow down to steal a look, I can't help but frown.

It isn't a text.

New AirTag in range.

And there are now two dots on the map.

Either it must have glitched, or it's picking up another AirTag connected to my phone.

My stomach drops. The new tag is close. Really close.

In fact, it's just up ahead.

The original AirTag I sneaked into Russ's jacket is now inside the house. This new one, though...

'... but how is that possible?'

I peer up the lane. As far as I can tell, this new dot isn't in the house. It seems to be hovering next to it. In the garage.

Why would they have a tag in their garage? Or, should I say, why would my phone be picking it up? It should only be picking up the ones I've assigned to me.

Unless...

Did Petunia take Olivia's coat without me realising it? I placed a tag in the hem of her coat as soon as I realised Frankie was making plans to leave. But if Petunia had taken it, surely I would have known. The tag would have activated earlier if the coat was in Petunia's car all along.

Oh no.

My heart rate spikes as I try to convince myself that this means nothing. Sometimes AirTags glitch. Sometimes they pick up random stuff. And there is a chance that Petunia did accidentally pick up Olivia's coat out of habit, and I didn't realise she'd done it. After all, I didn't check my phone while we were at Bramley House. Couldn't risk it. That has to be it.

It doesn't mean that she has anything to do with Frankie and Olivia going missing.

But... she has been remarkably calm throughout all of this. I put it down to her being a heartless witch, but what if...

... no.

It can't be.

She was with me.

Unless she's... hiding them? Took them here for some reason? But that makes even less sense. If that was the case, then why would Russ be so angry?

A whole host of awful possibilities flashes through my mind. Frankie, locked in a room.

Frankie, dead, awaiting burial.

I shake my head to clear the images away. No. Petunia might be terrible, but she'd never resort to anything like that.

Unless...

... Russ is her special baby boy. Always has been. It doesn't matter what he's done, he's always innocent, always the victim.

Except none of that is true. He isn't one of the good guys, and he never has been.

At first, I was flattered. No, scratch that – I was head over heels in love. That's the thing when you're being groomed, the dirty little secret that no one wants to talk about, let alone admit. At the time, it doesn't necessarily feel like abuse. It feels like love. Or, at least, what you assume love feels like. It's only afterwards, once you wake up and realise what's actually going on, that it clicks into place.

And by then, it's too late.

It's all too late.

My skin crawls at the memories. I was so young, so innocent, until Russell Minetti came into my life. What he did.

What he still does...

But I can't think about that. My time will come. Right now, I have to work out what's going on with this tag.

As I get closer to the house, I can see Russ and Petunia's cars out in the drive. But the dot isn't over either of them. It's definitely in the garage. Which means the tag isn't in either of their cars.

So why the hell is it in the garage?

I can't sit here figuring this out. At some point someone is going to notice me idling in the lane, so I shift my car into reverse and back out until I can do a U-turn and make it back to the main road.

I park up in a nearby passing spot. My whole body flares with goosebumps. This could be an innocent mistake. Upset at the disappearance of her granddaughter, Petunia took her coat. For comfort.

But then why leave it in the garage? Why not take it inside?

Also, I don't remember seeing the coat when we got home.

It wasn't hanging up, and it wasn't in Olivia's room. I'd gone to the bathroom to surreptitiously check on it, and there was nothing on my screen. If it had still been in the house, it would have been picked up by my phone. I figured then that they must have been out of range.

That Frankie had managed to get away.

Because that had been the plan. To give her the time. All I've wanted to do for the last few weeks is tell her that I'm on her side, that I always have been. I'm literally here because I know her husband. What he's like. He might deny it, might pretend that he's a doting husband and father, but the truth is he's a monster: a pampered, spoiled monster who has never had to face the consequences of his actions.

A spoiled monster I was planning to expose all along.

The problem was, when I got there, things were even worse than I thought. And so I tried to speed things up. Tried to drive her away, even if it meant I looked terrible while doing it. I kept telling myself that it would all be worth it in the end.

Now I'm not so sure.

Indecision cramps my guts. I could call the police. But what would I tell them? As far as I'm aware, Russ hasn't even reported her missing. He'd make something up, and I'd look like an idiot while also showing my entire hand, something I can't do; not without knowing for sure that Frankie is safe and well.

Maybe an anonymous tip? That might alert the relevant authorities that something's not right. But, again, what if that puts Frankie in even more danger?

I stare at my phone, willing it to tell me more, but the dots remain dumb circles on my screen. One in the house. One in the garage. Just sitting there.

Maybe I should drive up there? Go and see if they're okay. Make an excuse. Say I was worried about how upset Russ is—

One of the dots moves.

It's the one in the garage.

And it's coming down the lane towards me.

I fire up my engine and put my phone on the dash. I know you're not supposed to use your phone when you're driving, but I'm also aware that I only have a small window before whoever is driving the car could be well out of range if they go in the opposite direction. If they come in this direction, then I'll just have to hope they don't spot me. I grip my steering wheel, the adrenaline coursing through my body making me light-headed. I shake my head. I have to focus. I can't lose them.

I have to find out what's going on.

Thankfully, whoever is driving takes a left at the top of the lane, meaning they are heading in my direction. I turn my headlights off, trusting in the overgrown hedgerows and my car's small size as a large black truck-style SUV sweeps past me.

The dot goes with it.

A sickening feeling of dread curdles in my stomach as the SUV's tail lights disappear around the bend. I turn my headlights back on and begin to follow, carefully. Even without the tinted windows, it was too dark to see who was driving. It could be any of them, or all of them; it could even be none of them. But it doesn't matter. It's too late to back out now. No matter how this ends, I'm involved. If nothing else, I have to confirm that Frankie got away, and the AirTag in the car is just some horrible coincidence, the universe playing one last trick on me before I can finally breathe again.

Following someone when you don't want them to know you're there is harder than I thought it would be. I can't follow too closely, because they'll spot me, but at the same time if I hang back too much, I run the risk of losing them. The AirTag signal helps, but it doesn't have infinite range, and whoever is driving is going at a fair clip. As we drive deeper into the countryside, the roads turn unfamiliar. There aren't any houses around here, so there's a good chance no one has driven down here in ages. Another turn down an even narrower side road, and the feeling of dread grows heavier. As far as my map is concerned, this particular road ends in a track, which ultimately leads to acres and acres of private woodland.

The perfect place to hide something.

Or someone.

I switch off my headlights again and drop back even further to keep a decent distance between us. If I get too close, whoever is driving will absolutely spot me, and I can't think of a way to wriggle out of why I might be following them down here. It doesn't take long before the road turns into a single track lane, and the SUV slows to a crawl. It's at this point that I realise there's no turning back now; quite literally, given how thickly the trees are growing either side of me. The darkness takes on a suffocating edge as I peer ahead, hoping nothing leaps out in front of my car, and there are no deep potholes to get stuck in.

The whole time, the little red dot creeps on, deeper into the woodland.

The road is nothing more than a rocky track now. I continue rolling forward. Up ahead, the dot turns right, and continues into what looks like green empty space on the map. Whatever is out there, even Google Maps doesn't know what it is. My stomach drops another notch.

None of this is good.

Finally, after carefully navigating a few potholes, I come across an open gate. I check my phone. According to the dot, that is definitely the direction they took. The track beyond is even less maintained than this one, to the point I'm not sure my car could manage it. I chew on the inside of my lips, racked with indecision. Should I get out and scout ahead? Last thing I need is to get stuck up there. What if it's a complete dead end? What if the driver is up there, waiting for me? What if they've spotted me and are laying a trap? At least on foot, I might be able to hide in the tree line a bit. But what if they've done what they came here to do and try to leave, only to find my car blocking the gate? It doesn't matter where I move it to, it's going to be in the way. And there's no way to disguise it, or drive it off the track – the trees and shrubs grow far too thickly here.

In the end, I decide it's not worth the risk. If there's nothing here, then whoever it is doesn't need to know I was following them. And if there is? I'll cross that bridge when I come to it.

Aware that time is not on my side, I kick the car into reverse and make my way back down the lane, then make a U-turn as soon as it widens back out.

It doesn't take me too long to find an entrance to another service road that's cut off by a locked gate. It only goes in about fifteen feet, but it's enough. I pull in as close as I can to the trees, hoping the dark and that famous Minetti arrogance will do the rest.

Before I get out, I check my phone. The dot has gone. My heart judders. Damn. That means it's either out of charge, or out of range.

Or it's been found, and has been smashed.

No. I can't think like that. It has to be one of the other options. It must be.

The alternative doesn't bear thinking about.

FORTY-FOUR

Frankie

We owe a debt to our distant ancestors. 'Trusting your gut' is something that often gets dismissed as mystical woo-woo by those who pride themselves on being seen as practical, but that gut feeling is there for a reason. Some people call it a sixth sense, others call it luck, but whatever it is, it's helped keep our species alive for thousands of years.

I really wish I'd learned to listen to mine five years ago.

I can't hear the person upstairs anymore. But I don't think they've left. There's a heaviness to the air, one that keeps me from shouting, one that even silences Olivia's whimpering; both our guts are telling us to be quiet because there's a predator around, and we need to hide.

I all but fold myself around my daughter as I hear the scrape of bolts being drawn back. I glare defiantly. Whoever it is, I want them to know I'm not going down easily.

The door opens with a disappointing whisper. I'd at least expected a small creak. The general gloominess means I can't make out who is in the doorway, but I instantly recognise the scent. Cedar with notes of amber and vanilla.

Russ's favourite cologne.

I don't know whether to run to him or faint on the spot. It's Russ. Russ is here to save us! He must have made Jasmine tell him everything. He's here. Everything is going to be all right.

Except... he's not moving. He's just standing there. He hasn't said anything, either. But then again, neither have I. Maybe we're both in shock.

I manage to drag myself towards him.

'Russ... please... She chained me up... Take Olivia. I don't know if there's a key or something, but...'

Russ cocks his head to one side, studying me. Olivia lets out a terrified squeal and shuffles herself around me, so she is clinging to my back, as far away from her father as she can be without letting me go.

'No, Papa, no, no, no, Papa, Papa hurt Mama, no, no...'

'Pumpkin, it's okay, it's just Papa. Papa won't hurt you—'

The penny drops.

Everything she's been saying now makes sense. She didn't want her father.

She was trying to tell me it was her father all along.

'Oh, Frankie.' Russ hunkers down in front of me. I try to scoot backwards, but with Olivia on my back it's nigh on impossible. 'I really wish it didn't have to come to this, but here we are.'

'W-what? W-why?'

'Why what? Why are you here? What am I doing? What have you done? Why am I doing this? Come on, you need to use your words.' He grins, and I realise with a deep sickness that he's *enjoying* this.

'No, Papa, no!'

'Olivia?' Russ says sharply. 'Mama and Papa are having a talk, so I need you to shut up.'

'We don't use that phrase,' I say, more out of habit than anything else. 'It's damaging.'

'Oh, for pity's sake, everything's damaging according to you. Don't go out, Russ, where were you, Russ, don't say that, Russ... always nagging, never shutting up, always accusing, criticising.' He gestures to me, a look of disgust crawling over his face. 'You know, Mum was right. She always said she had no idea what I saw in you. I mean, at first, you had youth on your side, did as you were told. But then you had the brat and really let yourself go. I miss the old days. Do you remember? We used to have so much fun.'

'Funny how I remember you constantly cheating on me and then gaslighting me into thinking I was going mad.'

'Oh, everyone's so quick to chuck that stupid phrase around these days. The problem with women like you is that you don't get men. We need variety. And you had the best. You were the one I was living with, the Queen Bee, but no, that wasn't good enough, was it? You wanted to have complete control over me as well—'

'Don't you dare try to make out I'm the bad guy. You were the one cheating! And if we're on about controlling behaviour, what about all my friends? My family? You made sure to cut them out of my life. Hell, you even made me get rid of my cat.'

'That's because cats are disgusting animals, and you paid more attention to the damn thing than you did me half the time.'

'So I had to get rid of it because you were insecure... you know what, that doesn't matter. What matters is that you're going to untie me. I have absolutely no idea what the hell you and your insane mother have cooked up together, but I just want this to end. You want a divorce? You've got it. I'll move to Australia, patch things up with my brother. You'll never have to see me again... What?'

Russ is shaking his head and chuckling, like I've said something adorably stupid.

'Oh, Frankie, you always were naive. I suppose that's what attracted me to you in the first place. So young.' He raises his hand and tries to touch my cheek, but I jerk my head away before he can reach me. Behind me, Olivia lets out a cry. 'I thought if I got you young, you wouldn't have a chance to change. I'd be all you knew, after all. But, and it pains me to admit this, I was wrong. You did change. And now you've reached your expiration date. Time, as they say, for a new model.'

'And I suppose that "new model" is Jasmine?' I know I shouldn't antagonise him, but my hurt temporarily outweighs my fear. 'Was that the plan all along? Or did you decide after Mummy Dearest made you go to that dinner?'

Russ says nothing, just laughs again. A red-hot, visceral hate surges within me. I don't love this man. Did I ever? I must have done, once, but from this moment onwards, I despise him.

'Answer me,' I say, as reasonably as I can. 'It's the least you owe me.'

'Oh, I'm sorry? It's the least I owe you? That's rich. I provide a decent house, holidays, every little trinket to keep you happy, let you have two kids—'

'*Let me?*' I can't keep the incredulity out of my voice. 'I thought you'd had the vasectomy! I didn't know you'd chickened out.'

'The fact that you even thought I would entertain having a vasectomy shows your disrespect. There was no way I'd neuter myself, like an animal. But I had to shut you up somehow. And yes, I was disappointed when you fell pregnant so quickly, but then I thought, it's okay. Maybe you'll have a boy this time. But no. You couldn't even manage that. You have no idea how disappointed my parents are. My father, specifically. Two kids, and no grandson? If I'd known earlier you were having another girl, I'd have told you to get rid of it.'

My arms reflexively cover my bump protectively. Oh my God. The thallium. It all makes sense now. They were going to make me miscarry. Poison me and the baby. My stomach convulses as Sprout, my darling little Sprout, decides now is a good time to exercise her right to be acknowledged and play a staccato against the inside of my ribs.

My poor, precious daughter, already hated by the one man who is supposed to love her unconditionally.

I realise with mounting horror that the only thing I can do now is try to get us out of here alive.

'But that's not an issue now, is it?' Russ continues, seemingly oblivious to my distress. Was he ever aware of it? Or was he always pretending? 'I'll inform the police in due time. Tell them you left me, that I don't know where you are. Women do that. Just up sticks and leave. They won't suspect me. And even if they do, I'll just tell them that you've been ill. Mental health issues. That I'm so worried, because you've taken our daughter, that you're pregnant and you've found it so very hard this time around. And everyone will wring their hands and say, "Oh no, how terrible, that poor woman, that poor man." People have to pretend to care, you see. But deep down, they'll think you're just another one of those women who thought they could have it all, and then snapped. Of course the police will look for you. I'll give them a few places to investigate. And if one of them is by a lake and they just so happen to find a washed up plush frog... so sad. We did everything we could to help you, but it wasn't enough. Or maybe that's a bit too elaborate. I haven't made my mind up yet. If you make things too complicated, the risk of making mistakes increases. Afterwards, I'll play the suitably bereaved husband, maybe move out of the area because it's all too painful and that will be that. New life secured.'

He's staring at me, all trace of amusement gone. Only a

cold, blank seriousness remains. I read somewhere that out of all professions, surgeons were in the top five most likely to be psychopaths. And while I always secretly believed that to be accurate – some of Russ's colleagues are awful – I never thought he was one of them. But he is. In fact, he's probably even worse. Because he's learned to hide it. The veritable wolf in sheep's clothing.

It takes me more than a moment to gather my wits. When I open my mouth, a sob escapes. I have no control over it. I've just been told my husband means to murder not only me, but my children too. All because he's bored of us. He has deemed his desires more important than our lives.

The quintessential family annihilator.

'Russ,' I manage, tears streaming down my face. 'You don't have to... you can... we will... I'll leave. I won't chase you for anything. No child support. No maintenance. You'll never hear from us again. We'll change our names. It'll be like we don't exist to you—'

He gives me a wry smile and shakes his head, almost like he's a shopkeeper trying to tell me he's sold out of something, rather than listening to his wife trying to bargain for her and her children's lives.

'Frankie, come on. After all I said about complications?'

'But Russ, please, this isn't like getting rid of the cat—'

'Well, no, of course not. I just wrung the cat's neck and chucked it out with the trash. If I did that to you, I'd be in a lot more trouble. But the sentiment is the same. Anyway. Busy bee. Got to go and practise my sad face.'

FORTY-FIVE

Jasmine

Nearly there.

I take in a huge breath, hoping I might steady my nerves.

It doesn't work.

The ground is uneven and muddy, making my progress up the lane slow. I've stuck to the verges so I won't be as noticeable to someone driving towards me – just a quick skip and I'll be behind a tree.

I check my phone again. This time, it isn't just the red dot that's out of signal – everything is. I'm on emergency calls only, and I reckon even that's only if I'm incredibly lucky.

I didn't even realise I was pregnant. Not until I started bleeding. At first, I thought it was just a particularly bad period. I've always been irregular, always had bad cramping, but this was next level. It just wouldn't stop, and the pain... it was a lot, even for me. When I went to the doctor to try and find out what was wrong with me, I couldn't believe my ears.

Miscarriage.

Of course I know the statistics. How they are far more

common than people realise. That sometimes women who have them hadn't even realised they were pregnant. But my issue wasn't with any of that.

My issue was that I'd never slept with anyone. Like, ever. If I'm being honest, sex kind of scared me. I went to an all-girls' school. My 'boyfriend' was a man in his thirties, who swore he was happy to wait until I was ready. I thought he respected that, respected *me*.

How wrong I was.

To say I didn't know what to do after the miscarriage is an understatement. It ate at me. That he would do something like that. Even worse: he thought he could get away with it. I threw myself into my studies, determined to become the kind of woman who could eventually stand up to him – and be believed. But then he got married. Had children. Even worse: had a *daughter*. The man who stole my innocence. My trust. My self-esteem. My blood ran cold when Amanda told me. I felt so helpless, so utterly useless. I had to say something, *do* something – but what? If I spoke out now, people would question why I'd left it this long. Why I hadn't gone to the police. All those little excuses we use to shame women into silence.

But then I found that website.

I reach the gate. The path beyond is nothing more than tyre tracks in the mud. I'm glad I didn't take my car down here; there's no way it would have coped. The truck, on the other hand, clearly had no issues. The disorganised sprawl of deciduous woodland soon gives way to the more austere order of tall pines, and I'm left with a sinking feeling that if I do see the truck coming back up the track, there might not be much in the way of cover to hide me, as there isn't a lot of undergrowth. But it's far too late to worry about such things now. In for a penny, in for a pound, as my granny used to say.

I creep by the edge of the track, my senses on fire, every single one of them straining for any hint that someone might be out there, ready to pounce. But everything is quiet. Eerily so. At least in the woodland back by the road I could hear the odd bird call. Here, under the pines, everything is pin-drop silent.

This place gives me the creeps. It feels utterly abandoned, more like a crypt than a wood. There is a sinister air about the place, an edge that fills me with a different kind of unease. Maybe it's the way the trees grow in such regimented lines, or maybe the way the drifts of dead pine needles that gather around their trunks absorb all sound. Whatever it is, it's enough to make my skin crawl, and I find myself keeping low to the ground, making myself as small as possible. This place feels wrong, and I can't wait to get out of it.

A light flickers up ahead. I freeze. Is it a torch?

No. Something else.

Headlights.

My heart leaps into my throat and beats wildly as I duck down and half run, half crawl away from the track, trying to find some cover. All the while I'm waiting for the lights to flood around me and a voice to demand why I'm there. I find a rotted, moss-covered stump that I think will disguise me if I hunch up into a ball. I plaster myself against it, my fingers crammed into my mouth, my pulse thrumming in my ears as the headlights sweep through the trees around me, illuminating everything that was once secret in the dark.

Everything, that is, except me.

I stay crouched for a good while, not daring to move until the lights fade and the sound of the engine has completely died away, and even then it's only to peek over the top of the stump to check that the coast is indeed clear.

Silence settles over the pines again. A cold breeze has picked up, making me draw my jacket around myself. I still don't have anything that even resembles a whisper of a signal, so I'm totally blind as to whatever might happen next. For all I know, whoever that was could be going to get reinforcements. A sudden fear judders through my body as I realise the enormity of what I have taken on. If I'm right, and Frankie is here...

I still have seventy per cent charge on my phone. There's no signal, but I could run back and call the police. But what would I tell them? No. I have to keep going. I need to check out this place, make sure Frankie isn't here. And if she is, well, that's when I make the call. Then it's out of my hands.

Given the amount of charge I have left, I flick on the torch function and pick my way over the spongy ground. There's no point in breaking my ankle on a hidden root. I follow the fresh tyre tracks until I reach another gate. It's locked up with a chain and padlock that are starting to rust. If I hadn't seen it with my own eyes, I'd be wondering if I'd taken a wrong turn, but I can still see the tyre marks in the mud, along with a mess of fresh footprints.

A barbed wire fence swamped with brambles and stinging nettles is strung either side of the gate, but that too is rusted and old. The footprints in the mud lead off to the left, and about fifteen feet away from the gate, I can see that the wire has rusted through completely. This is clearly how they got in. I climb through the gap, careful to avoid the nettles.

On the other side there is some kind of abandoned yard, with stacks of mouldering logs and rusting pieces of machinery dotted around it. It must have once been a logging yard, closed down, probably by the pandemic.

Something unpleasant flips in my chest. The land isn't public, and I'd wager no one has been here for years.

It's the perfect hiding spot.

The feeling only gets worse when my phone illuminates the dilapidated remains of an old storage building in the far corner of the yard. There are fresh footprints in the soft earth around it.

This is definitely the place.

I dither a little by the door. Should I call the police now?

But I have no signal here, even the emergency signal is rubbish. If Frankie is in there, she might not have much time, and I'd have to run back down the road to call someone. And even if I do call, would they take me seriously? How long would it take them to get here? What if whoever was here before comes back? They could get here before the police come. They could simply be going back to collect something. And even if that's not the case, someone is going to realise I'm not home. All it takes is for someone to feel a bit paranoid and decide to come and check.

I take in a deep breath, hoping it might calm my nerves. All this dithering is just wasting time. If Frankie is in there, I have to help her. She is my priority. All I have to do is confirm it, then we can go straight to the cops. Once I have confirmation, they have to take me seriously. There will be no doubt, no fobbing me off. That's it. All of this could be over within the hour.

With that weirdly comforting thought, I take in a deep breath, pull open the rusted metal door and step into the dank interior of the utility building.

FORTY-SIX

FIVE YEARS EARLIER

Frankie

I haven't told my parents that Russ and I are back together. I want to see how things go first. I know how Dad feels about him, and I want to make sure this is a proper 'thing' before I broach that subject again. Due to this, I've asked Russ to stay away while my parents are visiting. It's just easier, I said. And he agreed.

So when my doorbell rings at eight thirty, I'm more than a little bit miffed.

'Hey, gorgeous,' he says, handing me a bouquet of flowers. He never arrives empty-handed these days. Says the least he can do is show me how much I mean to him.

'Russ, I said no to this weekend. My folks are here.'

'Oh, what? I thought that was next weekend.' He runs his hand through his wet hair. It's raining pretty heavily, and I can see he's soaked through.

'No, it's now. They're inside. We went out for a meal and now we're just settling in for the evening.'

Russ blows out a long sigh.

'Can I just come in for a minute? To ring for a cab?'

'Did you walk here?'

'Well, yeah. I thought we might go for a drink.'

'Look, I don't know, I don't think this is a good idea—'

'Frankie?' It's my dad, calling from my living room. 'Is everything all right?'

'Yeah, Dad, it's fine,' I call back. 'Don't worry.'

But it's too late. Dad's already in the hallway, looking concerned.

'Who's out there in this weather...? Oh.' Dad's tone changes from curious to deadpan. 'Why is he here?'

Before I can contrive an answer, Russ has jumped in.

'Hello, Brian, how are you? You're looking well.' Russ strides into my flat, his hand outstretched. It's clear Dad hasn't gathered his thoughts before Russ is shaking his hand, asking him all kinds of inane questions, guiding him back to the living room.

Mum is a little warmer towards Russ, asking him how his 'doctoring' is going. Russ chats like he's been invited, leaving me to panic in the corner while Dad glowers at the TV. He manages to keep his mouth shut while Mum makes pleasantries, but just as I think it's going to be okay after all, Russ spots the bottle of scotch on the side. I don't like scotch, but my dad does. So does Russ.

'That's a nice Speyside,' he says. 'Mind if I join you in a wee dram?'

He doesn't give Dad a chance to reply and pours himself a generous measure before leaning over and topping Dad's glass up.

Big mistake.

The thing about my dad is that he is a proud Yorkshireman. He likes gravy with his chips, never says no to a brew and always calls a spade a spade, no matter who he's talking to. Subtlety has never been his strong point.

'All I want to know is why you're here.'

Russ takes a sip of his drink and smiles indulgently at me.

'Isn't it obvious?' When Dad's glower intensifies, Russ looks surprised. 'Hasn't Frankie told you? We're back together. Have been for a couple of months. She's insisted we're to take it slowly, but I'm hoping we'll move back in together at some point soon.'

I wince, waiting for the outburst. But it doesn't come. Mum is now glaring at Dad, who is back to staring at the TV. He drains his glass of scotch.

'Mother, another,' he says, and Mum jumps to it.

This is not good.

But that doesn't shut Russ up. He continues to jabber on, telling my parents about him finally passing and becoming a surgeon, and how us getting back together basically means his life is perfect... Mum tries to be polite, and I try to smooth things as much as I can, even though all I want to do is run out of the room to get away from the inevitable argument that is brewing. If only Russ would shut up. Watch the TV quietly.

But that's not Russ's style.

I'm not even sure what the tipping point is. All I know is that one minute Russ is talking, the next, Dad is up out of his chair, red-faced and sweating, shouting about how Russ needs to leave me alone, that he knows his game and he'll just end up using me again. Russ acts shocked, like he can't believe that Dad would think such things, much less say them.

And then he turns to me.

'I know Frankie is on my side,' Russ says. 'I must say, I am rather disappointed. I thought we'd all moved on.'

I stare at Russ, dumbfounded. Mum looks like she wants to cry.

Dad sets his empty whisky glass down with a very final thud. Russ smiles.

I hold my breath.

'Cheryl. We're leaving.' And with that, Dad storms out of the room, with Mum in tow. I can hear her begging him to calm down, to do it for me, but Dad's untouchable.

'She lied to us, Cheryl! Lied to us about that slick bastard!'

The next thing I know, the front door slams.

I stare at Russ.

He's still smiling.

By the time I can move, my parents are long gone. I'm hoping Mum can calm Dad down, make him see sense.

'It's okay,' Russ says. 'He's always been very controlling, especially when it comes to you. Can't stand the thought of another man in your life. It's horribly common. Don't worry, He'll come round.'

But he doesn't come round.

He doesn't have a chance.

Russ has left by the time the police turn up.

I knew something was wrong. They were supposed to be staying with me for the weekend, so I assumed they'd gone for a walk. It's still raining and Mum doesn't like getting her hair wet.

They've been gone far too long.

The police officer informs me that there's been a collision. Two cars. Head on. Dad died at the scene. Mum's still alive, but is in a critical condition. They can take me to the hospital to see her.

Dad, furious at Russ, had obviously decided they were going to go home. They didn't get very far. He hit another car carrying a family for four. The driver and one child survived. The passenger – the mother – and her two-year-old didn't.

When you lose someone in such a sudden, senseless way, grief is almost incomprehensible. My father was in his late fifties; hardly an old man. But couple that with the loss of other, totally innocent lives? And the fact that it was his fault? I still don't understand it. Still can't begin to work through it.

Neither could Mum. She lasted six months after Dad's funeral. Hardly anyone came. Until he shattered that family and gained the title of 'drunk driver', he had been popular. Afterwards, no one wanted to admit ever knowing him. She couldn't handle the guilt. My brother found her. A bottle of gin and her antidepressants, all at once. That's when he moved to Australia.

Said it was my fault.

And it was my fault.

FORTY-SEVEN

Frankie

I sag back down next to Olivia. Is this my penance? My punishment? For taking Russ back? For not stopping my father from leaving that night?

Is this what it was all leading up to? Russ always said that we were made for each other, that no one would ever keep us apart. I thought it romantic then.

I don't now.

After the deaths of my parents, he became my rock. My only lifeline in a warzone of my own emotions. I spent some time in hospital. I spent some more time in another hospital. I thought he'd get bored of me, go and find someone who was a lot less hassle, but he didn't. He stuck with me.

And I healed.

Except... did I? Or did he use this as a chance to mould me? I'd been broken, and I thought he'd help fix me. But looking back, it was more like I was being trained. No more weekends away with my friends. No more visits to my family up North, not that they had much interest in seeing me after what Dad did. New job, one Russ arranged an interview for, working in HR with a friend of his in a company owned by a friend of his dad's. Quickly pregnant, so I had something to look forward to.

Every single aspect of my life, now controlled by him. My friends. My family. My job.

Everything.

Nausea swirls, and it has nothing to do with the baby. Russ has been playing with me like I'm a doll, and now he's bored with me, he's broken me and is chucking me away.

Because he has a new dolly to play with now.

That's when it hits me. The full weight of despair.

He isn't coming back. I've been thrown away. *We've* been thrown away. He doesn't even have to dirty his hands, just leave us down here to wither away to nothing.

I bow my head, tears sliding down my cheeks. Olivia reaches up and cuddles me, crooning 'Mama' into my neck. I rock her, as much for my comfort as for hers.

I can't let her starve. I won't. As hard as it will be, I'll either figure a way to escape, or we'll go out on our own terms. I'm not going to give him the satisfaction of making this final decision for me.

Dust rains down on me from above. Now the light has gone out, my heart jumps as I imagine spiders skittering over my skin. But then I hear the soft tread of unmistakeable footsteps.

Someone is upstairs.

Crap. Maybe I was wrong. Maybe Russ is back. Maybe he's not going to just forget us, leave nature to take its course. Maybe he just went back to fetch a knife, or a hunting rifle, or a cricket bat, or... or... I don't know, what do husbands usually use to murder their families? I scoop up Olivia and scoot back into one of the dark corners, shielding her from any possible attack. Maybe he'll have second thoughts if he kills me first. She's young enough not to remember it. She might even be able to scrape together something that resembles a normal life.

The footsteps stop. I strain my ears, but hear nothing. The silence, already unbearable, tears me apart. Come on, you piece of shit. Just get it over with. What you're doing is already despicable; you could at least pretend you're not enjoying it.

Another sound, just on the edge of my hearing, a soft scraping, as if something is being dragged across the ground. Then a slight creak.

Then nothing.

I shrink back, trying to make myself as small as possible, as if I might be able to mould myself into the wall. The sound of the bolts on the door leading to our little slice of basement hell is like a shotgun in the dark; my heart thuds painfully as I hold my breath. Even Olivia is silent, her tiny body a tense ball underneath mine. Sprout, sensing my obvious terror, is fighting for her life, kicking at the walls of what was once her sanctuary, now her prison, and I wrap as much of the chain that connects to my ankle around my fist as I can, because no matter what happens next, I am not going down without a fight.

The door slides open, and I'm momentarily blinded by a bright, white light. I grit my teeth, readying myself.

And then the world crashes in as someone says something I was not expecting.

'Oh my God, what has he done?'

FORTY-EIGHT

Jasmine

It takes me a moment to orientate myself. There's not much in here. Nothing suspicious, anyway. Rusted equipment leans against white-washed brick walls that are generously speckled with years of mould. Old crates, their wood softened by damp and insects, are stacked on top of each other, their labels too tattered and water-damaged to be read.

And that's it.

I'm totally stumped. I don't know what I was expecting, but it wasn't this. But it's definitely the place. Whoever was driving definitely came in here. Maybe they picked something up. Like, I don't know, a ransom, or a payment, or maybe a receipt. Or maybe this has nothing to do with Frankie at all. Maybe she got away, and this is just a strange coincidence.

I sweep the beam of my phone's torch around, wishing I'd brought a proper flashlight with me. Phones are useful in a pinch, but I need something stronger. I pace slowly around the building, looking for something, *anything* that might hint at why someone would come here, but again come up empty-handed.

There's nothing in the crates, nothing behind the old equipment, nothing *in* the old equipment, nothing on the shelves. All that's left is ripping up the floorboards to see if there's anything there...

Hang on a sec.

I pause and focus my meagre light on a spot near the back of the floor, beside one of the larger crates. In the gloom, the dusty floor looks a dull grey, and the cobwebs covering the crates resemble shrouds.

The floor near this crate is still dusty, but it has a groove in it, and rather than being anchored to it, the cobwebs flap in the draughty space.

My stomach does a little flip as I creep closer. Now I have my eye in, I can see more. Ghostly footprints, near the groove.

And now I know what I'm looking for, I notice matching handprints in the dust on the crate.

I put my phone down and brace myself. The crate shifts easily. I slide it across the floor, then peer behind it.

There's a trapdoor cut into the floor.

I scoop up my phone and pull the trapdoor open. It lifts easily, revealing stone steps that lead down into an inky blackness.

I swallow down my fear.

Time to find out exactly what the Minetti family are hiding.

I didn't specifically go looking for it. I didn't even know these kind of sites existed. I was actually on a forum for survivors of my kind of abuse.

It's a horribly large community.

It was there that I found out about the private website, where powerful men gather to brag and plot.

It was there I found out that Russ was an active member.

It wasn't just me. There have been others. Innocent teenagers, all falling for the dashing doctor schtick.

All of them being drugged and abused.

I physically threw up the first time I read his gloating posts. I don't know if he was talking about me, or about some other poor unfortunate, but it was enough for me to vow that, no matter what, I would stop him. And if I ruined his life in the process... that was just an added extra.

That was when the network recruited me.

I've baited men like Russ before. It's a horribly effective strategy. Sometimes their partners know and contact us to find irrefutable proof of their actions. Other times, the women are totally oblivious. Those are the ones I really feel sorry for.

Frankie was one of those women.

So when Amanda told me her brother needed a nanny, I knew this was my chance.

I could help save her... and ruin him.

After all, they say revenge is a dish best served cold.

The spiral steps are made of stone and smell like damp earth. I try the light switch at the top of the stairs, but it's long dead. I reckon this was probably a storage cellar of some kind, and given how well it's hidden I imagine it very well may have been built for less than honourable purposes. What those might be, I don't even want to guess at.

I can't hear anything at all as I creep down. The intense silence makes my skin crawl, and the feeling that nothing good has ever happened down here grows stronger. I sweep the beam of my phone around, taking in the mineral deposits that have collected on the walls. The steps are slick with moisture, so I'm extra careful where I put my feet; the last thing I need is to slip and break my leg. Then I round the final twist to find a metal door, its rivets rusted, its bolts drawn shut.

This has to be it. There is literally nowhere else to go.

There are no locks, so I draw the bolts back. They are

surprisingly well maintained. When I push the door open, it's whisper-quiet. For some reason, this unsettles me more than if it had creaked.

The first thing I notice is the reek of ammonia and I cover my nose with my jacket sleeve as I direct my light all over the room. It's dark in here and, disturbingly, there are signs that someone might have been here recently.

Crates. A bucket.

A chain.

My stomach, already pretty low, sinks even further.

I take a step inside. My skin prickles.

What the hell have they been up to...?

Slowly, I keep the light moving, looking for signs that might help me work out what on earth is going on. Then, seemingly out of nowhere, someone screeches '*You BITCH!*' And the next thing I know, something shoots out of the dark and barrels into me, knocking me over. The back of my head cracks against the stone floor and I momentarily see stars. But before I can catch my breath, my assailant is on me, trying to pummel my face with their fists.

Panic sets in immediately and I flail wildly, raising my hands up in a vain attempt at protecting myself. All the while, the spectre screams at me, calling me every slur under the sun, grappling with my hands, trying to hit me with a length of chain. But she's uncoordinated and completely out of control, so it doesn't take too much for me to grab her by the wrists.

Finally realising she can't hit me anymore, she pants as she glares at me, pure hatred in her eyes.

'Oh my God. Frankie?'

'Like you didn't know,' she spits.

'It Ja'min, it Ja'min, it Ja'min!' Little Olivia, now hysterical, runs out of the darkness. She's filthy but I don't care as she flings her arms around my neck. I let out a sob of something that is half relief, half sheer horror as I scoop her up and hold her close.

'No, Olivia, get away from her!' Frankie screams, but Olivia isn't listening. She's clinging to me like her life depends on it, and I'm clinging back because I know mine absolutely does.

'Frankie, please. I'm not here to hurt you. Please, I want to help—'

'Like hell you do.' She raises the chain in a threatening manner, but doesn't use it. 'Put my daughter down.'

'Frankie, I know you're—'

'*Put my daughter down!*'

'Frankie... Frankie, please... Just listen. That's all I'm asking. For you to listen. That's it.'

Conflict crawls over Frankie's face. Her fury is plain as day, but at the edges of it there is also hurt, worry and, most prominently, fear. She raises the chain one last time, then realising she can't hurt me without harming her daughter, she lets out a huge, sobbing sigh and finally sits back, pushing her hair out of her face. She looks dreadful: tired, sick and terrified, but there is a feral glint in her eye that tells me provoking her would be a very, very dangerous thing to do.

Olivia's grip is tight and desperate. My first instinct is to ask what has happened, but I don't need to. I know what has happened. I'm just not sure I can take it all in.

Because I was right. In fact, I was more than right. I was right the moment I took the job. It wasn't my imagination. She was in danger. *Real* danger.

More danger than I'd thought she was.

'Olivia,' Frankie snaps. 'Come here. Leave her alone.'

'No, Mama, it Ja'min!' Her joy at seeing me is so pure, it brings tears to my eyes. The kids know. I just wish her mother could see that.

'Yes, I know, now come on, away.'

'Look, Frankie, I know—'

'YOU need to SHUT UP.' Her change in tone makes Olivia jump, then cry. 'Olivia? I won't say it again.'

But Olivia is so traumatised, she can't hear her.

'Frankie, please, just hear me out—'

'I don't have to listen to a word you say.' She winds the length of chain around her fist, and I realise with no small measure of horror that it is locked around her ankle. 'You come into my life, steal my husband, plot with his family to replace me—'

'I... what? Who do you think wrote you that note?' I don't like raising my voice because it rarely helps, but I don't have time to talk her down. I have no idea how long we've got, and now I've found her, I need to contact the police as soon as possible. 'Who wrote it? Telling you to leave, that you were in danger.'

She jerks back a bit at that, a small frown of confusion creasing her brow.

'What? How do you know about that? But you—'

'And the money. Who do you think left you that?'

'... B-but the smoothies, you were poisoning me—'

'What?'

'The poison. The thallium. The stuff you were putting in my smoothies.'

'The what?' I have absolutely no idea what she's talking about. 'I've never even heard of the stuff.'

'Oh, that's convenient—'

'Frankie, I swear, I have no idea what you're talking about. Do you think I'd let Olivia taste them if I was poisoning them?'

'You... you let Olivia try them?'

'Of course I did. It's just fruit and veg. Nothing harmful. Unless...' My heart drops. 'No. He didn't... the water. I used a special watering can. He must have put it in that. I was literally watering the plants with poison. Oh, Frankie, this is all such a mess. I'm so, so sorry.'

'What...? How...? I don't...' Frankie blusters for a bit, looking confused, before her expression hardens again. 'I found the key to your room in Russ's bedside cabinet. I know he was using it to see you in the night. I heard him. Going upstairs. When I was in the dining room.'

'Yes. He did. And I told him to get out.'

I could tell her about the other stuff. About our history. Our *real* history. But not now. Frankie doesn't need any more evidence that her husband is a textbook psychopath. She's already got plenty.

'I only locked it at night,' I say, as gently as I can. 'When Russ was home.'

'But... the bracelet...'

'He bought it for me, for my eighteenth birthday.'

'Yeah, but the photo, in your journal, and all that secret stuff—'

'Frankie, we can talk about all of this once we're out of here and you're safe. Needless to say, your husband and I have a massive amount of history. That photo was taken when I was only eighteen. He was thirty-six. I was a kid. He started grooming me from the age of fifteen. And I'm not the only one.'

'But... but... why? Why come back? Why take the job if he hurt you? Why hurt me too?'

She's crying now. I don't think she's realised. All I want to do is gather her up and take away her pain, but I can't. Because he groomed her too.

He groomed all of us.

'He always said you were the one that got away. And that enraged him. He saw you breaking up with him as a personal failure, and he was never going to stand for that. I only know this because I snooped on his phone. I know it was wrong, but I needed to figure out what was going on. It didn't take long. There were photos. Of you. He kept them. Explicit ones.' Her face falls as I tell her this, making me wonder if I can tell her the other things I found. Because there weren't just pictures of Frankie on his phone.

There were pictures of me. Passed out and naked.

A swell of shame rises within me, but I dash it back with a wall of anger. No. This is not my shame. It's his. He did this.

No more secrets. Frankie deserves to know.

'There were also pictures of me. Pictures I had no idea he'd taken, in situations I knew nothing about. Because he was drugging me. I found a small bottle of GHB in his pocket.'

'What? I don't... I...' Frankie trails off, pain etched into her face.

'I'm sorry, Frankie, I truly am. By the time I headed off to university, I was just happy to never have to see him again. But then I heard that he'd married you, and that you had a kid – a daughter, no less – and you were having another child. Too many red flags. I knew I had to help.'

'So why didn't you just tell me? Why this huge elaborate scheme?'

'Would you have believed me? If I'd come to you and said "Hi, Frankie, just to let you know that your husband is an absolute monster and you might want to think about leaving him as soon as possible, okay?" You'd never have believed me. Plus, Russ had no idea I'd figured out what he was up to. So I had to be careful. I had to keep you safe, but also get you out of the house without Russ knowing what I was doing. I could expose Russ once you were safe. Never in a million years did I think he would resort to this.'

Her shoulders sag.

'I'm sorry, Frankie. I was going to explain everything. I even made sure Petunia kept to that stupid afternoon tea thing to give you time to get away.'

'You knew what I was planning?'

'Of course I did. I saw what you bought. I made sure the piggy bank was in a place where it would get smashed so you could take the money. I booked the accommodation for you. I was going to meet you out there, direct you to a women's shelter.'

Frankie slumps back, every line of her body screaming defeat.

'But why?'

'It's simple.' I hunker down in front of her. 'We can't let men like him win. And there are lots of them out there. After what happened to me, I thought I was alone. But I wasn't. I found a community online, one that works to help women in our situations. They scour the deeper parts of the internet, looking for places where men like Russ congregate, where they share tips and conquests. Where they plot and scheme. People think they don't exist, that we're just being paranoid, but they do. There are men out there who truly hate women while pretending to love them, and they're not all basement-dwelling trolls. They're lawyers and politicians, police officers and, yes, even doctors. They are men who exploit their position of power to get what they want, then further exploit it to ensure that no one believes the victims.'

'What am I going to do, Jasmine?' Frankie's voice is small, almost childlike. Gone is her former fury, replaced by a devastation so profound she can barely speak.

'First off, we get you out of here. Then, we speak to the police. Then we make as much noise as we can. People are going to listen, Frankie. We aren't going to give them any choice.'

FORTY-NINE

Frankie

I can't think. I can barely breathe.

Jasmine.

In a way, I was right. She was there to ruin my marriage and break up my family. Only not in the way I suspected. And she's right. If she had told me this before, there's no way I would have believed her.

But now, after all of this, I believe every word.

She has shed the sweet, naive skin of the girl who came to look after my daughter. Before me now is an indomitable young woman, once broken, now reforged, like iron. I can tell there is more to her story, and I dread to think what it might be. What my husband, the father of my daughters, might have done to her to make her this way. She could have stayed away. Washed her hands of us. Said that we weren't her problem, much less her responsibility.

But she didn't. She saw the warning signs. And she acted.

She's the closest thing to my very own guardian angel.

And I thought she was trying to kill me.

The more she reveals, the more my stomach clenches in revulsion and shame. But there is no blame in her, not towards me. There never was. I can see that now. It was all an act. An act to get me to leave – not to destroy my marriage, but to save me from it. So when she says she's going to get us out of here, I believe her.

Right up until I hear the clapping.

We both turn our heads towards the open door like startled deer. Olivia runs behind me and cowers, whimpering.

The slow clapping continues as Russ saunters into the room.

'Well, *that* was quite a tale,' he says, with a drawl. 'Story time with Princess Jasmine. Shame no one will ever hear about it.' He stops clapping and his eyes narrow. 'You left your car up the lane, you stupid bitch. It wasn't there before, so I knew something was up. Then I found this' – he holds up a small plastic disc: an AirTag – 'in my coat pocket. It didn't take much to figure out what you might be up to. You know, an intelligent person would have just called the police, but no, you had to be the heroine of the piece, didn't you? Such a pity. Never mind, it makes my life easier. The distraught and mentally disturbed wife, so driven by jealousy and her own personal demons, not only kills her daughter, but also takes out the young and beautiful nanny who she felt so threatened by before killing herself in a tragic murder-suicide. It almost writes itself—'

'You're a monster,' Jasmine growls. Her fists are clenched, her teeth gritted. 'Why do you want to do this?'

'I thought you summed it up pretty well, actually. She' – he points at me – 'thought she was in charge. And that's not the case. No one leaves me. No one humiliates me. And you humiliated me, Frances. In front of my parents, no less. In front of people who respected me. So you had to be taught a lesson. The plan was to humiliate you in front of your parents, but as luck would have it, your father took that into his own hands, didn't he? I wasn't expecting that at all. I mean, I did spike his scotch with a few drops of GHB – which I'd been planning on using on you, I might add – but I wasn't expecting him to drive. I mean, wow, that was foolish... Sorry, love, are you all right? You look like you've seen a ghost.'

The room spins as the breath is knocked from me.

Dad. He shouldn't have been driving. But he hadn't had that much. I knew he hadn't.

His drink had been spiked. By Russ.

Russ killed my father. And, by proxy, my mother.

All that consoling. All that 'I'm your family now'.

It was him, controlling me.

And all through this, he is just standing there, a grin on his face, because he is *enjoying* it, like a magician finally indulging himself, showing off how he pulls off his cleverest tricks.

Next to me, Jasmine lets out a feral growl and launches herself at him. Surprised, Russ yelps and swings at her. They both lose their balance, with Russ quickly gaining the upper hand. He's much bigger than she is, and years of going to the gym means he's pretty fit for a guy squeaking over forty. But Jasmine is fighting hard. She's going for his eyes, trying to dig her thumbs in, but it's not going to be enough as Russ wraps his hands around her throat with terrifying ease.

And all I can do is watch. It's like I'm not even there.

'No, Papa!' Olivia screams. She crawls over and tries to wrench Russ's arm away. He pays her no attention and elbows her hard, knocking her down. A bright bloom of red splashes across her forehead as it strikes the ground.

I come back into my own body with a brutal bump.

He hurt my baby.

Both his hands are back around Jasmine's throat as I gather up the slack on my chain.

He HURT my baby.

She's making choking noises now, and her face is bright red.

He HURT my BABY.

I swing the chain around my head, once, twice, to build momentum.

Then I smash it with as much force as I can into the side of Russ's head.

He yelps as the chain connects with a thud, drawing blood. It's not enough to knock him out, but it is enough to distract him. He lets go of Jasmine and raises his hand to the side of his head, wincing when it comes away bloody.

He gives me an almost comically confused look, and before he can say anything else, Jasmine rolls over, coughing and wheezing, and snatches up the slack of the chain. But she doesn't hit him with it. Instead, with a look of grim determination, she wraps it as tightly as she can around his neck.

And she pulls.

'Jasmine!' he gasps, but she doesn't let go. Instead, she jams her foot in between his shoulder blades and pulls harder.

He scrabbles at his own neck now, trying to speak, but only garbled squawks come out. I stand there, mesmerised, as Jasmine slowly chokes my husband, his face turning from pink, to red, to a deep, violent purple. He tries to worm his fingers under the chain to give himself some air but she grits her teeth and keeps pulling.

That's when I realise she means to kill him.

'Jasmine,' I say, as calmly as I can. 'Jasmine, you can't do this.'

'Oh yes I can,' she says. I try to ignore the tortured, bubbling wheezing now coming from Russ's throat.

'No, you can't. Because if you do, you'll be the one who pays, not him. What he did to you – to *us* – was terrible. But death is the easy way out for him. Make him face what he did to you. Make him pay in a way that will hurt.'

She glances over at me, and relaxes her arms, just a fraction. Russ takes advantage of this to draw in a long, rasping breath.

'But he deserves to die,' she whispers. She's crying now, huge, ugly tears born of years of pain. 'It wasn't just me.'

'I don't doubt you. But if you kill him, his other victims have no chance of closure. If we go public, he can't hide.'

'Public?'

'Yes. Police, the news, everything. We'll ask for other victims to come forward. Everyone will know that Russell Minetti is a predator.'

Jasmine wraps her hand around the chain once more, increasing the pressure on his neck. Russ's breath is now shallow; his eyelids are fluttering. He's close to passing out. A few more minutes of pressure, and he'll be dead for sure.

In the corner, Olivia is watching, her eyes huge, like an owl's. I wish I could have spared her this, but sometimes, you have to learn that the monsters are real, and sometimes they look just like us.

There is a moment when I truly believe she won't stop. But then I catch her glance Olivia's way. She looks back to me.

Finally, Jasmine nods and drops the chain.

Russ slumps to the floor. He's not dead – his heaving chest is testament to that – but he's not going anywhere soon. Jasmine shuffles forward and rifles through his pockets until she finds his keys. She tries each one on the lock around my ankle until it springs open.

Then she shackles it around Russ's ankle with a nasty smile.

'To stop him disappearing while we call the police,' she says, as if she needs to explain anything to me now.

It takes us a while to get up the stairs. We're all exhausted, and both of us take turns carrying Olivia. The cut on her head is largely superficial and is, ironically, in the same place as the one she'd had on Jasmine's first day.

Funny how these things turn out.

FIFTY

Frankie

Once we're out into the logging yard, we have what feels like the Herculean task of finding a phone signal. When the emergency call signal pops up on my screen, we both start crying. By the time we see blue lights flashing through the trees, I'm verging on hysterical. I'm just glad Jasmine is with me. Without her, I don't think I'd have been able to tell them who I am, let alone the rest of the details.

I don't remember much else about that day. Everything from the emergency services turning up to being put into a hospital bed is a total blur. They very kindly kept the three of us together on the same ward; I think they realised that if they didn't they were going to have a real problem on their hands.

I spent most of my time out of it. There was a touch and go moment when the doctors thought I might have to deliver Sprout early, but thankfully it never came to that.

Even after she was discharged, Jasmine stayed by my bedside.

We never once saw Petunia or Filippo.

Jasmine told the police where Russ was. She also admitted what she'd done. At first she said I had nothing to do with it, but there was no way I would let her take the rap for it all. When they questioned me, I made it very clear that Russ was trying to strangle Jasmine, and that we both subdued him in self-defence.

Once Russ was in a state to be interviewed, he admitted that he'd been spying on me all along. Had been telling his father of his suspicions. To my surprise and disappointment, Filippo had lent him his truck, and had been the one to help with the clean-up after the 'accident'. My car was discovered in the Minettis' garage, mangled at the back. Filippo had driven it and then had helped his son take us to the disused lumberyard to 'buy some time', as if Russ had made a mistake rather than committed a heinous crime. But then Jasmine went public with her story, and five other young ladies have also come forward with similar tales of grooming and, alarmingly, being drugged.

The final nail in the coffin was the thallium. I showed the police the photo of the bottle I found in the rubbish. At first they were a little sceptical – after all, how much worse could this tale actually get? – but a blood test confirmed it. The levels were high but not quite high enough to kill me, but that's probably down to me working out that something was wrong and limiting my exposure.

The police have since recovered the watering can Jasmine was using and had that tested, too. It came back positive for quite high levels of thallous chloride.

Naturally, Russ denied knowing any of this. He claimed it had been Jasmine, not him, who had poisoned me. That Jasmine was jealous. But by that point, no one trusted him. In the end, experts managed to piece together the likely method of delivery themselves. As a surgeon, one connected with heart stress tests, he had access to thallium. In a medical setting, it has its uses, but is strictly controlled as a radioactive element. In high enough doses, it can indeed be fatal, and repeated exposure over a short period of time leads to sickness followed by death. Their theory is that Russ was adding thallium to the water in the watering can, just as we suspected. It turns out, brassicas such as kale and spinach actually concentrate thallium, making such vegetables an effective source of delivery.

They suspect Russ already knew that.

I don't know what's going to happen next. There will be a trial, but even with that, there are no guarantees. Sadly, money talks, and the Minettis have plenty of it. But Jasmine assures me she has one last trick up her sleeve.

'The thing these people don't realise,' she says as she helps me pack my birth go-bag, 'is that I know people who have dirt on all of them. The network are watching them, and if one solicitor, one judge puts a foot wrong, they're all in for a world of hurt.'

I smile grimly at this.

'Good.'

EPILOGUE

NINE MONTHS LATER

Frankie

'Are you sure this is what you want?'

Jasmine is regarding me earnestly. There was a time when I would have hesitated. It's taken me this long to decide. But now I've made my mind up, I've never been more sure of anything in my life.

I smile at the waitress as she brings over our coffees. A decaf flat white for me, a macchiato for her and a babyccino for Olivia. I'm sticking with decaf because I'm breastfeeding now. I want to give little Cheryl the very best start in life that I can provide.

Jasmine gives me a warm smile as she takes a sip of her drink. We're going to miss her. In many ways I wish she could come with us, but that's not a decision for me to make. She has to live her own life now, forge her own path. I pull my coffee towards me and settle back. Baby Cheryl is, as always, clamped to my boob. This kid is always hungry, but she's otherwise a relatively easy baby. Apart from being a little low on the birth weight scale, she's pretty much perfect, despite everything she's been through.

My little miracle.

'T'ank you, Ja'min,' Olivia says, her little face scrunched up in concentration as Jasmine helps her with her babyccino. She takes a little sip, and doesn't spill anything. She's four now, but still can't say Jasmine's name properly. Not that I care. She'll get there.

'So, have you got everything?' she asks, as if she hasn't asked me this a thousand times before.

'I think so. It's not as if I'm taking much.'

'And you're sure this is what you want?' This has been a constant question, because I know she still feels responsible for all of us, despite being so much younger than me.

'I'm sure. I've spoken to my brother. He knows what happened. It was painful, but it's better. He's looking forward to seeing me, to seeing us. And I'm looking forward to a completely fresh start.'

Jasmine chews at her lips and stares out of the window, a sure sign that she's anxious. Aeroplanes line the edges of the airport, ready for their passengers to board. We're flying from Manchester rather than London, with help from the network. They helped with my legal fees, too. The organisation doesn't really have a name as such; they just refer to themselves as 'the network', a group of women who have been hurt by powerful men who use their status to abuse: men who either forgot, or most likely didn't even realise, that women are capable of becoming just as powerful as they are in their own right. The only difference is, where those men used their power and influence to abuse, these women use it to protect, because while people might like to claim 'it's not all men', it is all women: every single one of us has a story where a man's wants were deemed more important than our dignity. And to that end, the network has judges and lawyers, high-ranking police officers and politicians – and yes, even a few doctors – among their ranks. Jasmine has already told me that once she qualifies, she'll be one of them, a clinical psychologist helping children as well as their mothers. Keeping the next generation as safe as she can from the Russell Minettis of this world.

And speaking of Russ, his trial is due to start soon. I had worried it might delay my plans to start a new life in Australia, but the courts have agreed I can connect remotely. Since Jasmine was the one who actually choked him, she's the one his defence are trying to go for, not me. I think they realise trying to turn a jury against me is a complete non-starter, with or without the additional information on what Russ was up to. He kidnapped his pregnant wife and toddler daughter with the express purpose of either killing them or letting them die so he could escape an unhappy marriage. No matter how you slice that, it's not a good look. And then there are all the women who have come forward saying they, too, were groomed by him. Turns out, being a handsome and charming doctor gave him almost unfettered access to young women, be they nurses or patients. The sheer scope of his abuse is now being serialised in some of the more salacious weekend newspapers. It's going to be a long and hard road bringing him to justice, but I'm ready.

We're not going to let him win.

The Tannoy chimes, announcing that the flight to Melbourne will be boarding soon. A lump, never too far away at the best of times, swells in my throat. Jasmine looks at me, her eyes huge and watery.

I guess it's time.

I gather up our hand luggage, trying to pretend everything's fine, but as soon as I see tears rolling down Jasmine's face, I can't hold it together anymore. A sob escapes me and Olivia looks up at me, confused.

'Mama okay?'

'Yes, Mama's fine,' I say, and take her hand. 'We need to go on the plane now.'

'On the plane? Up in the sky?'

'That's right, all the way up in the sky!'

'And Ja'min coming?'

I pause. This is the bit I've been dreading.

'No, darling. Jasmine is staying here.'

'And Cheryl?'

'Cheryl is coming with us.'

'But not Ja'min?'

'Not Jasmine.'

'But—'

Jasmine hunkers down in front of her.

'It's okay, Olliebean. I can come and visit. But I have to stay here. You have to go and look after Mama and baby Cheryl.'

Olivia nods, then wraps her in a big cuddle, which Jasmine returns wholeheartedly. By now both of us are sobbing, much to Olivia's confusion. But that's okay. Little kids don't understand the implications of such things. She probably thinks she's going to see Jasmine tomorrow. Sadly, she'll probably have forgotten about her by Christmas. And in a way, I kind of hope she will have. Because if she's forgotten Jasmine, then hopefully there's a chance she might forget what actually happened with her father and be able to live something like a normal life.

We wander over to the security gate, tissues in hand. I produce our tickets – business class, of course; Jasmine told me that the network doesn't scrimp – and we share a last embrace. Just before we disappear down the corridor to Customs, Olivia looks back and waves. Jasmine waves back, and my chest caves in. But I still wave back. Because it's all I can do.

The girl I thought was going to ruin my life ended up being the best thing to ever happen to me. And I'm probably never going to see her again.

She was, after all, just there to help.

A LETTER FROM CLAIRE LUNN

First things first: thank you so much for reading *I'm Here To Help*. Thank you for being here, and therefore being part of my journey as an author. If you enjoyed it and want to keep up to date with all my latest releases, just sign up at the following link. Your email address will never be shared and you can unsubscribe at any time.

www.bookouture.com/claire-lunn

The thing with *I'm Here To Help* is part of it is real. Not the bad husband bit – thankfully he's a treasure. Nor the awful mother-in-law (I lucked out there, too). But the hyperemesis... that's written from experience. If you've ever had morning sickness, even for one day, then I totally empathise with you. It's rough. It can lead you to feel isolated and frustrated. Pregnancy does weird things to your body in the best of circumstances, without feeling like you went on a month-long bender as well. It's like your body isn't your own anymore. It's not an illness you can recover from. All you can do is grin, bear it and try to ignore the fact that even ginger beer tastes awful. Just grit your teeth and keep going, Mama!

I'll never forget that day. My in-laws were visiting from Devon, staying with us for the weekend. And I felt ill. Properly, if I move I'm going to throw up, ill. But I didn't want to ruin anything, so I kept quiet. My mother-in-law and I went shopping at Gunwharf Quays. She wanted to go to the Kipling bag shop, and then to Molton Brown. The shops were hot, and the synthetic scents of beauty products almost had me throwing up on my mother-in-law's shoes. Thankfully, things didn't go as badly as they did for Petunia that day.

Now, I'm pretty sure you don't want a blow-by-blow account of my first pregnancy. Let's just say I threw up every day, including the day I gave birth. Thankfully, her little sister was easier. I have no idea how I would have coped had it been the other way round – although my eldest, who was coming up for three at the time, did like to go into the kitchen and announce, 'Mumma, I just done wees,' just as I sat down to feed her sister (and her sister was ravenous; four-hour feeding sessions weren't unusual). In the end, I became very good at feeding on the go. All I can say is thank you, the inventor of the baby sling!

The other reason for writing this is a little more sobering. I can't exactly remember where I first heard it, but the most dangerous time for a woman in terms of domestic violence is while she is pregnant. This is compounded by the other most dangerous time: when you decide to get out. Every deck is stacked against Frankie, and while the story is one hundred per cent fiction, her situation isn't. I think it's important to spread awareness, and to keep our eyes on our fellow sisters. I am a teacher, and I've had to report some very serious situations to various safeguarding agencies; I had a duty of care then, and I have a duty of care now. So, if anyone needs help, or suspects someone else might, the following sites may help:

National Domestic Violence Helpline (UK): https://
www.nationaldahelpline.org.uk/

National Domestic Violence Hotline (US): https://
www.thehotline.org/

I hope you loved *I'm Here To Help* and if you did I would be very grateful if you could write a review. I'd love to hear what you think, and it makes such a difference in helping new readers to discover one of my books for the first time.

I love hearing from my readers – you can get in touch on my Instagram page and on Threads.

Thanks,

Claire

instagram.com/claires_nonsense

threads.net/@claires_nonsense

bsky.app/profile/clairesnonsense.bsky.social

ACKNOWLEDGEMENTS

First and foremost, my thanks and love to my amazing agent, Sandra Sawicka. If she hadn't shared my writing with Nina, this book wouldn't be here. She continues to believe in me even (especially) when I'm doubting myself, and I literally wouldn't be here without her continued guidance and support.

To Nina Winters, my equally amazing editor. The sheer faith you've had in me from the moment you read my writing has probably been one of the most affirming experiences of my life (the other? See above!). From that very first Zoom meeting, I just knew I was in exceptionally good hands. And then meeting you in London? Confirmation doesn't get much stronger than that. Thank you so much for seeing the potential in me and taking a chance; it means everything to me.

No book is an island, and the village that rallied around this book has been equally brilliant. (I'm not going to lie, I totally appreciate how organised you guys at Bookouture are!) From editorial manager Mandy Kullar to copyeditor Donna Hillyer and proofreader Emily Boyce, to Lisa Horton's amazing cover and Jess Readett and the marketing team's enthusiasm, this has been a team effort. I really feel *I'm Here To Help* found the perfect home from day dot. Thank you so much, everyone!

Then there are the people around me. My family, who are now used to me muttering to myself around the house. My husband, Grant, who supports me in every way (even when I'm jumping out of bed at 3 a.m. to write down the idea I've just had). My daughters, Lucy and Emily, who roll their eyes and tell their friends, 'Don't worry, she's talking to someone who doesn't exist again.' My mum and dad – I got there in the end! And Mum, you're okay, there's not too much swearing in this one (and yes, I did base the neighbours around Exeter Close!). My in-laws, especially my mother-in-law, Marilyn, who has more patience and grace in her little finger than Petunia ever will. You are officially one of the Good Ones!

Friends come in lots of different guises, both in person and online. There's Jane and Simon Colebrook, who I've known basically forever, offering boards to bounce off, demystifying tax stuff and general fun and games. Sofi Cosh and Katie Whiteley-Fuller, fellow English teachers, ready to talk books at any time of the day. Luke Walker, Chris Carpineti and Jenni Milward, who have been there forever with a shoulder or a celebration, depending on the day.

And finally, there are the new friends I will hopefully make through this book. Thank you for being here, reading this.

(Oh, and my cats, Hiccup and Tifa. Thank you for the purrs and cuddles... but not so much for the time you walked across my keyboard, Tifa, and the panicked couple of minutes that followed. Hiccup might be grumpier, but at least he never managed to delete my entire MS then sit there, smugly cleaning his paws.)

PUBLISHING TEAM

Turning a manuscript into a book requires the efforts of many people. The publishing team at Bookouture would like to acknowledge everyone who contributed to this publication.

Audio
Alba Proko
Melissa Tran
Sinead O'Connor

Cover design
Lisa Horton

Commercial
Lauren Morrissette
Hannah Richmond
Imogen Allport

Data and analysis
Mark Alder
Mohamed Bussuri

Editorial
Nina Winters
Imogen Allport